I0825360

A DEFIANT WOMAN

ALSO BY KAREN E. OLSON

MODERN TUDOR MYSTERIES

An Inconvenient Wife

BLACK HAT THRILLERS

Hidden

Shadowed

Betrayed

Vanished

TATTOO SHOP MYSTERIES

The Missing Ink

Pretty in Ink

Driven to Ink

Ink Flamingos

ANNIE SEYMOUR MYSTERIES

Sacred Cows

Secondhand Smoke

Dead of the Day

Shot Girl

A DEFIANT WOMAN

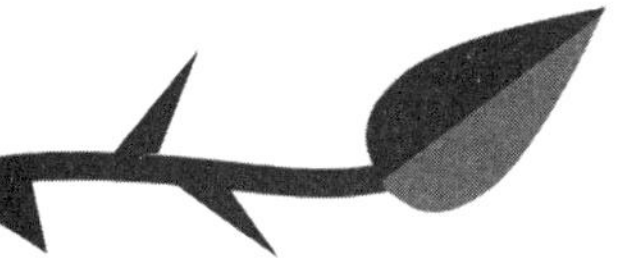

A MODERN TUDOR MYSTERY

KAREN E. OLSON

PEGASUS CRIME
NEW YORK LONDON

A DEFIANT WOMAN

Pegasus Crime is an imprint of
Pegasus Books, Ltd.
148 West 37th Street, 13th Floor
New York, NY 10018

First Pegasus Books cloth edition March 2026

Interior design by Maria Fernandez

Library of Congress Cataloging-in-Publication Data is available.

ISBN: 979-8-89710-054-5

10 9 8 7 6 5 4 3 2 1

Printed in the United States of America
Distributed by Simon & Schuster
www.pegasusbooks.com

To Chris, for everything

Changes in fortune make a woman stronger.

—Margaret of Austria

A DEFIANT WOMAN

PROLOGUE

NAN

The first text message came through at midnight. She had just come off her shift at the restaurant and was on her way home when the phone pinged.

We have your daughter.

She frowned, thinking of her son, who was spending the night with his friend Gabriel. The text must have been meant for someone else. She was about to delete the message and report it as spam when the second text came through.

This time, though, it wasn't a message but a photograph.

She squinted at the small screen and recognized the young girl with long red hair, dark gray eyes, a pointed chin, and high cheekbones.

The girl *was* her daughter. There was no mistake. She forced herself to breathe slowly, in and out, willing her heart to stop beating so fast and trying to sort this out. She couldn't let herself panic.

Who knew this was her number? She considered the people with whom she'd shared it: her son, Gabriel's parents, the restaurant.

She was distracted by the three dots pulsating on the screen, the indication that the person on the other end was typing.

Finally, information for a flight from Paris to Boston—in less than forty-eight hours.

If you're not on that flight, we'll know.

The threat lay beneath the words. Her hands began to shake. But as she tried to process it, she realized there was no real proof that they had her. In the photograph, the girl looked well, looked happy. For a moment, she was distracted by that. Had it been best that she'd left? What would the girl's life have been like if she'd stayed?

She shook the thoughts away. She'd asked herself those questions so many times over the past years and never had any answers. It was better to leave the past in the past.

Except now, the past was creeping into her present.

She'd been gone a long time. Long enough that she was no longer a threat to anyone. Yet it was clear that someone wanted her back in the States badly enough to take her daughter—or at least threaten her with the thought of that. Whatever this was, it couldn't be about money. If it were, they would have texted her daughter's father, who had plenty.

So, why? Why would someone say they'd taken her daughter and demand that she return?

What do you want? she texted back, her fingers feeling too large and clumsy for the tiny keyboard.

As she waited for a response, she again ran through the names of those who had this number. Her old friend Margaret Pole used to, but Margaret had died a couple of months ago. Had she given the number to someone? Margaret had always been trustworthy, but she'd also had a touch of dementia.

What she wouldn't give to forget the years before she came back to France. There was a time when she had everything she'd ever dreamed of: a husband whose empire stretched to every continent, who'd been devoted to her, wooed her for years, brought her into his business and gave her almost as much power as he had. When his divorce was finally granted and she became pregnant, she had believed she'd never have another worry again. She had the man she'd waited for, and they had a beautiful daughter. Her life was perfect.

And then it wasn't.

She could blame the infertility drugs; she should have been happy with what she had. She shouldn't have reached for more. But in the end, it was in his nature to wander, grow tired of her, find another woman. He'd cheated on his first wife with her, after all, so it shouldn't have been a surprise when someone else caught his eye.

But that was years ago now. She wasn't fighting for him any longer.

She had abandoned her husband, a powerful man she was convinced would kill her rather than give her what she wanted in the divorce. He'd taken their daughter, threatened that she'd never see her little girl again. The familiar guilt gnawed at her. She'd been a coward. She'd left her three-year-old daughter behind. Should she have stayed? Fought for her?

There was nothing she could do about it now. She'd made her decision. And she had a son. A boy for whom she'd sacrificed everything. She'd left before he was born, when he was still a mere flutter inside her. She went to the only place she felt safe, where she could disappear and no one would find her.

By leaving, she saved her son's life as well as her own—she'd never told her husband that she was pregnant—and Margaret kept an eye on her daughter, making sure she was well cared for despite not knowing what had happened to her mother.

She was supposed to be dead, but instead she survived.

She started fresh in a small city in France, where she took a culinary course and spent her days and nights in restaurant kitchens—far removed from the sophisticated wife and businesswoman she'd been. She was an unwed mother, as far as anyone was concerned, and she raised her son without the extravagant wealth she'd been accustomed to. They lived a simple, uncomplicated life.

Until now.

Because as the words appeared on her phone's screen, she knew everything was about to change.

Be on that flight or we'll kill her.

There were no more pulsating dots. Whoever was on the other end was done.

Police Investigate Disappearance of Billionaire's Daughter

MARTHA'S VINEYARD, MASS. (AP)—Elizabeth Tudor, 11, daughter of billionaire businessman Hank Tudor, has been reported missing. Police are investigating, and an Amber Alert has been issued.

Elizabeth, who has been staying at her father's estate in Tisbury, was last seen Monday afternoon as she headed to the beach to meet a friend, but she never showed up, according to police. She was wearing a white T-shirt, denim shorts, and white sneakers and carried a large white tote bag decorated with a yellow stenciled pineapple.

Police said Blanche Parry, 12, waited for her friend for half an hour, but when she received a text allegedly from Elizabeth saying she couldn't meet her, Blanche went home. She said she wasn't aware her friend was missing until Elizabeth's half sister, Maril Tudor, came to her house looking for her.

Ms. Tudor told police she watched Elizabeth head to the beach but did not report her missing until 10 P.M.

"I spent four hours looking for her," a distraught Ms. Tudor said. "After the beach, I drove everywhere, searching for her. She's vanished."

Mr. Tudor could not be reached for comment. Police said he is on the island, assisting in their investigation.

Elizabeth is the daughter of Mr. Tudor and his second wife, Nan, who disappeared eight years ago while staying at the same property with her daughter, who was three at the time.

A headless body of a woman was found nearby, but a DNA analysis indicated it was not the second Mrs. Tudor.

Police are asking that anyone with any information about Elizabeth contact them immediately.

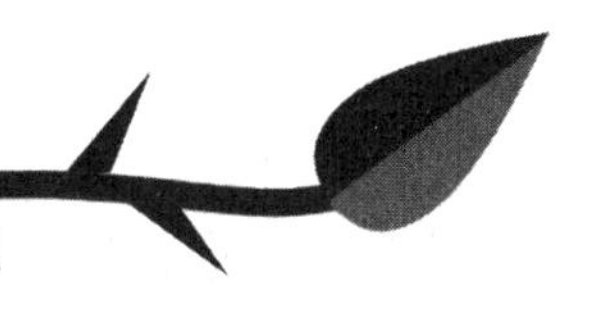

PART I

1
KATE

Kate Parker Tudor glanced at her watch and wondered why it took so long to make a coffee. Five people were in line ahead of her. She resisted the impulse to tap her foot impatiently. The baristas were making coffee for the absent people, the ones who had ordered online and would swoop in, grab their cardboard cups off the counter, and give those in line a smug smile. Granted, she could have ordered online for pickup, too, but that always felt like cheating, somehow. She was perfectly capable of walking three blocks to the coffee shop and ordering in person. Except every time she did, she regretted it.

It wasn't as though she didn't have the time. She had all the time in the world these days, days that stretched lazily from one to the next, without the stressful pressure of the job she'd had for the past three years. She'd been Hank Tudor's assistant, a high-powered position for the high-profile CEO and owner of Tudor Enterprises, an international multimedia corporation.

And then she'd married him. Hank Tudor, the billionaire who'd been married five times previously, his last wife brutally murdered and found decapitated on his Greenwich, Connecticut, property.

They'd had two weeks of wedded bliss before Caitlyn Howard's body was discovered and two more weeks before Kate left him. That was two months ago. Since then, he had communicated with her only through his lawyer, Thomas Cromwell. He said he didn't want a divorce, but he couldn't be bothered to talk to her face-to-face.

Kate finally reached the counter. She ordered a decaf latte, a remarkably simple drink but one she knew would take at least another ten minutes to make. She moved to the side to wait.

"Kate?"

She resisted the urge to turn. There must be another Kate. She'd taken the sublet on the Upper West Side specifically because she didn't know anyone in the neighborhood, although it was possible someone had recognized her because of Hank. She hoped that wasn't the case.

"Kate?" the voice came again from behind her, a deep baritone.

Reluctantly, she glanced around. It wasn't a stranger. Even though it had been years, she still recognized him: tall and well built under the dark suit jacket, tousled dark hair—a tiny touch of gray now around the temples—bright blue eyes, sharp jaw, and a wide grin.

"Tommy?" She couldn't believe it. "Tommy Seymour?"

"Of all the gin joints in all the towns in all the world, she walks into mine."

"Yours? Do you live up here?"

He put his hand over his heart, feigning dismay. "I'm devastated you haven't been stalking me all these years."

Kate felt herself blushing. It had been a long time since she'd done that, although she couldn't help but see his bylines out of Washington. He'd always wanted to cover politics, and she'd been happy that his journalism career went the way he'd hoped. He'd been her first—her first friend at Columbia, her first love, her first, well, everything. And now, here he was, standing in front of her in the coffee shop. She never thought she'd see him again—especially in New York. When had he moved back?

"Of course, I know what *you've* been up to," he said without waiting for a response. "Mrs. Tudor." He gave a short bow.

She shook her head. "No, no, Tommy. With you, I'm just Kate." She was acutely aware that it sounded like she was flirting with him. *Was* she flirting? Could Mrs. Hank Tudor flirt, even though she was separated from her husband?

The barista interrupted her thoughts by calling out, "Kate!"

Kate grabbed her cup off the counter and thanked him, happy for the momentary distraction. She'd felt somewhat isolated these past weeks. Was that why she was so glad to see Tommy?

He was saying something.

"I'm sorry, what?" she asked.

"Why don't we get out of here? It's a bit too crowded and loud." He held out his hand to indicate she should go ahead of him.

Once out on the sidewalk, Kate again felt flustered. She took a sip of her coffee. It was too hot and burned the top of her mouth. Served her right for stalling. But Tommy Seymour had always made her weak in the knees, and she wasn't sure she wanted to know whether he still might be capable of it.

"It's okay, Kate. I know what you've been going through," Tommy said kindly, his eyes locking with hers. It unnerved her, as though he were privy to all her secrets. But he couldn't possibly know she'd found Caitlyn's diamond engagement ring and phone in Hank's carryall, how her husband didn't have a real explanation for why he had them. While the police had closed the case on Caitlyn's murder—the man who'd killed her was dead now, too—she still didn't know if Hank had played a role in it.

What Tommy probably meant was that he knew about Caitlyn's death and how it had come so soon after Kate's wedding—not to mention that she had been shot by Caitlyn's killer—but she was tongue-tied as she struggled with how to respond.

Her hesitation prompted him to pivot. "So, what are you doing here? In this neighborhood, I mean."

She gave him a small smile. "Walking." It seemed the simplest and easiest explanation. He didn't have to know she was living two blocks away in a two-room sublet instead of with her husband in his opulent Central Park West penthouse.

"Remember how we walked all the way to Chinatown for dumplings in the rain that time?" He grinned.

"Because the subway line broke down, and we didn't have cab fare," she added, smiling at the memory.

He snorted. "Well, you certainly have the cab fare now."

Was it her imagination or did he sound a tad bit resentful? On one hand, she couldn't blame him; she was married to a billionaire. But on the other hand, *he'd* never asked her to marry him. He broke up with her right before graduation and then headed off to Europe with Molly Fitzroy, leaving her with a broken heart. It was a long time before she got over him; she'd married her first husband on the rebound. A big mistake.

Kate stood up a little straighter as she tightened her hold on her cup, her mouth set in a grim line. "Yes, I suppose I do have the cab fare."

Tommy chuckled, his eyes twinkling. "No need to get your back up, Mrs. Tudor."

She couldn't help herself. Kate relaxed, smiled back, but then felt her cell phone buzz in her trousers' pocket. She pulled it out to check the caller ID. "I've got to take this," she told him.

He nodded. "I understand." He probably thought it was Hank. "Maybe we could meet up sometime. Take a walk down memory lane. We can get a pastry at the Hungarian bakery. Like old times." He produced a pen and scrawled a number on her coffee cup. "Don't lose it," he said, grinning as he sauntered away.

Kate's phone was still buzzing as she stared after him. He hadn't even given her a backward glance, and she was surprised that she'd hoped he would. Absently, she answered the call.

"Hi, Anna," she said. Anna Klein, Hank's fourth wife. "What's up?"

"Have you seen Lizzie?"

"No, why would I?" As far as Kate knew, Hank's daughter Lizzie and her younger brother, Ted, were still at the house on Martha's Vineyard with their half sister, Maril, at least until they were packed up and sent back to their boarding schools for the fall semester.

"I just thought I'd check with you." Anna's voice was laced with stress.

"What's going on?" Kate had started to walk again but stopped now, her hand gripping the phone. Something was definitely wrong. And Anna's next words validated her concern.

"Lizzie's missing."

2

"What do you mean Lizzie's missing?" Kate asked.

"She was supposed to meet a friend at the beach, but she never showed."

Kate didn't like the sound of that. Lizzie was almost twelve and a lot more mature than most girls her age, but she was still a child.

She had another thought that caused her to take pause. Lizzie's mother, Nan, had disappeared from that very same house on Martha's Vineyard eight years ago, and no one had seen or heard from her since.

"How long?" Kate asked. "I mean, how long has she been missing?"

"Since yesterday. Maril called me last night. I came out to the Vineyard this morning." Anna had been a surrogate mother to Hank's children since her short marriage to their father, so it wasn't a surprise she'd gone to the island to help look for Lizzie and take care of Ted. "There's no sign of her, Kate."

"You don't think she ran away, do you?"

"That's what the police think."

"But not you."

Anna was quiet a moment, then said, "No." Something lingered in her tone, though, that Kate couldn't pinpoint.

"Why not?"

"It's just, well, it reminds me a little of Joan."

Anna's wife, Joan Carey, had vanished two months ago, not long after Caitlyn Howard's body was found, and hadn't turned up—dead or alive—since. All the police had found was one of her sneakers with blood on it. Everyone was assuming Joan had been killed by the same man who'd killed Caitlyn—and shot Kate in her apartment.

"Will Stafford is dead," Kate gently reminded her. "He can't hurt anyone anymore." It was cold comfort, though, and something she'd been repeating to herself on a daily basis.

"I know, it's just . . ."

Anna wasn't convinced that Joan was dead. Or at least she couldn't let herself believe it.

"For now, Lizzie's the focus, okay?" Kate said softly.

"I know." Anna took a breath. "Hank and Cromwell have brought in a private investigator."

"Are they sure they want to go that route?" Kate asked.

"What do you think?"

Kate realized how ridiculous her question was. Of course they would hire their own investigator. It was the way Hank Tudor operated. He wasn't a fan of the police, and he had a lot of resources at his fingertips. Anyway, the more people looking for Lizzie the better.

Kate resumed her walk back toward her apartment. She took the last drink of her coffee and was about to toss it into a trash can on the corner when she saw Tommy's phone number scrawled on the side. After only a moment of hesitation, she dropped the cup in the can.

"Is there anything I can do?" Kate asked, instantly regretting the question. What if Anna wanted her to go to the Vineyard? Was Hank there, too? He must be, but she couldn't bring herself to ask about him. She wasn't ready to see her husband, although the longer their estrangement went on, the easier it was to accept that perhaps their marriage was over.

She touched her abdomen as though she had felt the baby inside her. She hadn't told him about the pregnancy yet, but she didn't want that to be the only reason they reconciled.

"I don't think so," Anna said, and Kate let out a sigh of relief that she hoped wasn't audible. "I just wanted to check in with you."

"I'm sure she's fine," Kate said, although a tinge of worry was growing. "Keep me posted, okay? And, really, if there's anything I can do . . ." She felt confident repeating the offer, since this time she knew she wouldn't be called on for anything.

"Will do," Anna said, ending the call.

Kate tucked her phone back in her pocket. If she were still Hank's assistant, she'd be on the front lines, coordinating with the private investigator and making sure the media wasn't getting too close.

The media. She hadn't asked Anna about that. Stopping again on the sidewalk, she took out her phone and did a simple search. The *Associated Press* had posted a story about Lizzie's disappearance an hour ago. If she hadn't been out getting a coffee and running into Tommy Seymour, she probably would have seen it before Anna's call.

Tommy. He was a journalist. Was it a coincidence that she'd run into him? Did he know about Lizzie? Was that the reason he showed up out of the blue? Kate felt a strong urge to confront him, ask him if he had an ulterior motive.

She glanced back at the trash can where she'd dropped the cup with his number on it. No, she wasn't going to go back for it. It was in the garbage now, and that's where she needed to leave it. If she made a big deal about it, he'd figure there *was* a story and wouldn't let it go.

And even if it had truly been a random encounter, it had been too long and too much had happened in the years since she'd been with Tommy to revisit any sort of relationship—even a casual one. Kate didn't think she could ever be casual about Tommy, even now. Too much water under that bridge.

Her mind drifted as she walked, not even hearing the traffic that passed her. Living in the city had made her immune to its sounds.

If Lizzie had run away, where would she have gone? She was on Martha's Vineyard. There was no way to get off the island except by boat or plane, although it would be easy enough for someone, even a child, to walk on board the ferry that went to the mainland at Cape Cod. But then what? Where would the girl go from there?

Kate wasn't convinced Lizzie would leave on her own without a good reason. But she was hard-pressed to think of what that might be. Hank's children had everything they wanted. Or did they? Their father was hardly ever around. Lizzie's mother had abandoned her, and Ted's mother had died from complications after his birth. They had seen a string of stepmothers come in and out of their lives. While Anna and Joan had filled the gap, the children were still sent away to school—and then Joan vanished. As she thought about it, it struck Kate that she wasn't blameless, either, and a rush of guilt overcame her. While Kate had stepped away from her marriage, Lizzie would see only that Kate had left her, too. Considering all of that, maybe it wasn't such a stretch that Lizzie might run away.

There were stories all the time in the news about girls disappearing, but they were always just faces and names. Not girls Kate actually knew—and, yes, cared about. Because despite being estranged from her husband, in the short time she'd spent with Lizzie, Kate had enjoyed her company. Lizzie was sometimes far too serious, but she had a playful side and was very protective of Ted.

Kate wondered how Ted was handling this. He and his sister were close, despite their four-year age difference. She hoped he was okay. She'd been so distracted when talking to Anna that she'd neglected to ask about him.

The apartment wasn't too far, just another block. She considered stopping at the corner market at 110th and Broadway for some oranges. She'd had a craving for them all summer, and the juicer in the kitchen had come in handy. But she'd gone only half a block when a long black limousine slowed and then pulled up against the curb next to her. The door swung open, and she did a double take. Her husband's attorney, Thomas Cromwell, got out.

"What are you doing here?" she demanded.

Cromwell gave a snort. "Nice to see you, too, Mrs. Tudor."

Kate crossed her arms over her chest. "What do you want?" she asked, although after her conversation with Anna, she was drawing lines between this surprise confrontation and Lizzie's disappearance.

"Time for you to go home to your husband. This"—he waved his arm around—"little excursion of yours is over."

3

Kate bit down her anger. "It's over when I say it is," she hissed at him, glancing around to make sure she wasn't overheard, but none of the passersby were paying any attention to them.

Cromwell shook his head. "Not this time. He needs you back."

His tone had changed slightly, and Kate heard his concern. Despite herself, she softened.

"It's Lizzie, isn't it?" she asked, aware of the anxiety in her voice.

"So, you've heard."

"I just talked to Anna."

"I should have known," he said. *No fraternizing between wives*, he'd said when she and Anna had become close earlier this summer.

"I'm glad she called. I wouldn't have wanted to find out on TV or on the internet." She hesitated, then added, "She wanted to know if I'd seen Lizzie, but I haven't."

Cromwell didn't respond, merely indicated she should get into the limo. Kate froze.

"I'm not going to bite," he said. He wasn't a man who showed his emotions, but the worry that was etched in his forehead abated her apprehension. While Kate didn't entirely trust Cromwell or his tactics as Hank's attorney, she knew there was a heart lurking somewhere inside him. She'd had a rare glimpse of it when he told her about his wife who'd died of breast cancer, and she could see a flash of that humanity in his eyes now.

She got in and settled into the leather seat.

"We'll stop at the sublet, and you can pack a bag," he said, tapping on the glass between them and the driver, and the car eased back onto Broadway. "We'll take the jet from Teterboro to the Vineyard."

Kate had figured Cromwell would take her to Hank's penthouse on Central Park West, so this was a surprise, but she should be thankful he hadn't already gotten into the apartment and packed for her.

While she had a momentary flashback of the forced togetherness in Greenwich after Caitlyn's body was discovered, she looked forward to seeing Anna again. The two women had formed an odd connection as they were sequestered at Anna's inn, next door to the crime scene.

"Do *you* think Lizzie ran away?" she asked.

He was quiet a moment, then said, "No." Something lingered in his tone, though, that Kate couldn't pinpoint.

"Why not?"

He pursed his lips, clearly weighing how much to tell her. Finally: "There's been a ransom request."

Kate frowned. "Anna didn't say anything about that."

"No. She doesn't know."

"Why not?"

"The fewer who know, the better."

"So why tell *me*? I'm not even living there." As she said it, she realized just how removed she'd become from her husband and his family.

Cromwell leveled his gaze at her. "This is why you have to come back," he said.

Kate was confused. "I'm not exactly sure why. Does Hank want me to help with the press?" She again thought about Tommy Seymour and how he'd shown up out of nowhere after all these years. It was a good thing Tommy had left when Anna called—and before Cromwell arrived. It wouldn't be good if Cromwell—and, by extension, Hank—discovered she'd been talking to a journalist. That was worse than a little flirting with someone from her past.

"No. But if someone can take Lizzie . . ." Cromwell's voice trailed off.

Kate realized the implication: then someone could take *her.* Hank was worried about her, about her safety. But where had he been two months ago when Will Stafford broke into her apartment and shot her? In Dubai, that's where, after they'd had a fight. And after she'd discovered Caitlyn's phone in his carryall.

"He doesn't want anything like that to happen again," Cromwell was saying, reading her mind.

"I don't understand, though. If there's been a ransom request, why do the police think she ran away?" Even before she finished asking the question, she knew the answer, and Cromwell confirmed it.

"We've been instructed not to tell the police." Cromwell's tone was steady, but she could hear frustration rumbling beneath his words. "We've hired a private investigator."

She didn't let on that Anna had already told her that. It made more sense now, not to rely on the police.

"When is the payoff?" Kate asked. Was *payoff* the right word?

"Don't worry about that, we've got it under control."

It certainly didn't seem like they had anything under control. Lizzie had been kidnapped.

"How much is the ransom?" she asked.

"Five million."

She gasped. Not that Hank couldn't afford it—of course he could—but just hearing the amount was shocking.

Cromwell leaned toward her, his elbows on his knees, his eyes locking with hers. "You need to tell him."

"Tell who what?" Kate asked, suddenly suspicious that Cromwell *had* seen her with Tommy.

He gave a short snort and shook his head. "You can't hide it much longer." His gaze moved to her abdomen.

Instinctively, she crossed her arms, guarded now for a different reason.

"What are you afraid of?" he asked.

How to explain? Did she even have to?

"He had nothing to do with Caitlyn's death," Cromwell said definitively, as though he knew it for a fact.

Kate had lain awake at night, wondering. Neither her husband nor Cromwell were strangers to getting their hands dirty when necessary. While they may not have killed Caitlyn themselves, hiring Will Stafford to do it would not have been out of the realm of possibility. The police had discovered a large deposit of cryptocurrency in an account Stafford had, although they couldn't trace its source.

Caitlyn had also been pregnant when she died, and Hank was the father of her baby. He had arranged an "appointment" for her—one she clearly didn't want to keep—and suddenly she was murdered.

"He'll be happy about the baby," Cromwell said, interrupting her thoughts. "He loves you."

But Hank hadn't come to see her in two months, even though he knew where she was living, so she wasn't convinced.

Cromwell's phone pinged, and he shifted around in his seat as he answered. Kate was happy that someone else had his attention. She didn't want to think about Hank, not now, when Lizzie had been taken. She shivered with the thought.

Kate attempted to reassure herself. Hank would pay the ransom; the girl would be with her father soon. Kate certainly wouldn't want to be whoever had taken Lizzie. Hank's wrath and punishment wouldn't be worth five million when it was all over.

"Are you sure?"

Cromwell's sharp tone caused her to look over at him. Was it about Lizzie? Kate's heart began to beat faster.

"Let me know as soon as you can," he instructed the person on the other end of the conversation before ending the call. He shook his head, gave a short laugh. He seemed flustered; curious, because it was a state in which Kate had never seen him before.

"What is it?" Kate asked.

"Nan Tudor."

"What about her?"

"She's back."

4
NAN

Nan Tudor handed her passport to the customs agent, watching him closely as his eyes moved from the photograph to her face. Did he recognize her? It had been so long since she'd used her own name, eight years now. When she'd left the country, she'd had false documents, thanks to a connection her husband didn't know about. He'd prided himself on thinking he knew all her secrets, but he didn't know everything. She'd made sure of that. Just in case. There were a lot of possible "just in cases," which was why she'd kept her real passport and had it renewed at the embassy in Paris.

The customs agent slid her passport back toward her. "Welcome home," he said gruffly, his attention already moving on to the gentleman behind her in line.

Home. That was no longer accurate. The longer she'd been away, the more Nan didn't think she'd ever come back to the States.

When she'd first left, she'd expected her husband to look for her. The body she'd left behind didn't share her DNA, and she knew it wouldn't take long for everyone to realize she was still alive somewhere. She could have been found if he'd really tried. But Hank had merely gone through the motions of looking for her, proving that she'd made the right decision.

Hank divorced her in absentia and had married four times since. So far there had been six wives; one had come before her. He'd divorced Catherine to be with her—although it had taken seven long years, thanks to Catherine's tenacity and firm belief that Hank was hers and hers alone. In retrospect, Nan wished Catherine hadn't given up. It would have saved them both a lot of anguish. But her children were a reminder that she and Hank Tudor had shared an idyllic life—for a little while at least.

While Harry's resemblance to his father had grown stronger with each year, she pushed it aside with the conviction that he never had to know Hank Tudor, never had to know that she'd escaped a marriage that almost destroyed her. But her son was getting older—he was eight now—and starting to ask questions. Nan was vague in her answers, only telling him his father was American and they were divorced. Both of which were true. She wasn't sure how long she could hold him off, though, before the questions became more persistent.

As she wheeled her carry-on behind her, tucking her passport into her bag, she realized that this trip was most likely the catalyst for the truth—at least some of it.

She felt her phone buzz and pulled it out of her pocket. A text.

Take the shuttle to the rental car terminal.

She didn't recognize the number it came from. Each of the texts she'd received had been from different numbers.

Nan had made the flight reservations as instructed by the anonymous texter two days ago. She couldn't take any chances that they wouldn't really kill her daughter if she didn't come back—although she still wasn't convinced Lizzie had actually been taken. She had seen nothing online about an abduction of Hank Tudor's daughter, and because of his status, if it had happened, it would most definitely be reported. Someone was toying with her.

She supposed she could have reached out to Hank: *Surprise! I'm alive and well, and, by the way, how is Lizzie? Can I talk to her?* No, it was less complicated to follow the instructions, take a few days out of her life, and make sure her daughter was okay before disappearing again. She grieved the death of her friend Margaret, who had been her lifeline to Lizzie ever since she'd left.

As she'd made the arrangements for the trip and for Harry's care—she had no idea just how long she'd be gone—Nan found her initial fear replaced by anger. She had her suspicions as to who was behind this, and she was almost certain a confrontation was expected. She had to be on guard, and it was possible if she played her cards right that she could slip in and out unscathed.

Nan made her way toward the signs leading to ground transportation. She didn't need to go to baggage claim. She had only this one suitcase. She glanced around, trying not to be obvious, but *someone* was following her every move.

A shuttle to the rental car center was waiting at the curb when she emerged. She hefted her carry-on up the stairs and kept it by her side rather than putting it with the other suitcases in the front of the bus. Within minutes, the driver shut the doors, and the shuttle began to move. She still didn't know where she was going; the invisible person on the other side of the texts was pulling all the strings.

Her phone vibrated again. Now the text contained a link. Normally she didn't like clicking on links—who knew whether it would put a virus on her phone? But since she already had an unknown person stalking her, what would it matter?

The link was to an *Associated Press* story. Elizabeth Tudor was missing; an Amber Alert had been issued.

Nan bit the inside of her cheek to keep from crying out. It was true. It was real. Someone *had* taken her daughter. She'd been hoping that it was just a façade, a trick to get her to come back, and that her daughter wasn't really in any danger at all.

Do you want to know where you're going? the next text read, and an image of a map popped onto the screen.

Martha's Vineyard.

She really *was* going home.

But then she realized something. Frowning, she clicked on the news story again.

According to the story, Lizzie had gone missing yesterday. But Nan had gotten the first texts instructing her to leave for Boston *two* days ago. When Lizzie was still safe at home.

5
CATHERINE

The flight had landed on time. By now, That Woman should be getting into her rental car and starting the trip to Martha's Vineyard, which the map application showed should take a little less than three hours—as long as she caught the ferry from Woods Hole on time.

Catherine shut her laptop and poured herself another cup of coffee, despite the butterflies in her stomach. The plate with the untouched slice of toast sat on the kitchen island beside her.

"You should eat something, Mrs. Catherine," Lourdes said as she came into the kitchen.

"I'm not very hungry this morning," she admitted. It wasn't the first morning she'd skipped breakfast recently, and she wondered if she shouldn't force herself. Lourdes already knew about her agoraphobia. It wouldn't do if she also suspected her of anorexia. Lourdes had a habit of reporting back to her daughter, and the last thing Catherine needed was to have Maril preoccupied with her eating habits. Maril already spent more time than she should trying to get Catherine out of the house.

The funny thing was, after years of isolating herself within these walls, she'd started venturing out. So far, no one knew about her short trips to the store, to the beach, to the library. It wasn't as though anyone would recognize her these days, her invisibility shielding her like a cloak. Her time as Mrs. Hank Tudor was long over, but she still believed that Hank would return to her so she could rightfully take her place beside him again. That was the reason why she'd begun to leave the house. Hank needed a wife who didn't rely on Xanax to step across her own threshold.

Catherine had also begun an exercise regimen. She'd lost a few pounds, but mostly she relished the feeling of being stronger physically. She debated joining a gym—what better way to acclimate to outside life? But when she thought more about it, she realized that she'd have to be gone too long, and she wasn't ready for that yet. Instead, she consulted videos on the internet, invested in weights and yoga mats and a rowing machine. Lourdes was curious about her new home gym, which she'd set up in one of the spare rooms upstairs, and Maril was ecstatic.

"Mummy! I could come over and work out with you!"

While pleased with Maril's enthusiasm, "working out" together wasn't part of the plan. She gently let her daughter down by saying that her optimal time to exercise was midmorning, and of course Maril would be at work.

As Catherine carried her coffee into the den, she pondered the changes she'd been making in her life the past couple of months. Hank was still separated from his sixth wife; Catherine wondered why it was taking so long for him to divorce her. In her weaker moments, she'd debated reaching out to him, but she wanted to make sure that the break with Kate Parker was permanent before doing so. He'd jumped from wife to wife so quickly, and the timing had to be just right.

She also had to make sure that Nan was truly out of the way. While it had been more than eight years since Hank's second wife had disappeared and he'd had four wives since, Catherine wasn't confident that if she returned, Hank would discard her. Being separated from his sixth wife meant he was back on the market. Catherine had seen how Nan had once turned her husband's head, how besotted with her he'd been. That Woman had bewitched him. There was no guarantee that she wouldn't do it again. Catherine's hate for the woman still simmered, and she recognized that Nan might again be a strong opponent in the fight for Hank's heart.

Especially since the woman had had his son.

Catherine's heart had sunk when she'd learned about the boy. Hank already had three children, but to discover he had another could be too strong a draw. That was why she'd gotten rid of Caitlyn Howard, who was carrying his child.

And why That Woman had to suffer the same fate.

6
KATE

Kate always knew Hank's spies were everywhere, but that they'd actually found Nan Tudor after all this time seemed impossible.

Still, it appeared to be true. Cromwell's expression, while usually so guarded, had shown his surprise—and a touch of fear. She believed him. Yet what did this mean, if Nan Tudor was really back? Back from where? And where was she now? But Cromwell had grown quiet after his pronouncement and refused to say anything else. Kate fidgeted with annoyance and frustration. Had Hank known where Nan was all this time and that's how he knew she was "back"? Kate had spent enough time working for Hank and being part of his world to know that if he didn't want her to know something, she wouldn't. And she'd also learned that it might be best not knowing.

But this. This was different. This was a wife he'd once loved even more than he'd loved Caitlyn. Even more than he might have ever loved *her*.

That made her take pause. Did it even matter now?

"How do you know this, that she's back?" Kate's eyes held Cromwell's, but she couldn't read what he was thinking.

The surprise was gone, and he gave her a slow, condescending smile. "You know better than to ask questions, Kate."

She wanted to say, *Well, you brought it up*. She wouldn't have known anything otherwise, if he hadn't been caught off guard. This was not expected—and not welcome—news.

"What do you think it means?" She couldn't help but press.

"She's been gone a long time" was all he'd say, turning back to his phone, where his fingers were frantically texting with someone. Most likely Hank.

Kate forced herself to think about this practically. If Nan had been in hiding somewhere, what would cause her to reemerge now?

Lizzie. It had to be Lizzie. That was the most logical reason. The press had already reported it; it was more than possible that Nan had seen the story and decided she had to look for her daughter.

But that raised another question. Nan had abandoned her daughter as well as Hank. So why would Lizzie being missing change anything?

Nan had left long before Kate had begun working for Hank, although their affair and marriage had been extensively examined in the public eye. All Kate knew about the woman's private life came from a diary that had inadvertently come into Anna's possession—a diary that Hank clearly did not know about. Nan had been scared for her life, scared that her husband was trying to kill her, so she left. The diary had no mention of any friends to speak of—were there any? Since Hank had hired a private investigator to try to find his wife when she vanished, Kate had to assume that anyone Nan knew had been interviewed. And yet no one had come forward with any information about where she might be.

But now she was back.

If Kate were still Hank's assistant, what would she do? First, she'd make sure the media didn't find out. That would be the last thing Hank would need right now, what with Lizzie's kidnapping. While a missing daughter was already fodder for the press, the sudden appearance of that daughter's mother after more than eight years in hiding might overshadow everything.

Kate could see it now: headlines in all the media outlets, the gossip would be nonstop.

Second, she'd make sure Hank's current wife didn't find out, either.

Well, it was too late for that.

It was ironic that Cromwell, Hank's most trustworthy employee, had been the one to tell her. Of course he'd been caught off guard, but Hank wouldn't see it that way. Kate wondered if she should be worried for Cromwell. Hank was known for his ruthlessness and how quickly a friend could turn into an enemy.

But then she remembered: he was *Tom Cromwell*. He'd survived worse. Hadn't he?

The limo slid into a convenient spot just a couple of doors away from the brownstone where Kate was subletting her apartment. Cromwell seemed just as surprised as she was that they'd arrived so quickly. What did Cromwell know about Nan's disappearance? It was almost as though he really had thought she was dead and the fact that she wasn't was unnerving him.

The rumors about the headless body of a woman found near Hank's Martha's Vineyard house had swirled for years, and even though the police had used DNA to eliminate Nan Tudor as the victim, it didn't dissuade people from believing it was her. But something Kate had heard just two months ago—*money can cover anything up*—made her also question whether the so-far-unidentified woman might actually be Nan—and whether her husband might have had something to do with her death.

But if Nan Tudor was alive and well, then her doubts about Hank were for naught. And if he'd been telling the truth about that, then maybe he really wasn't responsible for Caitlyn Howard's murder, either.

She desperately wished that were so. She didn't want to be so wrong about the man she'd vowed to love until death.

The chauffeur came around to the side of the limo and opened the door. She paused on the sidewalk when Cromwell got out with her.

"He told me not to leave your side," he explained, and Kate knew he was talking about Hank. Maybe her husband really *was* worried about her safety after all. Still, having a babysitter irked her. She'd been alone long enough—before Hank and during the past two months—that she was perfectly capable of packing her own bag and bringing it down to the car herself.

She took two steps at a time, with Cromwell on her heels, until she reached the second floor, where she let herself into the apartment. She left him in the living room as she went into the bedroom to pack a bag. She pulled the suitcase out of the closet, then hesitated. How long would she be gone? How much should she bring?

Erring on the side of practicality and comfort, she set out a couple of pairs of jeans, a fleece, three T-shirts, and two sweaters. She was certain there weren't any formal dinners on the agenda. The white canvas sneakers on her feet were the only ones she'd need.

As she folded and packed, she wondered how long it would be before she wouldn't be able to fit into the jeans any longer. They were already getting a tad tight.

Cromwell was standing in the middle of the living room with the phone to his ear when she came out. He cocked his head toward the door, still murmuring to whoever was on the other line. Kate was used to this, used to ignoring phone calls and conversations she had no part in, so she started back down the stairs, hearing Cromwell shut the door firmly behind him.

The driver took her bag, and she was about to get back in the car when Cromwell put his hand up.

"Change of plans," he said. "You'll be going to the penthouse after all."

"So not the Vineyard?"

"You'll leave later today."

"Are you staying with me?" Kate didn't like the idea of being cooped up at the penthouse with Cromwell, even though there was plenty of room and they probably wouldn't even have to see each other.

Cromwell gave a short snort. "No."

It hadn't been a silly question, had it? "But I assume that someone will be watching me."

"Yes."

He said a few words to the driver, who glanced briefly at her and then nodded. Kate remembered how her life had been orchestrated by her husband, both before and after they married. She wished she could go back in time, to just a half an hour ago, when she'd unexpectedly run into Tommy Seymour, who, while having broken her heart, was uncomplicated.

She was thinking this as she climbed back into the limo—and saw Hank sitting in the seat across from her.

"Hello, Kate," he said softly.

7

Kate forced herself to keep her expression neutral, but the sudden appearance of her husband after two months threw her off. She struggled with what to say: *What are you doing here? Why aren't you out looking for your daughter? Why haven't you called or come to see me? Did you have anything to do with Caitlyn's murder? How do you and Cromwell know Nan Tudor is back?*

Instead, she said calmly, as though they'd run into each other at a cocktail party and were making small talk, "I thought you were on the Vineyard."

He gave her a smile. It was the one she remembered from their most intimate moments, the one that had always made her knees grow weak. It wasn't fair that those memories could still be conjured when there was so much that needed to be sorted out between them—if they even wanted to sort them out.

"I had to come back to the city unexpectedly."

"What about Lizzie?"

"It *is* about Lizzie."

"You don't think she's in New York, do you?" Kate wasn't sure if Cromwell was supposed to tell her about the ransom request, so she decided to see if Hank would tell her himself.

"I had to talk to the bank. I told Tom to update you on the situation."

She shouldn't have expected Cromwell would tell her anything that Hank didn't want her to know. Except, perhaps, about Nan Tudor.

"You have to get the money," she guessed.

He nodded. "We were given thirty-six hours, and I hope it won't take longer. It's a lot of money. A lot of logistics to work out."

Hank was talking to her as though no time had passed, as though they hadn't been living apart with no communication.

"They want it in cash?" She couldn't keep the surprise out of her voice.

"Some of it."

"Only some?"

"A million."

It would be easier to make a wire transfer for the full amount to an offshore account somewhere, an account that couldn't be traced. Asking for cash seemed rather old-fashioned, not to mention risky. There would have to be a drop-off, which meant a possibility that whoever was demanding the money could be caught.

"Are you sure?" she asked. "I mean, are you sure that they'll let her go once they get the money?" And then she had another thought. "Are you sure they even have her? Maybe she really did just run away."

Hank pulled out his phone and tapped the screen a couple of times before turning it so she could see it.

A photograph of a girl with duct tape over her mouth and a blindfold covering her eyes. Kate wanted to say it could be anyone, but she recognized the fiery red hair pulled back to show off the distinctive widow's peak and the small mole above her left eye. It was Lizzie. And it terrified her.

"My god, Hank," she whispered, looking up at him. She saw it now, the fear and worry in his eyes. She was certain her own matched his.

Hank shoved the phone back into his pocket. "We've been told we'll get instructions on when to make the wire transfer and where to deliver the cash, but as of now, this is all we know."

He was speaking in the plural, like he did when he was discussing a business transaction. It was probably easier for him to look at it that way, to try to keep his emotions out of it, but she heard the slight tremor in his voice.

Instinctively, Kate reached across and put her hand on his knee. "I'm so sorry."

He grasped her hand and held it tight. "Nothing you can do about it. But I want to keep you close."

"I'm not going anywhere," Kate assured him. Was it an empty promise? Was she saying that only because he was vulnerable, because his daughter had been taken? She decided not to think about that; she only wanted to help him get through this. That had been her job, after all, helping him get through various crises for the past three years.

She shifted to the seat next to her husband, and he put his arm around her.

"I've missed you," he whispered in her ear.

She had an urge to tell him about the baby, but this wasn't the time or the place. He had to focus on Lizzie, get her home before Kate told him he was going to be a father again.

His phone buzzed with a text message, and he pulled his arm away, turning in his seat, dismissing her. What had she expected? Kate moved back to the seat across from him, the distance between them more than merely physical. His fingers were moving on the screen as he tapped out a return message, not even glancing up at her. Was it about Lizzie—or Nan?

The thought startled her. Yet the more she thought about it, it really couldn't be a coincidence that Nan Tudor might have returned just when her daughter went missing. Kate wasn't inclined to believe in coincidence, and this one would be a big stretch.

Hank tucked his phone back in his pocket, but they'd been interrupted, and his attention was still elsewhere.

"Was that about Lizzie?" she asked tentatively.

His head snapped up, and he seemed almost surprised to see her there. He shook his head. "No," he said.

"Was it about Nan?" She was taking a risk bringing this up, but she couldn't keep her curiosity at bay.

Hank's mouth twitched, but she couldn't tell if it was anger or amusement. "You always knew things before you were supposed to," he said. "How do you do it?"

Kate shrugged, but she didn't say anything.

"I assume Cromwell told you."

"It was only because I was there when he got the call," she explained. "He was in shock." Maybe that was an overstatement, but not by much. "He told me before he realized what he was saying."

Hank leveled his gaze at her, as if daring her to ask for more details. She wasn't going to give him the satisfaction, even though she wanted to.

Finally, he sighed. "Nan came through customs a little while ago at Logan."

The airport in Boston. "From where?"

"Paris."

That wasn't a surprise. Nan Tudor had spent several years in Paris and always wanted to return, at least according to the journal she'd kept. Since Hank didn't know about the journal, Kate pretended that this was news to her. "She's been there the whole time?"

Hank shook his head. "I have no idea."

Kate weighed her next question carefully. "Then how do you know she came through customs?"

"We've had someone on payroll whose job it is to know things like this."

Kate thought about her own situation. How, despite moving into a sublet farther uptown, she was sure Hank had been keeping track of her movements. She'd sensed that she'd been followed on several occasions but didn't give it much thought. Hank knew where she was, and if he wanted to see her, he could.

But now, something else dawned on her. If he'd had her watched, he must know that she'd had more than one appointment at the obstetrician's office—and what those visits would mean. Cromwell obviously knew, so Hank must, too. He was waiting on her to tell him. Maybe it *was* time. Kate opened her mouth, but before she could say anything, his phone buzzed again. She sighed with relief as he turned his attention back to his phone.

Kate gazed out the window and watched the city pass by. She thought about the oranges she was going to buy and wished she had one right now. Would there be food at the penthouse? Hank rarely ate at home; anyway, he'd been at the Vineyard and possibly traveling before that. It was likely he hadn't stayed at the penthouse in a while. She hoped someone had thought ahead to stock the kitchen for a couple of meals.

Immediately she chastised herself for thinking about food when Lizzie was being held captive somewhere. But, she rationalized, they had to eat.

Hank cleared his throat loudly, and she looked back at him. His eyes were dark.

"What's going on?" she asked.

"Why don't you tell me why you were talking to a journalist?"

8

Hank was looking at her expectantly. Cromwell must have seen her with Tommy on the sidewalk after all.

"He wasn't a journalist," Kate explained. "I mean, he is a journalist, but we were friends in college. We ran into each other in the coffee shop. It was nothing." As she spoke, she realized she was omitting a lot about her relationship with Tommy Seymour. Hank didn't have to know their entire history, although if she were to hazard a guess, he already knew enough about her college beau. Background checks and investigations weren't just for employees; wives were subject to the same scrutiny.

Hank studied her face, as though looking for a lie. She didn't want to say any more; otherwise, it might look as though she was protesting too much.

"A college *friend*?" he asked warily.

"Yes. We were at Columbia together." What did he expect her to say? If he wanted her to admit that she and Tommy had once been lovers, he was going to have to ask directly. She wasn't going to make it easy for him.

"You know he works for the *Associated Press*?"

She sighed. "Yes. He covers politics in Washington."

Hank shook his head. "Not anymore."

Kate frowned. "What do you mean?"

"You don't know?"

Hank was teasing her like a cat with a mouse, and she didn't like it. But she was curious about Tommy, and Hank seemed to know *something*.

"He's been temporarily reassigned. Apparently, he had an inappropriate relationship with a female source." Hank leaned back in his seat and watched for her reaction.

She wasn't going to give him the satisfaction. Instead, she rolled her eyes. "He was always a ladies' man," she said, her tone belying the emotions she was feeling. Tommy could be so stupid about women, although she was sure that when they were together, he hadn't strayed. She would have known if he had.

"As long as you're not going to see him again," Hank said softly, the threat beneath his tone.

Kate bristled. "It's not as though you've been around," she snapped, unable to stop herself. "Two months. It's taken two months and the abduction of your daughter to see me?" She was aware her voice was getting louder with each word. She took a deep breath. "I don't want to go back to the penthouse, Hank," she said. "Why don't you just put me on the jet so I can go be with Anna? She needs me."

Hank studied her face for a few moments, and it frustrated her that she couldn't read him. Finally, he tapped on the window between them and the driver, and it rolled down. "You'll drop me at the penthouse and then take Mrs. Tudor to Teterboro," he told the driver. He punched a number into his phone. "Get the jet ready. Yes, she's going now after all."

He ended the call and turned to her. "Is that what you wanted?" he asked.

Kate hadn't meant to lash out at him. That wasn't productive. She'd forgotten how to handle him, how she should make him feel as though he was the one in control—even when he wasn't.

"You know, Kate, when this is all over, when we have Lizzie back, decisions have to be made." Hank was looking at her expectantly, and she nodded but didn't say anything.

The limo was pulling up in front of their building on Central Park West. It struck her how close it was, how close she'd been to Hank all this time. When the car eased against the sidewalk and stopped, Hank brushed past her, pushing the door open, not waiting for the driver. When he was outside, he leaned in.

"I'll see you on the Vineyard," he said, then stepped away, the door shutting and leaving her alone.

Kate glanced out the window, but Hank had already disappeared into the building. She suddenly wanted to tell the driver to bring her back to her apartment, forget about the airport. While she was concerned about Lizzie, she was certain Hank would find her, bring her home, and whoever had taken her would be caught. Kate had no place in Hank's world any longer. She'd gotten used to her life in limbo, not making any decisions about her marriage. She longed for her apartment, where she could curl up with a good book or get some writing done. She'd started writing a novel, something she'd always wanted to try, to see if it was something she could do after years of writing for other people. She liked living alone, and since she'd been married to Hank for only a couple of weeks before she left, it was what she was comfortable with.

Maybe she *should* tell him she wanted a divorce. Stop all the procrastinating. But something was holding her back—and it wasn't just the baby. She'd spent three years with Hank, and during that time she'd seen a side of him that he rarely allowed others to see. He could be tender, loving, and, yes, even vulnerable. He'd tapped into a passion that she had never experienced with anyone else. But considering everything that had happened, was that enough? The seesawing emotions made her dizzy. She could blame it on being pregnant, on the hormones, but those were just excuses.

Her phone buzzed in her pocket, and she was glad for the interruption. When she fished it out, she saw that it was Anna again. While Hank hadn't told Anna about the ransom request, Kate wondered if she should.

Anna had suspected *something*, not certain that Lizzie had run away, like the police had indicated.

"Yes, Anna?" she asked when she accepted the call.

"Can you talk?"

"Yes. I'm actually in a limo, on my way to the airport. Hank wants me to join you out there."

"Why?"

"Hank thought it would be best if I was there."

"He wants to keep a closer eye on you, you mean," Anna said. "Because he doesn't think Lizzie ran away, and he wants to protect you."

Anna obviously was putting two and two together. "He's considering everything" was all Kate was able to say before Anna spoke again.

"Well, he might want to reconsider that she might have run away, and I don't think you have anything to worry about."

"What does that mean?"

"I think Lizzie has been in touch with her mother."

9

ANNA

Anna wasn't used to feeling like a jumble of nerves. She'd always prided herself on how calm she could be, even when life's stresses piled up. But ever since Joan's disappearance two months ago, it was as though she was wound tighter than a rubber band, ready to snap at any moment. And now Lizzie was missing.

She glanced over at Ted, who was digging holes in the sand with his toes as he stood on the beach, hands clasped behind his back, his face unreadable. She'd tried to talk to him this morning, ask him how he was doing, but all she got was an eye roll. He hadn't spoken since they'd discovered Lizzie was missing, but Anna wasn't ready to call in the child psychiatrists just yet. It was perfectly normal for a little boy to have this reaction when his sister disappears. She just hoped that Lizzie would return soon so everyone could get back to normal.

What was "normal" anyway, though? Her life certainly hadn't been normal since her wife had vanished into thin air, leaving nothing behind but a bloody sneaker.

She wished that she'd been out here with Maril and the children all summer. Hank had asked her to stay, but she went back to Greenwich with Kate, worried that if she was gone, Joan wouldn't know where to find her if she returned. She hadn't considered that her absence might be seen by Lizzie and Ted as a sort of abandonment. Lizzie's mother had already left her; she was the only mother Ted had truly known. Anna's guilt rose. Would Lizzie have gone missing if she'd stayed? It had been selfish of her to leave.

Anna also hadn't considered Maril, how the woman had to turn to fully remote work while caring for her half brother and sister.

"My job is in jeopardy," she'd told Anna last night over her fourth glass of wine on the back porch. "Daddy wants me to quit. Says I'm 'more useful' to him here," she added with air quotes. "He's never wanted me working with his companies. At least not since he divorced my mother. I've thought about resigning. It's not like I haven't had other offers."

Anna was surprised Hank was so easily dismissing his oldest daughter. Maril had recently brokered a merger with a company that was on the forefront of artificial intelligence and, according to news stories, would "bring Tudor Enterprises into the twenty-second century." Maril's deal would bring in billions; she was clearly an asset. But she was also the daughter of his first wife, who had made his life more than difficult—and Maril was collateral damage.

Anna made sympathetic noises, but then something snapped in the other woman.

"I'm getting so tired of trying to prove myself to him. I've spent months on that deal, and without me, it never would have happened. But instead of thanking me, appreciating me, here I am, because this is where he wants me. *You* should have been here," she said angrily. "It's not like you have any responsibilities anymore. I mean, your wife is dead, and you don't have any children of your own."

Anna was taken aback by the attack. She'd always gotten along with Maril. But she chalked it up to the fact that Maril could be feeling guilty about Lizzie. It was on her watch that the girl went missing.

"If you want to leave now, it's no problem," she said softly. "I can take care of Teddy."

Maril glared at her. "You still don't get it, do you? You and I? We don't make those decisions. We're like pawns in his own personal game of chess. He moves us around as he sees fit." She gave a short snort before adding, "Someone needs to change the game."

She'd pushed back her chair and fled the room, leaving Anna alone to look out over the water and the sliver of orange along the horizon.

They were all on their last nerve, she told herself, although Maril had a point. Hank did control their lives—yet Kate had left him and Lizzie was missing. The game had already changed.

Anna had gathered up the wineglasses and made her way into the kitchen, where she washed and carefully dried them before putting them in the cupboard. She stood for a moment, listening, as though expecting to hear Lizzie's voice, Ted's laugh. But the house was still, quiet.

Sometimes she wondered if she couldn't sense Nan Tudor's ghost in the hallways. Nan was everywhere in this house. That could be another reason why Maril was so tense. Nan had replaced her mother in Hank's affections. He'd cast them both aside to pursue the wild and beautiful Nan. Lizzie looked mostly like Hank, with her red hair and long, lean limbs, but her large, dark gray eyes were Nan's. Did Maril see Nan every time she looked at her sister?

Lizzie was only eleven; she wasn't responsible for what had happened before she was born. Anna could only hope Maril wasn't holding it against her.

Anna checked her phone to see if Hank had reached out. He'd left suddenly to go back to the city, no explanation. She assumed it had something to do with Lizzie, which was why she'd called Kate to see if she'd seen the girl. Anna wouldn't put it past Lizzie to make her way to New York on her own if she was so inclined. But Kate hadn't seen her, hadn't even known Lizzie was gone.

The police had left, too, presumably to keep looking, but so far no one had turned up any clue as to where Lizzie had gone. It was possible she was still on the island somewhere. There were no sightings at the ferry, which was the most logical way for the girl to get off the island—if that had been her plan. There hadn't been any sightings anywhere.

Anna climbed the stairs and went into Lizzie's room. The police had been here, searching for anything that might help them locate the girl. When Anna had arrived, she, too, went through the dresser, the closet, even looked under the mattress—who knew where an eleven-year-old girl would hide something? Nothing had changed since the last time she'd been in here. She stood, surveying the double bed with the white duvet cover, the lace curtain floating in the breeze from the open window.

No use in standing there, so Anna made her way down the hall to her room, where she'd stayed at the start of the summer. Her suitcase sat unpacked on the chair in the corner, so she began putting her clothes in the drawers. She might as well get comfortable; she had no idea how long she'd be here.

The bottom drawer was stuck; the wood had most likely expanded with the summer's humidity. Anna yanked on it, and it slid open with a squeak that grated on her. She'd have to find some oil. As she began to push it closed again—why bother putting clothes in there if it would be difficult to open—she heard a thud. She tugged the drawer open further to see a cell phone with blue painter's tape stuck across its back. Anna took it out and turned it over. Maybe this was the reason the drawer had been stuck.

She ripped the tape off the phone and pressed the power button. It lit up with a series of notifications of text messages. There didn't seem to be any password protecting a sign-in, and Anna tapped one of the messages. It filled the screen immediately.

I used to sing to you in French. Do you remember? You were so small, but you were so smart.

What was this? Who was this? There was no name attached to it.

But there was a name on the response: Lizzie.

I remember. I speak French and I'm taking Latin and Spanish and Mandarin, too. I love languages.

The next two texts were in French. Anna didn't know the language, so she skipped to the most recent texts.

I want to see you. I have to see you. This one was from Lizzie.

You can't tell anyone. You have to leave the phone, because they might be able to track it and follow you, and they can't know about me. Can you do that?

Tell me where.

The Vineyard Haven Marina. The boat is called Perseverance.

10
LIZZIE

When I wake up, I can't get my bearings. I've got a little headache, and my arm is sore. That's right, they gave me a shot. I felt it sting, and then my head got all fuzzy.

I hear seagulls squawking and the soft hum of a motor. There's a gentle rocking motion. I must be on a boat. If I concentrate, I can hear waves slapping against the hull. I hope I don't get seasick. I haven't been on many boats in my life, but I've seen *Titanic* and the idea of a vast ocean with no land in sight is terrifying. Not to mention the fact that I'm blindfolded, my hands and feet tied, and something stiff covers my mouth. If the boat sinks, I won't be able to swim. I imagine myself floating, unable to save myself. Unable to breathe.

There's nothing for me to do except think about how I'm going to die.

I really thought I was going to see her. That she was the one who was texting me. But I guess when you're desperate, you see things that aren't there. I've tried not to think about my mother too much, but with Dad marrying Kate—I really hope this is his last wife—I've been thinking of her all the time. I have only brief memories: long dark hair, a gentle touch on my cheek, a low voice singing lullabies. Were they real? I don't know, but I cling to them. I don't have anything else.

When will they find me? Will they ever find me? People disappear all the time—my mother did. I've heard the whispers—*She's dead*—no one willing to say it to my face.

Since she's not here, like I thought she would be, then maybe she *is* dead.

Will they kill me and pretend I've run away? Was this what happened to my mother? Did someone take my mother, too?

A loud crash from somewhere startles me. Is it glass shattering? I can't tell. I hear voices, but they're muffled, like they're speaking into a pillow. I imagine them on deck, talking about where they're taking me. Where will they take me?

I left a clue. I couldn't walk up the gangway and onto this boat without leaving something behind. Just in case. I hope someone finds it.

I try to move my hands, but my fingers are asleep. What if my circulation is completely cut off? Would they have to amputate my hands? My heart begins to race. Would that be worse than drowning?

I can't breathe as I try to suck in air through my mouth. But whatever is covering it—some sort of tape?—is unrelenting and I start to choke. I close my eyes and try to focus. I can breathe through my nose, in and out. I count one, two, three, and the panic subsides.

I have to stay alive. Stay calm. Until they find me.

They have to find me, right? Dad will come looking. He has a lot of power, a lot of money. He loves me. Doesn't he?

It's not like he's around all the time. He works a lot, traveling all over the world. But that doesn't mean he doesn't love me. It doesn't mean if I was gone, he wouldn't miss me.

More voices. Louder now, but I still can't make out what they're saying. Not that it would matter. I'm not going anywhere on my own. Not like this. I concentrate on what's beneath me. I'm not on the floor, because it's soft. A cushion. I shift a little, my head knocking against something hard. The wall? I hate that I can't see. Was this how Helen Keller felt? I read about her in school. Helen Keller had learned how to use her hands to communicate.

Suddenly, the engine sputters and falls silent. What's happening?

Footsteps clamor toward me, and a hand grabs me under my arm and jerks me up so I'm sitting.

"Do as you're told, and you won't get hurt." The voice is thick and raspy, unrecognizable.

So far, though, no one has told me to do anything. But it isn't as though I can tell them that, so I sit, unmoving, waiting for instructions.

"Okay, I think that's good," I hear.

What's good?

The hand pushes me back down onto the cushion, and the footsteps move away.

I'm alone again.

But this time, I recognized the voice. And a new terror pulses through me. The voice belongs to a dead woman.

11
NAN

When Nan arrived at the rental car kiosk, she discovered the car had been prepaid with a credit card with her name on it. All she had to do was agree to keep it on the same card she'd made the reservation with and that she'd fill up the tank before returning it.

Would she be returning it?

The attendant led her to a small sedan that had been reserved for her. Since whoever was texting her had managed to bypass the security on her phone and could locate her, she was willing to bet that there was also a tracking device on the sedan. She thought about the nameless, invisible person sending her the texts. Whoever it was knew her, knew what she was like. Would they really think she'd follow all the rules? Maybe, because of Lizzie. But learning that this was all put in motion before Lizzie had gone missing had changed things.

Nan pointed at the car next to the sedan. "What about that one?" she asked.

The attendant hesitated, glancing at the paperwork on her clipboard. "I've been instructed to give you this car," she said, indicating the sedan.

"I prefer that one," Nan insisted.

The attendant finally shrugged. "Fine."

"Do you have to change the paperwork?"

The woman gave a short snort. "Not at all. Usually, we just tell people to pick the car they want."

Nan took the key and settled into the car, familiarizing herself with the controls before pulling out of the parking spot. She made her way to the exit, handing her paperwork to the attendant in the booth before he lifted the gate, and she drove through. Her phone pinged with a text message, but she ignored it. It was more than possible the texter realized she wasn't driving the assigned car, but she wasn't going to worry about that.

Up until now, she'd been acting on pure maternal instinct, but perhaps she needed to take a breath. Step back and look at the situation a little more objectively.

It was one thing to send ominous messages to lure Nan back to the scene of the crime, so to speak; it was another to actually take the girl. Hank would be trying to find Lizzie, and it was more than possible he'd find her before Nan even showed up on the Vineyard. Hank had resources at his fingertips. He had *people*. He had Tom Cromwell. The man behind the man. He'd shown up at her door, full of threats if she didn't agree to Hank's divorce terms.

"Hank's being generous," Cromwell had told her all those years ago, with that evil glint in his eye. "If you agree, you'll be able to see your daughter from time to time."

In retrospect, she should have signed the agreement. But at the time, it had felt worse than never seeing her again, and Hank would have taken Harry, too. She'd have been left with nothing.

Her phone pinged again with another text. Nan continued to ignore it.

Through her friend Margaret, Nan had hired a private investigator in New Haven when she wanted to get proof that Hank was cheating on her. She'd needed some leverage in the divorce, but as it turned out, Hank was covering his tracks too well, so there was never any evidence. What was the investigator's name? He'd been incredibly discreet, considering who his client was.

Nan got off at the next exit and pulled into a gas station parking lot. She glanced briefly at the texts that had come in:

You'll regret what you're doing.

And then a picture of Lizzie, blindfolded and her mouth covered in duct tape. Nan's heart jumped into her throat, and she bit back tears. Maybe she shouldn't be going off script. Maybe she should resist her urge to rebel and just go to the Vineyard as directed. Give herself up to save her daughter.

She took a few deep breaths, trying to regroup. It wouldn't hurt to see if she could get someone to help her. Help Lizzie. Granted, she was sure Hank had hired his own people, but the more help, the better. Right?

Nan typed "private investigator" and "New Haven" into the search engine on her web browser. And there it was. Wyatt Investigations.

Nan clicked through to the website, relieved that he was still in business. But he'd been fairly young back then, maybe mid-thirties, about her age. She hit the link for the phone number.

"Wyatt Investigations," the receptionist said.

"Mr. Wyatt, please." Nan's tone was that of the woman who'd run one of Tudor Enterprises' multibillion-dollar businesses, who had spearheaded a women-in-management initiative that was still being implemented. It was as though the woman she'd been for the last eight years had disappeared. She wasn't sure even her son would recognize her right now.

"May I ask who's calling?"

"No, you may not."

She heard a catch of breath on the other end, but then after a moment, "Please hold." The woman should be used to clients who demanded anonymity.

There was no music on the line as she held, her hand gripping the phone and hoping what she was doing was the right thing, in more ways than one. Financially, she didn't have a lot of extra money these days; working as a chef in small restaurants kept a roof over their heads and food in the house, and she and Harry didn't need much more than that. But Nan Tudor did.

Finally: "Wyatt here. May I ask whom I'm speaking to?"

"Mr. Wyatt," Nan began, with no hesitation. "Is this a secure line?"

A short chuckle, then, "Yes. How may I help you, Ms. . . . ?"

"Savoy," Nan said. "Louise Savoy." It was the name she'd adopted when she left, the one that she felt most comfortable with these days.

"What can I do for you, Ms. Savoy?"

"I have a delicate matter I'd like you to handle."

"I'm used to delicate matters," he said. "Shall we set up a meeting?"

"It's rather urgent." She swiped her phone screen to look at the map on the navigation app. "Would it be possible for you to come to me, say, within a couple of hours?"

"Where are you?"

"I can meet you in Providence." She checked her phone again and named a small Italian restaurant she remembered from years ago.

"This is highly unusual." But she could hear the curiosity in Wyatt's voice. "I'll be there under one condition."

"What's that?"

"Tell me what this is about. It's a long drive just to get fleeced."

Nan took a deep breath. She had to give him something or he wouldn't show up. "Margaret Pole was a close friend of mine." She wasn't willing to say any more over the phone.

For a moment she thought the call had been dropped, because he didn't say anything. But then: "I only did one job for Maggie," he said softly. "I'll see you in two hours." And he ended the call.

12
KATE

When Anna explained about the text messages on the phone she'd found in the dresser, Kate immediately thought of Nan Tudor and how she was "back."

"You have to tell Hank," she said.

"He's not picking up. I left a voicemail. But I really wanted to run this past you. This has thrown me for a loop."

Kate understood how it could. She'd had Anna read her the texts twice, just because she wasn't sure she'd heard properly.

"Do you really think Lizzie's mother could be alive?" Anna's tone was incredulous. "It's impossible, isn't it?"

Maybe not as impossible as you think, Kate thought. Before talking to Anna, she'd been skeptical that the woman who'd come through customs was really Nan; it might be a case of mistaken identity. But Anna's discovery made it more believable. Still, she was unwilling to tell Anna what she knew about Nan. Hank valued her discretion, and this was sensitive enough that she'd stay quiet for the time being. Kate felt guilty because she didn't like keeping secrets from Anna, although this wouldn't be the first.

"You don't think that Lizzie met her mother on this boat and they sailed away together somewhere, do you?" Anna asked.

"Anything's possible, and we have to look at everything and everyone," Kate said, although she was thinking that since Nan had just gotten into the country, Lizzie had not found her mother on the boat—if that's where she'd gone. And if she had gone there, who did she find? Had Nan sent someone ahead?

She recalled the picture Hank had shown her. Kate had a hard time believing that a mother would do that to her child, which made her think someone else might be involved.

"Since you couldn't get through to Hank, I can go talk to him in person. I'm not far." Before waiting for Anna to respond, Kate tapped on the window between her and the driver. The window slid down. "Can you take me back to the penthouse?"

She saw his frown in the rearview mirror. He wasn't supposed to do anything Hank hadn't instructed him to do.

"It's important," Kate told him, using her public relations voice.

After a second, he nodded, the window rose, and he moved into the next lane to turn around.

"Are you sure you're all right with this?" Anna was asking. "I mean . . ."

Kate knew exactly what she was asking. Anna was more than aware of the tension between Kate and Hank these days, but this was something that needed to be addressed quickly, so she said, "No worries. Can you send me screenshots of the texts? I can show him. We have to keep this between us, though. He can decide what to do with it." Hank might not be happy that Anna had shared the texts with her, but since Kate already knew about Nan, she hoped he'd be okay with it.

The limo pulled up in front of the building just as Anna's texts came through. Kate texted her back with a thumbs-up emoji before the driver opened the door. She gave him a short nod as she stepped out of the car and headed into the building. If the doorman was surprised to see her after two months, he didn't indicate it.

As the elevator rose to the penthouse, Kate felt her stomach start up in knots. She'd told Anna not to worry, that she'd take care of this, but it wasn't like she and Hank were on the same page on things any longer.

He was standing on the other side of the door when it slid open. "What's going on, Kate? Why are you here?"

She'd expected that the concierge downstairs would alert him that she was on her way up.

"Anna's been trying to reach you, but she hasn't gotten through, so she called me," Kate said as she stepped past him, through the foyer, and into the spacious living room. It was exactly as she'd left it, the abstract paintings she hated taunting her. She hadn't been here long enough to replace them.

She felt Hank's hand at the base of her back, his touch momentarily throwing her off. He moved even closer, and her heart began to beat a little more quickly. But then she remembered why she was here. Kate spun around and away from him, her phone in her hand. She held it out for him to see the screenshots. "It seems that Nan may be communicating with Lizzie."

Hank took the phone and scanned the texts, his expression unreadable. "Where did you get these?"

"Anna found a phone in a dresser at the Vineyard house. It was hidden, taped to the bottom of the drawer."

Hank's eyes narrowed slightly.

"I figured since I knew about Nan coming back and Anna didn't, it would be better if I told you about this first. Anna will have questions."

He nodded. "You're right, of course." His eyes hadn't left the phone.

"Do you think Nan sent Lizzie to that boat?"

Hank finally looked up at her, and she could see the anger simmering in his eyes. "She won't get away with this," he whispered, more to himself than to Kate, as he turned his back to her and walked away.

Kate watched until he disappeared around the corner, and she heard the door to the den slam shut. She stood awkwardly, uncertain what to do. Should she go back downstairs and get in the limo and head to the airport? Hank still had her phone, though. She wanted it back, but she knew better than to knock on the door and ask for it.

Kate crossed the room and slid the glass door open, stepping out on the terrace that overlooked Central Park. She could barely hear the street sounds from up here, the blue sky touching the treetops.

"Where is he?"

The loud, guttural voice came from behind her, and Kate turned to see Cromwell standing in the doorway. Hank must have immediately reached out to him about the phone and texts.

"He's in the den."

Cromwell went back into the penthouse, and she moved to the railing, letting the breeze caress her face. She debated whether she should just leave; she was certain the limo driver was still waiting for her. The jet was ready to go. She didn't really need her phone, did she? The phone was merely an excuse. It was more her curiosity about the situation that held her back. If she hung around, maybe she could glean some information as to what was going on.

Again, the irony of being Hank Tudor's wife rather than his assistant meant she wasn't privy to everything that was going on any longer. She wondered where Lindsey, Hank's current assistant, was, and if *she* knew about Lizzie and the ransom request. No, probably not. Hank and Cromwell would keep that one close to the vest. So maybe Kate wasn't as irrelevant as she'd feared, since Hank had told her about it.

A cacophony of voices interrupted her thoughts as she made her way back inside. Hank and Cromwell, their voices raised. Not in anger, but frustration.

"What's going on?" she asked.

They both turned to look at her, seemingly surprised to see her.

Hank took a step toward her. "I didn't realize you were still here."

Kate shrugged nonchalantly—or she hoped it appeared that way. "I thought perhaps we would all go to the Vineyard together when you're ready. No use taking two jets at this point." It sounded like she'd had it planned all along. "Anyway, I need my phone."

Hank exchanged a look with Cromwell that she couldn't read. He held out her phone, and she took it; the tension in the air was palpable. She should have left. Was she being too presumptuous? No longer an assistant—and, maybe, no longer a wife.

"You're right about the jet," Hank said, "but it'll be best if you go on ahead to Anna and Ted."

Kate could read between his words: Faced with this new information about a boat called *Perseverance*, he had to put his resources and time toward that. If he could find Lizzie, perhaps he could capture the kidnapper and not have to pay the five million.

While she wanted to know more, it wasn't realistic to expect that, so she put her phone in her pocket and nodded, starting toward the door.

To her surprise, Hank followed her. He leaned down, his fingers caressing her waist as he brushed her lips with his. "Thank you," he whispered, his breath hot against her ear.

And then he turned, toward Cromwell, away from her.

Kate had stepped out of the lobby and onto the sidewalk when she felt her phone vibrate. Maybe Hank had changed his mind. She glanced at the text that had come through.

Meet me at the Hungarian bakery. I've got information, and I'll only give it to you. Old time's sake.

13

Kate glanced over at the waiting limo as she contemplated Tommy Seymour's text, which indicated that theirs had not been a random encounter, as she'd suspected once she'd learned about Lizzie's disappearance. He had sought her out. How had he found out where she'd be? How did he get her cell number? She hadn't given it to him; he'd written his number on the coffee cup, which she'd promptly discarded.

Regardless, Kate couldn't help but admire the way Tommy had always been able to get people to tell him things without realizing what they were doing. He was an exceptional journalist. His recent suspension was more about how he couldn't keep it in his pants—that wasn't new—than how good he was at his job. And if she knew Tommy, he was doing everything he could to get a story that would put him back in his editors' good graces.

Finding Hank Tudor's daughter would definitely be that story.

Kate had promised Hank she wouldn't have anything to do with Tommy, but she was tempted. Tommy said he had information, and it was more than possible he actually did. He had sources. Yes, Hank had the best people on this, but it didn't hurt to have more, did it? And while she'd been distant from Hank and his family these past two months, she did want to do what she could to bring Lizzie back safe.

Not to mention that this was something she could control, like the days when Hank relied on her to take care of things. She was comfortable in that role, and right now she realized just how much she missed it.

Still, she wasn't about to go meet Tommy. And despite her sudden craving for an almond croissant, she wasn't naïve enough to think that a trip down memory lane was meant merely to conjure old feelings, but rather to trick her into giving him a story. She debated texting him back, but she didn't want anything in writing, so she called him.

"Hey, Kate," he said before she could say anything.

She might as well jump right into it. "What sort of information do you have?"

"What, no foreplay?" His voice was smooth as silk, as though her own flirtatious behavior earlier gave him permission to continue where they'd left off. It threw her a little, remembering how it used to be between them, the easy banter that always had a tinge of sexual innuendo even before they'd started sleeping together.

Kate pushed her memories aside. "The information?" she prodded.

"Can you meet me?"

"Come on, Tommy. That's not possible. I'm on my way out of town." She paused a moment. "By the way, how did you get my cell number?" she asked.

He laughed. "There's an app. All I needed to do was put my phone near yours."

Technology was moving faster than she could keep up. She vowed to keep her cell phone tucked away. "The information, Tommy," she said, pivoting back.

He didn't respond right away.

"Are you still there?" she finally asked.

"Yeah." Did she sense a hint of disappointment that she wasn't going to play along? Before she could consider that further, he continued. "Okay, I know about your stepdaughter. How she's missing. I also heard she didn't run away. She was kidnapped."

Someone on the inside must be feeding him information, since the police didn't know about the kidnapping. But who? Hank paid his people well to keep quiet, but disloyalty was always possible if someone was disgruntled.

"Where did you hear that?" Kate asked. She wasn't about to give anything away, especially to Tommy.

"I can't divulge my source," he said. "But I'm going to the Vineyard. I thought you should know."

"You thought you'd warn me, you mean." Hank wouldn't be happy about this, and she was already trying to figure out how to handle it. How *was* she going to handle this? Tommy on the Vineyard—along with Hank, who had already made it clear she was not to have contact with her old friend. She didn't have any doubt that Tommy would barge right into their lives and play up his tie to Hank's newest wife. There was a day when she would have admired his moxie, but that was when she wasn't directly involved.

"Maybe you'll give me access?" he asked. This was what he was after: access to Hank, to the family, to get quotes on the record.

"You know better than that," she said sharply.

"A favor for old time's sake, Kate?"

"You wouldn't need a favor if you didn't screw up. You shouldn't have slept with a source," she chided coldly.

"What can I say? I made a mistake."

He didn't deny it or say he'd been in love, or even in like.

"I can't help you, you know that."

"Come on, Kate. Do a guy a favor."

"You have to tell me where you heard this."

Silence for a few seconds, then he said, "If I tell you, will you give me access?"

"I can consider it," she said. "That's the best I can do, under the circumstances."

He was quiet again, weighing whether he could trust her. Finally: "I got a tip."

She laughed. "That tells me nothing. You don't even know if it's true." If she were honest with herself, she'd hoped that he *did* have something credible she could bring to Hank.

Kate could see the driver of the limo, now standing next to the open door, watching her, waiting for her. She started to walk toward the car, ready to end this futile conversation.

But his next words made her stop short.

"What I hear is, Nan Tudor came back from the dead and kidnapped her own daughter."

14
NAN

Nan surveyed herself in the restroom mirror. She'd worn her hair the same way for years now: pulled back in a ponytail. It was easier to manage when working in the kitchen. She recalled how often she used to go for blowouts, highlights, her hair falling in soft layers around her face. She peered more closely and saw the crow's feet and lines in her forehead, things she might have taken care of with Botox back in the day but were now souvenirs of everyday life and natural aging. She no longer wore makeup, and her clothes were a hodgepodge of jeans and T-shirts that were covered daily with a chef's coat, so it didn't matter what was underneath.

But that was her life in France.

Nan pulled the ponytail loose, her dark hair sweeping past her shoulders, and she fluffed it out as much as she could with her fingers. She couldn't remember the last time she'd had a trim, but she'd have to work with what she had. Looking more closely in the mirror, she spotted a couple more silver strands among the dark. If she were still married to Hank, she would have made sure to cover them up, but these days she rather liked the silver, a sort of badge of honor. She took the makeup bag out of her carry-on and carefully applied foundation, blush, mascara, and a red lipstick she'd bought at the airport.

Digging further into her carry-on, Nan found a clean pair of dark jeans and a white, V-necked T-shirt. She quickly changed, and while it was her usual uniform, she transformed her look with a brightly colored Hermès scarf and a black blazer. Red heels replaced the sneakers.

When she looked in the mirror again, Nan Tudor saw the woman she used to be, but instead of feeling nostalgic, she longed for her son and the life she'd built from nothing. And then she zipped up her carry-on, slung the Birkin bag she hadn't been able to get rid of over her shoulder—what did it say about who she used to be that she salvaged the bag rather than her daughter—and stepped out into the restaurant.

She had time to put the carry-on into the trunk of the rental car and get seated at an outdoor table with a glass of white wine before she saw him approach on the sidewalk.

Nan had never met Thomas Wyatt, but the tall man with the dark mop of hair and closely cut beard had clearly recognized her as he approached. He waved off the hostess, indicating he was expected. Sliding into the seat across from her, Wyatt narrowed his eyes and studied her face.

"It *is* you," he said.

There was a time when she was akin to celebrity, glamorous and on the arm of one of the richest men in the world. She had been used to being in the spotlight, and even though she'd conjured up that old self with some makeup and a chic look, his reaction confused her and she almost turned around to see whom he was addressing.

"I heard about Maggie," he said before she could respond. "I was sorry to hear it. She was a formidable old gal."

Nan bristled a little at the description of her old friend but had to admit that it was accurate. "I hadn't seen her in a long time," she said.

"You haven't seen anyone in a long time," he said, then turned to the waitress who was hovering. "Club soda and lime," he instructed.

Nan raised her eyebrows, and he grinned. "I'm driving."

It had been a long time since a man looked at her the way Wyatt was looking at her, and she'd forgotten how powerful it made her feel.

"I assume this is about your daughter," he said.

For a moment, she was puzzled. How would he know? But then she remembered the *Associated Press* story. It had probably gone viral by now, all the media outlets getting their desired clicks.

"Your husband has hired an investigator to find her. He's apparently not fond of the police." He hesitated, then asked, "So, why am I here? What are *you* looking for?" His eyes locked with hers.

He hadn't waited for her to say anything until now, but as his club soda was placed in front of him, he leaned back in his chair. It was clearly her turn.

Nan took a sip of her wine, reminding herself not to appear nervous. "I'd like a separate investigation to find my daughter," she said. "My ex-husband doesn't know I'm here, and I'd like to keep it that way."

He nodded. "I understand. But he's hired the top firm in the country; I'm small potatoes compared to them. Why do you think I can find her?"

It was a good question. When Margaret had hired him, it was to find evidence of Hank's affair with Jeanne, give her ammunition in the divorce. But Hank had covered his tracks so well that Wyatt hadn't discovered anything.

"Margaret spoke highly of you. She trusted you," Nan said, and that was enough. It had to be enough. She didn't have anyone else to turn to. "And then there's this." Nan took her phone out of her bag and pulled up the texts, handing it over to Wyatt.

He frowned as he scrolled through the messages. "You started getting these a couple of days ago?" he asked, looking at her now.

Nan nodded. "Before she was reported missing. But I didn't know that until I got to Boston and saw a news story."

He let that sit between them for a few moments before he spoke again. "Someone lured you here by sending you a threat about your daughter."

She nodded again.

"So, you thought it was about *you*?"

It sounded so selfish to hear him say it like that.

"But she's actually missing?" Wyatt asked, getting to the heart of why she'd called him.

Nan nodded. "Yes. Apparently so. I need you to help me find her. I know Hank's people are good, but you're under the radar. Whoever took Lizzie won't be expecting someone other than Hank to be looking."

Wyatt kept scrolling through the texts. "Why take her if you were already on your way and whoever wanted you here could have just taken *you* when you arrived?" he asked.

"That's the question, isn't it?"

Wyatt handed her back the phone. He took another sip of his club soda. "As I see it," he said, putting his glass back down, "once I find your daughter, I'll also find out who's after *you*."

"Oh, I already know who's after me," Nan said with a smirk.

He laughed then. "Why the hell do you need me, then?"

Nan leaned forward, her elbows on the table, and she stared into his eyes. "Because if it's who I suspect, the person who's orchestrated this tried to have me killed once before, and I have to make sure she never gets another chance."

15

CATHERINE

The girl was still missing, but there was no report of a kidnapping. Hank was keeping it quiet, which is what she would have done, too, under the circumstances.

Catherine had not been completely on board with the prospect of a ransom request, but the argument had been made that it would give more credibility to the situation—and she grudgingly agreed.

She hated leaving things up to others; she didn't like not being in total control. But she'd been convinced it was best this way, this one time.

It was possible the police and the investigators would make their way here to question her about what she knew about Maril's movements in the past couple of days, since the girl had been under Maril's watch when she vanished. Catherine could truthfully say she hadn't seen Maril, had only spoken to her by phone. *She's been on the Vineyard, minding Hank's children.*

Surprisingly, Catherine found herself worried about the girl. She remembered Maril at that age, on the cusp of womanhood, and the girl didn't have a mother to help guide her through all the changes she'd experience mentally and physically. Yes, she had Anna Klein, who did seem to love Hank's children, but Anna was struggling with the loss of her wife and hadn't been with them all summer, leaving the job to their older half sister. It wasn't fair of Hank to ask Maril to give up her life until Anna could pull it together, and Catherine had heard the frustration in Maril's tone when they spoke. Knowing her daughter, Catherine was afraid that Maril wasn't as nurturing as she could be under the circumstances.

She tapped her fingers on the arm of the sofa and thought about the diary that was hidden upstairs in her safe. The girl didn't know her mother had written down everything about her life with Hank. Catherine had debated destroying it, but something held her back. Was it the thought that if *she'd* kept a diary, she'd want Maril to have it at some point? No. She didn't want Maril to know all her secrets, and that girl didn't need to know everything about *her* mother's life, either. She didn't need to know that her mother had stepped into the middle of a marriage and tore it apart for her own pleasure and desires. Catherine was protecting her. Someone needed to.

Still, she hadn't gotten rid of the journal.

It was time to reassert her authority, make it clear who was really in charge of this operation.

Catherine had been careful with communication since she'd pulled Joan Carey out of Anna Klein's house. Joan hadn't been happy about the timing. The woman had actually fallen in love with Anna Klein. Catherine hadn't expected that. She'd had to gently—and then not so gently—remind Joan of her commitment. It was too late to bring anyone else in—and Joan knew too much. In the end, Joan had "vanished," her bank account that much richer—funny how it always came down to money—and her loyalty relatively intact. Catherine continued to have lingering doubts about the woman, however, and had to handle her delicately. At least until she was no longer useful.

Catherine made her way upstairs. She unlocked the door to the room that held her bank of computers, the room Lourdes wasn't allowed to enter. Catherine spent her mornings here, trading. She hadn't expected to take to it like she did; she'd begun by mainly targeting Tudor Enterprises' stocks, manipulating them in a way that might worry the man who thought his empire was untouchable. As she became more skilled and confident—and successful—Catherine began branching out, feeding her offshore accounts with money made off her husband's rivals as well as his companies. Hank had no idea how much wealth she was amassing; his paltry alimony allowance was merely pin money these days. This house had been part of the settlement, and she'd paid off the mortgage without his knowledge, owning it outright now. Catherine had become more than adept at hiding her tracks.

Once upon a time, her husband had appreciated her intelligence, her business acumen. She'd built Tudor Enterprises side by side with him—only to be cast aside when That Woman turned his head.

Catherine had spent too much time ruminating about what had gone wrong in her marriage before she finally decided to take matters into her own hands and take back what was hers.

She ignored the screens—she'd already done her trading for the day—going straight to the walk-in closet and pulling up the rug in the back corner to reveal the small safe below. Punching in the code, she heard a loud click and opened the door. Nestled inside was the diary. She pushed it aside and took out the burner phone that lay underneath.

She didn't bother leaving the closet, just hit "1" and waited for the call to go through, letting it ring three times before hanging up.

Catherine again questioned whether keeping Joan on was the right decision. She could end up being a real liability. Perhaps Joan's "disappearance" *should* be made permanent. It wouldn't be difficult; in fact, everyone thought she was dead anyway. It might be tricky about how and where, but she'd never run from a challenge.

The phone buzzed with an incoming call. Catherine frowned. This was not protocol. She accepted the call.

"Yes?"

"They know about the boat."

16
NAN

Since she'd left, Nan had kept her secrets close. She had woven a new life where lies became truths. She wasn't naïve enough to think that when this was all over, she'd be able to go back to that life. At least not as Louise Savoy. She would have to tell Harry who she was, who his father was. But not today.

Nan told Wyatt just enough. He sat, his eyes closing and opening during parts, not seeming shocked when she told him she'd been afraid Hank would kill her rather than give her what she wanted most in the divorce: her daughter. She glossed over the violence—he didn't need to know the details, just that the threats were there—but recounted seeing the woman murdered on the beach and realizing it could be to her advantage.

"I saw the sword," she said, recalling how it had glinted in the moonlight. It all happened in the shadows, as though behind a curtain. A headless woman might be mistaken for her—at least long enough for her to escape. And that's what she did.

She'd squirreled away some money; she had falsified documents that were real enough to fool the authorities. So she went to central France, took a culinary class, and decided to become a cook while she waited for her son to be born.

Wyatt's eyebrows rose at the mention of Harry, but he said nothing.

"I kept in touch with Margaret, who kept me informed about Lizzie," Nan explained. "But it wasn't until right before Margaret died in the house fire that she told me we'd had it wrong." She paused for a moment. "It was Catherine. That's who tried to kill me. Catherine Tudor."

Wyatt sat up straighter, his eyes wide. "You're sure?"

Nan gave him a small smile. "I only have it on Margaret's word." She reached into her bag and pulled out an envelope, handing it to him. "It's all there. The last letter she wrote me." The letter telling her how Hank's first wife had discovered where she was and warning her that she should disappear again.

Wyatt took the piece of paper out of the envelope and scanned it, nodding as he did. "She had dementia."

"Some," Nan admitted. "But I believe her. She wasn't delusional."

"She didn't have any proof."

"No."

Wyatt turned the envelope over. "She had your address."

"Well, a post office box. But if someone wanted to find me, it wouldn't be impossible."

"Do you think she gave it to anyone?"

"Not deliberately." Nan hesitated, then continued. "I think whoever set her house on fire managed to find it."

Wyatt's eyes widened further. "That fire wasn't ruled arson. You think it was?"

"There was a woman," Nan said, not answering his question. "She showed up in town. I'd already decided to move because of Margaret's warning. But this woman wanted an English-speaking guide since she didn't speak French. We would be gone in a few days, so I didn't think it would do any harm to say yes." She stopped, again feeling foolish for this decision. She should have known better.

"And . . ." Wyatt prompted.

Nan took a deep breath. "It was fine, we left, never saw her again, at least not in person. But not long after, I saw a picture online. It was her. It was definitely her."

"Who?"

"A woman named Joan Carey. She was married to my ex-husband's fourth wife."

Wyatt leaned forward. "She disappeared two months ago."

Nan nodded. "Right about the time I met her."

"That's not a coincidence."

"No."

They let that sit between them for a few moments. Wyatt was so quiet that Nan began to doubt whether she'd made the right call in trusting him. It had been so long, though, and if she wanted him to help her, she had to tell him her story and what she knew about Joan Carey. Not that she knew much at all. Joan had lied to her about everything except her first name. She'd said that she was taking an extended vacation after a nasty divorce and was thinking about buying a second home in France, a place that could be a respite for her. She hadn't asked Nan many questions about *her* life but had seemed very interested in Harry and the fact that Nan had no husband. In retrospect, she shouldn't have engaged at all, but it was only three days, she'd told herself.

Nan had packed up their things, and she and Harry left in the early morning. She hadn't told the restaurant about their departure—that was part of the plan, just in case anyone came around looking for her. She'd already had a job lined up; it was remarkably easy to find work in a kitchen. Harry was at that age where making friends was easy, and they settled into their new life as though the old one had never existed.

She didn't like admitting that she sometimes searched Hank's name on the internet, but that's how she saw the news stories about Joan Carey's disappearance—and the discovery of his fifth wife's decapitated body, killed the same way Nan was supposed to be.

Wyatt sat back in his seat and studied her face. She felt herself blushing a little under his gaze. She told herself it was because she was a little jet-lagged and had had a glass of wine.

"Do you think Joan Carey had anything to do with your daughter's kidnapping?" he asked.

Nan nodded. "I think she's working for Catherine Tudor. I think she missed her chance in France, and this is a way to lure me here."

"You didn't change your cell number when you moved?"

It was a reasonable question. "I never gave her my number. We met at allotted times. She asked for it, of course. But I never gave it to her."

"So how are you getting these texts?"

Nan had been considering every possibility but there was only one way she could think of. "Margaret had this number. Because of her dementia, she probably had it written down. So, when my address was discovered, my phone number was, too."

Wyatt took a small pad of paper and pen out of his jacket pocket. "Can you give me the numbers you're getting the texts from?"

She recited them, and he wrote them down.

"There's no guarantee that I'll find out anything about them. They may be AI generated, but it's worth a look," he said, almost apologetically.

"I understand."

Wyatt chewed on his lip and nodded as though to himself. "You have to go to Martha's Vineyard. I'm going with you."

Nan frowned, and he grinned. "Oh, not *with* you. I'll have my own car." He paused, then asked, "I assume you can pay me?"

"Yes. Whatever your fee is—and expenses." It might take everything she had, but there was a job at home, and her life wasn't extravagant. She'd make it work to make sure Lizzie was safe and to stay alive to get back to Harry.

"Whoever's texting you told you what car to take but not where to stay on the Vineyard?" Wyatt asked. "I can't imagine they'd think you'd go to your old house. I mean, your daughter's been taken, I'm sure there's security everywhere." He paused. "Or was that the plan?"

Nan shrugged. "I don't know. But while I was waiting for you, I made a reservation for myself at a motel in Vineyard Haven."

"Give me the name of the motel, and I'll reserve a room there, too." He hesitated a moment, then added, "I'm going to bring someone else in on this. The more boots on the ground, the faster we find your daughter."

Nan wasn't sure about trusting anyone else, but she assumed he knew what he was doing.

"His name is Mark Smeaton. He's good."

She hoped they were both good. Her daughter's life depended on it.

The ping of a text message coming through startled her. Nan had left her phone face down on the table. She froze a moment. Wyatt met her eyes and nodded. "Look at it."

Nan turned the phone over and saw the message, which was merely comprised of two emojis:

A girl's head and a sword.

17
KATE

While Kate had never been to the house on Martha's Vineyard, she *had* been to the island several years ago with friends after her first divorce. However, on that trip, she'd arrived with the throngs of tourists by ferry from Woods Hole, not at the small airport by private jet. And instead of carrying her own bag and walking to the inn where they'd stayed in Vineyard Haven, now she was picked up by a private car and whisked toward Hank Tudor's beachside estate in Tisbury.

She missed the simplicity of her life back then but had to admit to herself that being Hank Tudor's assistant and then his wife had given her a life she'd never thought possible—and she enjoyed it. Too bad she wasn't sure if it would end with a happily ever after.

Even though Kate was used to Hank's security detail, she wasn't prepared for the number of guards at the house. Two appeared out of seemingly thin air when the car pulled up, one opening the door for her and the other getting her bag out of the back. She shrugged her purse over her shoulder as she shimmied out of the limo. Another guard stood at the door of the house. Anna's outline was discernible inside as she watched Kate approach.

When the screen door opened, Anna's arms were suddenly around her, and Kate breathed a sigh of relief. Anna let go and led her through the foyer.

"That's a lot of security," Kate commented as they entered the kitchen, bright white and gleaming from someone's elbow grease. Probably Anna's, for lack of anything else to do. Anna was used to caring for a large house, since she'd run an inn in Greenwich.

"And there's a lot more that you *don't* see. Hank's not taking any chances," Anna said as she took two wineglasses out of the cupboard and a bottle of white from the fridge. She poured without asking if Kate wanted any.

Kate pushed her glass away. "I think I'll just have some ice water. Maybe a little lemon?"

Anna's eyebrows rose. "I've never known you to turn down a glass of wine," she said. "Unless . . ." Her gaze drifted to Kate's figure with the unspoken question.

Kate nodded. She should have confided in Anna two months ago, but she hadn't, and it was easier as time went on not to tell. "I found out in the hospital, you know, after what happened with Will Stafford," she said. "I had to process it. I haven't told Hank." As though that would make it better that she hadn't told Anna yet, either.

Anna didn't immediately react. After a few seconds, she said tentatively, "Are you happy about it?"

Kate's face fell and tears rushed into her eyes. "I don't know," she admitted. "I just don't know." It was the first time she'd said it out loud, that maybe this baby wasn't what she wanted. If she and Hank weren't estranged, it was possible she'd be overjoyed. But babies had never been on her radar; she'd never felt a biological clock. Now, however, she had no choice but to somehow come to grips with it.

Anna pulled her again into an embrace. "It's okay to have doubts. Especially considering everything that's happened."

Kate began to feel guilty. Anna had lost her wife, and Kate still had a husband and now a baby. She shouldn't be so selfish. She stepped away and wiped her cheeks with the back of her hand. "I'll figure it out," she said. "We have more important things to think about right now. Is there any word of Lizzie?"

Tommy's revelation about Nan Tudor being involved with Lizzie's kidnapping—if it was true—had shaken her. *Someone* had told him Lizzie had been kidnapped—that was certainly true. And he somehow knew Nan Tudor might be back "from the dead." Kate had hung up with a laugh that indicated incredulity, and the moment she'd gotten back into the limo, she'd called Hank. He hadn't picked up, though, so she'd left a voicemail that merely asked him to call her back when he could, that it was important. She still hadn't heard from him.

Anna was shaking her head. "No. Nothing yet. I assume Hank has gone looking for that boat, but I don't know anything about it. I've been here with Maril and Ted, who, by the way, hasn't spoken a word since Lizzie vanished. I've tried everything to get him to talk, but nothing. I'm really worried about him."

"You talking about Teddy?" Maril came into the kitchen and gave a side glance at Kate. "Where's Daddy? I thought he was coming with you."

"Change of plans," Kate said.

Maril frowned at the glass of iced water in front of Kate, cocking her head at Anna's glass of wine. "I'll take one of those."

Anna slid the glass originally intended for Kate over to Maril, whose eyes moved from Kate's face to the glass of water and back again. Kate could see she was making the connection as the other woman's expression hardened.

"Does Daddy know?" she asked.

"Not officially," Kate admitted.

Maril's mouth pressed into a thin line. She hadn't expected Kate to marry Hank so soon after his divorce from Caitlyn, most likely hoping he'd go back to her mother. That's what Maril and Catherine had been wishing for ever since Nan vanished. Now, however, with a baby on the way, maybe they'd both face reality: Hank was never going to reconcile with Catherine.

Anyway, her pregnancy was really none of Maril's business. There was a time when Kate thought they might grow closer—they were only a couple of years apart in age—but it was clear that would never be the case.

She decided to take the high road. "I hope you're holding up okay," Kate said. "Especially since you were here with the children when Lizzie, well . . ."

Maril's eyebrows rose, and she shrugged. "I don't know where she went that day. I shouldn't have let her go alone to meet her friend. But she was so damn stubborn."

Maril's use of the past tense took her aback, but then she dismissed it as a slip. Lizzie *was* stubborn and probably nagged her sister until Maril couldn't fight it anymore and allowed her to go. Although Maril could be just as tenacious.

"You must be tired," Anna said to Kate, clearly not wanting to go over the events of the day Lizzie went missing yet again. "Let me show you your room and you can freshen up a little before supper. I want to check on Ted anyway."

They left Maril alone in the kitchen and went through the front room to the stairway.

"Maril's been driving me crazy," Anna whispered when they were out of earshot. "She keeps asking if I know anything, which I don't, and I've found her creeping around like she's some sort of spy."

That wasn't a surprise. Maril had a habit of keeping her mother apprised of everything going on in Hank's household. "I'm sure she's reporting everything back to Catherine," Kate said, a bitterness in her tone that she didn't try to conceal.

Kate followed Anna up the stairs, unsure where her bag was until they reached a room at the end of the hall, and she saw it sitting on the white bedspread as though it had magically appeared there.

"I didn't know whether you would be sharing a room with Hank when he arrives," Anna said. "Will you?"

Kate shook her head. "I have no idea. I honestly hadn't even thought about that." And she hadn't. She told herself that Hank probably wasn't sleeping anyway, so the whole thing was moot until after Lizzie was found, but at some point, she was going to have to make a decision. It had been easy to put out of her mind while she was living separately, but the events of the last hours had proven that she was still—whether she wanted to be or not—Hank's wife.

That thought gave her pause. Tommy Seymour hadn't indicated that he knew she and Hank were separated. Granted, she and Hank had kept the separation under wraps, and it had not been reported. But Tommy *was* a journalist. And if he had information about Nan Tudor, it seemed odd that he wouldn't know about their estrangement. Or maybe he did. Maybe that invitation to the Hungarian bakery wasn't only about getting a story.

Kate's phone pinged. "It's Hank," she told Anna, glad he was finally calling her back. Anna stepped into the hallway, shutting the door behind her, giving Kate privacy.

"Hello, Hank," she said when she answered the call.

"I got your message. Things have been a bit busy here. What did you want?"

It was the best apology she could expect, under the circumstances.

"I just wanted you to know that the word on the street is that Nan kidnapped Lizzie herself."

He was quiet, then: "Who did you hear that from?"

She had to come clean. "Tommy Seymour. He wouldn't tell me who's saying that. He's coming to the Vineyard, and he wants access. I told him no."

"Well, it's not really your position to make that call one way or the other, is it?" Hank's tone was menacing. "I told you to stop talking to him."

"He got my phone number. I didn't give it to him." She felt anger rising. She didn't need him to remind her that she didn't have any power in this situation. "I just thought you needed to know." Kate didn't even attempt to keep the edge out of her voice.

She could hear Cromwell in the background, talking to Hank. Was she on speaker? Was Cromwell listening in? She'd had enough of this. Kate was ready to end the call, but Hank spoke before she could.

"This might be to our advantage."

"What?"

"Perhaps you *should* keep talking to him."

Kate was confused. "Why?"

"He could be useful. Find out who his source is. Make him promises of access if it comes to that."

Kate still didn't understand. "Why the turnaround?"

Hank was silent a moment, then: "Because that boat, the *Perseverance*? The one where Lizzie was supposed to meet her mother? It's registered to Nan."

18
CATHERINE

The sixth wife, Kate Parker, was on the Vineyard. Catherine should have known their separation wouldn't last.

And that wasn't even the worst of it.

The woman was pregnant.

Catherine had to sit down when Maril called to tell her. It was as though all her energy had suddenly left her body. It was a distraction she did not need.

Hank just couldn't help himself, could he? He had to marry all those women and impregnate them. It wasn't as though he wanted more children; he'd told her time and time again that it didn't matter to him that they'd had only one child. He really didn't want any more. Perhaps he was merely being kind after the two miscarriages, but she chose to believe him.

Maybe she should have just ruined him financially—that wouldn't be impossible, not with her trading skills. Did she really want him back?

Yes. He was her husband. He would always be her husband.

They were so much alike, she and Hank. Ruthless and passionate—and they'd been perfect together. Running the businesses, doubling and then tripling the Tudor Enterprises empire. Celebrating each takeover with champagne and lovemaking, the memory of which could make her blush, even now. He had worshipped her body—and she, his. He had taken her to places she'd never even dreamed of.

Was it wrong to want all that again? She was older now, some would call her "a woman of a certain age," and for a while she admitted that she'd let herself go. But now that she was exercising, taking better care of herself, when she looked in the mirror, she could see her younger self. The woman Hank Tudor had fallen in love with so long ago.

He couldn't have forgotten what she was capable of, either, since she'd been leaving him subtle reminders. Caitlyn Howard's body and that one on Martha's Vineyard were staged to remind him of James Stuart. How they'd found James's body in that alley, his head in the dumpster.

Catherine had seen the threat the moment she'd met him. The president and CEO of Stuart Holdings, James Stuart was as charismatic as he was cutthroat.

But James had made a mistake. He shouldn't have attempted the hostile takeover while Hank was away—and while she was in charge. Hank had signed the papers so she could run the business without his approvals.

Sometimes she wondered if she had gone too far, but James never would have stopped.

She and Hank never talked about it, but without her interference, Tudor Enterprises would not have survived James's maneuvers. And if Hank had made the connection between his wives and James, he hadn't come after her, hadn't told the police. That was most likely because Hank was well aware how she'd set it up—and how the evidence, if it ever came to light, would point to him and not to her.

She was sure he admired her tactics.

Hank needed a strong woman, and none of the others had been as strong as she was. He could love her again. She knew it. Knew it as well as she knew herself.

But a new baby. With the newest wife.

By all rights, Kate Parker should be dead. Will Stafford had shot her in the head. Too bad it was with a small-caliber bullet that only managed to give the woman a concussion.

Catherine considered the situation—two wives, one pregnant and another with a secret son—knowing she could afford no missteps. It was possible she could make everything work to her advantage. The reporter could be manipulated. The fact that he had a history with the sixth wife could be beneficial. Two birds with one stone, perhaps. Hank wouldn't like it that his current wife might be stepping out on him—and cooperating with a reporter.

Plant a few seeds of doubt and see what happens.

19

NAN

The next text came through not long after Nan boarded the ferry.

Vineyard Haven Marina

Nan glanced around as though she'd catch someone watching her, but the other passengers were engrossed in their own journeys with their own companions, and no one was paying her any mind. Whoever was on the other side of the text didn't know where she was—or if she was even going to the Vineyard since she hadn't taken the car she'd been assigned and couldn't be tracked. But by telling her to go to the marina, the texter was counting on one thing: Nan would eventually follow directions because it was about Lizzie.

She sidled over to Wyatt, who was casually leaning against the railing, overlooking the water, and slipped him her phone. "More instructions," she murmured.

He gave it back to her after reading the message. "Do you have any knowledge of this marina? Did you ever have a boat there?" His voice was low.

"Not there."

"But you *did* have a boat? Where?" He hadn't looked at her, and anyone watching would have to pay close attention to even see their exchange.

"The yacht club in Edgartown." She didn't bother telling Wyatt that the yacht was a whim Hank had right before Lizzie was born. Nan had liked the flashiness of having it, how it advertised how much money they had, how powerful it made her feel. Yet when Hank sold it, she wasn't sorry. A yacht wasn't a place for a baby, and she'd settled into motherhood, preferring to stay at the house with mornings spent at the beach. But that was irrelevant, too much information that Wyatt didn't need to know.

Wyatt took out his phone, tapping out a text of his own. "Smeaton can start looking into it. The marina. There's a reason they want you there."

"Maybe that's where they've got Lizzie?"

"Maybe." Yet his tone made her think he wasn't sure.

"Maybe Catherine means to have me thrown off the dock and drowned," she said with a chuckle.

Wyatt did look at her then. "Maybe."

He hadn't even cracked a smile. He was serious. Nan laughed out loud. "At least I'll have a witness with me."

"Glad you've got a sense of humor about all this," he said wryly.

"Not really, but I have to cope somehow," she admitted. "I'm worried about my daughter." Not to mention her son. She hadn't spoken to him since she'd left, and she'd been anxiously looking at her watch to gauge the time difference and when she could call him. They'd never been separated like this before, and she felt his absence keenly, hoping that he was well and that no one had decided to kidnap *him*, too.

Nan forced herself to stop thinking about Harry. He was safe with Gabriel and his parents. She wished Lizzie was as safe.

The thought made her take pause. Just how could she have been taken? Hank always had security teams on his properties. She couldn't imagine that Hank had eased up on that, especially in light of his fifth wife's murder. In fact, he'd probably added more security. What, then, had happened to Lizzie? The news story said she'd been on her way to the beach to meet a friend. Alone? Nan had a hard time believing that. And then she remembered reading that the man responsible for Caitlyn Howard's murder had been head of security at Anna Klein's inn. Who was vetting these people? Were they being vetted at all?

Nan pushed down her instinct to take charge, ask questions. She was never going to be making decisions in Hank Tudor's world again.

She turned her thoughts back to the most recent text message and wondered if bringing in Wyatt had been the best idea. Perhaps she should have just gone along with the mysterious plan and let the chips fall where they may, so to speak. But she was so close to the situation, and it was always good to have someone on your team who didn't have any skin in the game. Someone who could be objective, neutral. Wyatt certainly seemed to fit the bill—and Maggie had trusted him.

Nan turned to ask Wyatt if he had any thoughts as to what to do once the ferry docked, but he wasn't next to her any longer. Where had he gone? She walked along the deck and finally spotted him through the window, inside; he was on his phone. Probably talking to that Smeaton fellow.

The island was still out of sight, but as Nan stared across the water, she was distracted by an unexpected yet familiar thrill that ran through her. It had been a long time since she'd been to the Vineyard—she'd left in the dead of night—and at this moment, she felt as though she were coming home. She wished that once she disembarked, she could disappear among the vacationers and pretend that she was one of them. Pretend that she was discovering this island for the first time. In a way, she was. This time she wasn't Mrs. Hank Tudor but Louise Savoy from Paris. The only thing missing was Harry.

Harry would love the Vineyard, like she did. She could imagine him riding the carousel, where he could reach for the brass ring as he went round and round on one of the brightly painted wooden horses. He would delight in the gingerbread houses and the icy water of the Atlantic that swept across the beach, smoothing out the stones. Nan wished it wasn't only a daydream, that someday she could bring her son here.

She found a seat and wrapped her arms around her torso, warming herself against the cool ocean breeze and allowing herself to close her eyes. She hadn't slept much since she'd left Paris—no, since she got that first text—and the jet lag and time difference had begun to get the better of her, despite her determination to stay awake.

She didn't know how long she'd been asleep when she felt someone brush against her arm, startling her. But it was only Wyatt—and he was holding a couple of wrapped sandwiches and two bottles of water. He sat down next to her, handing her one of the sandwiches. "I hope you like ham and cheese."

"Not hungry."

"You didn't eat anything in Providence, and something tells me you might not have eaten since you left Paris."

He was right. Along with not sleeping, her stomach had been in knots for two days as she prepared for this trip. While she'd made sure she'd eaten so Harry wouldn't get worried, she'd barely touched the meals on the plane. A small roll and a cup of coffee right before landing was all she managed. That glass of wine in Providence had gone to her head, leaving her with a slight headache. A sandwich would probably set her to rights. Still, she wasn't sure she'd be able to keep it down.

"Just a couple of bites," Wyatt said. "We can't have you passing out."

"I'll be fine."

"Humor me."

She rolled her eyes at him but obeyed. She was hungrier than she'd thought.

By the time they were finished eating, the ferry was coming up on the dock, so they dropped the sandwich wrappings in the trash on their way to the hold where the cars were parked. They were discussing whether to go directly to the marina or to check into the motel first when Wyatt took his phone out.

“Smeaton,” he said by way of explanation, reading a text that had come through. When he was done, he looked at her.

“Well, it seems that Nan Tudor *does* own a boat—and it’s docked at the Vineyard Haven Marina.”

20

The motel was plain but serviceable. The clerk ran Nan's credit card and handed her a key with hardly a look before giving cursory directions to her room. Even though she was eager to head to the marina, as soon as she stepped inside the room, she began shedding her clothes and headed for the shower. Nan let the hot water wash away the hours of traveling. She'd been going nonstop since she'd left home, and the fatigue had worn her down; the shower reinvigorated her.

She had been confused when Wyatt told her about the boat. "Nan Tudor doesn't exist any longer," she said. "How could she possibly own a boat? Not to mention that Nan Tudor on her own couldn't possibly afford a boat." It felt a little strange to refer to herself in third person, but Nan Tudor *was* another person, another lifetime ago. And the one hundred thousand dollars she'd managed to escape with had barely built her new life, after travel and rent and culinary school. If she could do it again, she would have put away a lot more money—but there still wouldn't have been enough for a boat.

Wyatt had given a snort. "Well, there's a boat registered to Nan Tudor."

Mark Smeaton was earning his keep to have found this information so quickly. But you could find out anything with a computer, especially if you knew what you were doing.

"How on earth could that boat be registered in my name? Someone's impersonating me?" Nan had asked.

"Not difficult to do these days, unfortunately." His phone had buzzed with another incoming text. "Smeaton says the registration was filed a week ago with the Coast Guard. He's trying to trace the title."

"Someone has concocted an elaborate plan." Nan had always known Catherine was devious, but this was far worse than she'd imagined. Buying a boat, registering it under her name, well, that was crazy. Not that she hadn't seen the crazy in Catherine, but she kept coming back to how long it had been. Catherine couldn't possibly think that Nan was still a threat, could she? But maybe time wasn't passing as quickly for Catherine. Maybe her life hadn't moved on.

For a moment, Nan had felt sorry for the woman. Until she remembered that her daughter had been taken—not to mention the attempt on her own life those years ago.

Wyatt was oblivious to her distraction and had begun reading from his phone. "A one-hundred-three-foot yacht is registered under the name Nan Tudor. It's called *Perseverance*."

It was as though someone had punched her in the gut. He noticed.

"That mean something to you?"

"I organized a masquerade ball for Catherine, when I was her assistant. I played the part of Perseverance." It was also the first time she'd met Hank, but she wasn't willing to tell Wyatt about that. About how their eyes had locked across the room. How he'd taken her in his arms and they'd danced as though they had known each other forever. She'd had enough champagne to let him kiss her—just once, but it was enough. He'd taken her breath away. And then she slipped away, like Cinderella, because he was Catherine's husband.

It had been the beginning for them, the beginning of their fairy tale, until it turned into a nightmare.

Nan pulled on a pair of black leggings and an oversized T-shirt and was towel drying her hair when she heard the knock at the door. Peering through the peephole, she saw Wyatt outside. He'd changed out of the gray suit trousers and into a pair of jeans, and instead of the white dress shirt, he now wore a green polo. She took note of the slight bulge under the gray blazer; he had a gun. She hadn't expected that, but she probably should have. He was an investigator, after all. She hoped he wouldn't have to use it.

Nan opened the door and let him in. "I'll be ready in a few minutes."

"You look fine the way you are," Wyatt said. "We don't want to attract too much attention." The implication being that Nan Tudor might be recognized; Louise Savoy, not so much.

"The text didn't say where the boat was," Nan realized as she pulled her hair back in her familiar ponytail, "so, how are we going to find it?"

"The text didn't say anything about a boat," Wyatt reminded her.

That's right. It didn't. The only way they knew about it was because Smeaton had told Wyatt. What would happen, since there was no explicit instruction, except "be at the marina"?

"So, it's possible that it's not even here."

"It's not."

Nan frowned. He sounded so sure. "How do you know that?"

"I called the dockmaster's office. She told me that the *Perseverance* left almost two hours ago. It wasn't long after that police arrived, looking for a missing girl on that exact yacht."

"But they were too late? The boat was gone?" Her spirits deflated. She'd imagined that Lizzie would be at the marina and she would be able to rescue her.

"We still might be able to find her." Wyatt held up his phone. A map was visible on the screen, with little red triangles. "This shows us all the boats registered with the Coast Guard. And a yacht that large would definitely be registered." He moved the map around with his fingers. "I haven't been able to locate it anywhere nearby, but I'll keep looking."

If the police were looking for Lizzie on the yacht, that meant Hank must also know about it. He would put all his resources into finding it, and with his money, he could charter his own boat or even manage to get the Coast Guard to help locate the *Perseverance*. Wyatt's app would be useless. And if

Hank knew about the yacht, then he very likely also knew it was registered in her name. By alerting the police that a missing girl might be on board, it tied Nan to her daughter's kidnapping. She said as much to Wyatt.

"Isn't the point of all this to make sure your daughter is found safe?" Wyatt asked. "Maybe you should just let your ex-husband rescue her, then the threat disappears and you can go home."

Everything he said made sense. But how could she explain to him that she desperately wanted to see Lizzie? If she did what the texter asked of her—that is, if there were any more instructions at all—it might mean she could put an end to whatever scheme Catherine had devised and she might be able to be a part of Lizzie's life again.

But then she realized: "I got that text after the boat had already left. Why do they want me there?"

Wyatt scratched his beard thoughtfully and shook his head. "No idea. Do you still want to go?"

Nan pondered the question. She had been lured to the island under the threat of her daughter's life. She had no reason to think that threat no longer existed because of the absence of a yacht she would never even have known about without Wyatt's help. She sat up a little straighter and nodded. "Of course. Let's see what she's got in store for me."

"You sure about that?" A tinge of worry laced his tone.

"Absolutely. They said they'd kill her if I didn't do what they said."

Wyatt chuckled. "But you did take a two-hour detour to hire me."

She shrugged. "Covering my bases."

As she followed Wyatt out, Nan had no idea what to expect. Would Catherine suddenly materialize? Would this be a showdown?

All she knew was, all of these theatrics were truly about *her*, with Lizzie caught in the crosshairs—and still missing. She couldn't stop thinking about the sword emoji in the text. That was the one that told her they were serious, reminding her what had happened on the Vineyard eight years ago—and that it was possible it could happen again.

21
LIZZIE

When they take the tape off my mouth, I scream.

"It's not going to do you any good," a voice says. It's a woman's voice, not one that I've heard before. "There's no one around to hear you."

I want to tell her that even if no one will come to my rescue, I want to scream. I want to keep screaming just to prove I can.

We must be somewhere out in the ocean—which is why no one will hear me scream, presumably. Who else is here besides this woman? Someone must be driving the boat, right? Is that the right word: *driving*? It's not like a car. *Piloting*, maybe? But that's a plane.

I have nothing better to do than debate semantics with myself. Maril thinks I'm some sort of freak because I know words like *semantics*.

I wish I had a dictionary. I love looking up words—and not online. I love the feel of the pages under my fingers. It's more real than looking at a screen. I don't tell anyone this, because then everyone will think I'm a freak, not just Maril.

I wonder where we're going. We eventually have to reach land, don't we? But then I remember a story about a ship that never docked anywhere, just sailed all over the world. Is that what's going to happen to me? I'll never go home, never see Teddy or Anna or Dad again.

My eyes are still covered, and my hands are still tied behind my back. But I feel fingers fumbling at my legs. They're taking off the binds. I kick out and make contact with something—her leg or knee or some other body part. But she doesn't indicate I've hurt her, even though I know I'm strong and probably have. I try to kick again, and a hand catches my ankle, holds it tight.

"Kick again and you'll be sorry," she hisses, and I feel something cold against my neck. A blade. "I don't want to cut you, but I will if I have to."

I stop. I'm not stupid.

She takes me to the bathroom. I've never felt such relief in my life. I've been holding it so long, but I didn't want to give them the satisfaction of wetting myself. I'm not a baby.

Afterward, I'm brought back to wherever it is I've been. I expect to have my mouth taped up again, but instead they give me a sandwich. It's ham and cheese. I hate ham, but I eat it anyway. I figure I have to keep up my strength, in case I can get out of here.

There were two people with me before, but now, it's only this one woman who's feeding me. She's not saying anything, but she breathes hard, like she's coming off a cold. Or maybe she's just nervous. She should be. If my father finds out who she is, he'll make her pay.

But the way I figure it, she's the one making him pay. I know about kidnappings and ransoms. I've seen *Miss Congeniality 2*—and everyone knows my father is rich.

I wonder how much I'm worth to these people. How much are they asking for? And then I have another thought: What if my father makes me pay back the money? I can hear him now, telling me that it would "build character" to "take responsibility." I am to blame for this. I believed that she was my mother, and he's not her biggest fan. I've stopped asking questions about her, because he won't answer. Anna didn't know her, so I can't ask her, and Maril, well, she hates my mother more than my father does. I've heard her talking to her mother when she doesn't know I'm listening.

My mother couldn't have been that bad, could she? I can't believe that. I wish I could talk to someone about her, someone who knew her and liked her.

The woman doesn't put the tape back on my mouth after I finish the sandwich.

"My arms hurt," I complain, and it's not a lie.

She sighs loudly but doesn't say anything. I hear her walk away, her footsteps soft in the carpet on the floor—she doesn't even say goodbye or good night, is it night?—and then a door shuts, leaving me alone again.

22
ANNA

Anna couldn't help but be a little hurt that Kate hadn't confided in her about the pregnancy. It wasn't as though she hadn't had the opportunity to tell her; Anna and Kate had been talking on a regular basis—about once a week—since Kate had moved back to the city earlier this summer. But as she recounted their conversations, they were mostly about Lizzie and Ted and Joan. Kate hadn't said too much. Anna had put it down to Kate being estranged from Hank and that she was still uncertain if Hank had had anything to do with Caitlyn's murder—despite Will Stafford—not to mention the fact that Kate had been shot, which was traumatizing although, luckily, not debilitating. So, Anna hadn't pressed, and Kate let her do all the talking.

It was going to be awkward when Hank returned, too, because Kate didn't even know if they would share a bedroom. Anna had readied a second room for Hank, wishing Kate hadn't let this go on so long. If Kate wanted a divorce, the baby would muddy the waters since she'd have to let Hank be a part of the baby's life. But while Hank deserved to know he was going to be a father again, Anna wasn't optimistic that he'd be any more attentive to Kate's child than he was with Lizzie and Ted. Was that the reason for Kate's hesitation?

Anna was happy she'd managed to get out of her marriage with no complications. Her relationship with Hank was amicable. She didn't mind being a surrogate mother to Lizzie and Ted, as she didn't have any children herself and she genuinely enjoyed the role. When she was with Joan, she'd felt she had a perfect life. Now she was slowly coming to the realization that she may never know what had happened to Joan and that she'd have to start rebuilding her life without her.

The house was quiet as night settled over it like a blanket. Anna had put Ted to bed, and wordlessly he dropped off after she read a chapter of *The Hobbit* to him. She'd watched his little chest rising with each breath and wished she had the words to comfort him. Maril's light was on; she was probably working. Anna hadn't seen her since supper. She'd noticed the tension between Maril and Kate. Kate should have known her pregnancy would not be welcome news to Hank's daughter, who already resented her father's predilection for wives.

Anna wouldn't be able to fall asleep—her insomnia had been worse since Joan's disappearance—so she made herself a cup of chamomile tea. She imagined Kate upstairs, unable to sleep as well, and wondered if she'd have company so she set out two mugs, just in case.

She almost dropped the kettle as the slam of the screen door made her flinch. Footsteps approached the kitchen until she saw Hank's silhouette in the doorway. She caught her breath, looking past him, hoping to see Lizzie, but he was alone.

"You didn't find her," she said flatly. Tears sprang into her eyes.

Hank shook his head. "The boat was gone before we got there."

"Is there any way to find it?" There had to be, right? Could they track a yacht the same way they track airplanes?

"We're working on it," he promised.

Anna wanted to ask about Nan Tudor, but she had to tread carefully. Hank didn't know that she'd had Nan's diary in her possession for a short time; he didn't know Nan had even written a journal. After reading it, though, Anna could believe that Nan had come back for her daughter, even after so long.

"Do you think it was really Nan who sent those messages to Lizzie?" she asked.

Hank nodded. "I do."

"But that assumes—"

"That she's alive." Hank finished her sentence. "She came through airport customs in Boston earlier today. So yes, she's alive."

"What?" Anna wasn't sure she heard correctly. "Nan really is alive?"

"Seems so."

"How do you know she came through customs?" she asked.

Hank raised an eyebrow. "I've got it on good authority."

Anna shouldn't even have questioned how. She now noticed the dark circles under his eyes. "You're not sleeping well."

He gave her a small smile. "Neither are you."

"That's nothing new."

"But it's for a new reason."

She crossed the room and reached around him into a cabinet, withdrawing a bottle of cognac. Without even asking if he wanted any, she took two brandy snifters out of another cabinet and poured each of them a short one, handing one of the glasses to Hank. He took it and sipped.

She lifted her own glass to her lips. The liquid burned her throat, settling in her chest, a warmth spreading through her.

For a few moments, they drank in silence.

When Hank finished, he put his empty glass on the kitchen island. "I've got some phone calls to make, some things to follow up on, so I'll be in the den. Try to get some sleep." He leaned over and gave her a peck on the cheek before leaving her alone in the kitchen.

As Anna picked up Hank's glass and rinsed it out in the sink, she thought about Lizzie's mother and this new information. Did Kate know about the woman's return? She hadn't said anything, so Anna wasn't sure if she did. But Kate hadn't told her about the pregnancy, so it was possible this was yet another secret she was keeping. Anna admonished herself for feeling left out. She shouldn't be surprised she wasn't in the loop. She'd isolated herself in Greenwich, waiting for her wife to come home.

Everyone thought Joan was dead, but Anna wasn't convinced. She was a very practical person but had the unexpected romantic feeling that if Joan were dead, she would instinctively know it.

And now that she knew Nan Tudor was alive and had reemerged after so long, it gave her a renewed hope. Nan had been gone eight years. Joan had been away for only two months. Could Anna wait eight years? Absolutely.

Anna absently dried the glass with a kitchen towel and stared out the window. Because of the darkness that had fallen, she could only see her own reflection in it. She'd lost weight this summer, and her eyes looked too big now that her face was thinner. Joan would tell her she was silly, why wasn't she eating more, keeping herself healthy and strong. Joan's voice often came into her head, talking to her throughout the day. Anna was careful not to mention it to anyone; no one would understand the comfort it gave her.

She supposed Kate wasn't the only one keeping secrets.

Anna put the glass back in the cupboard and when she turned again to the window, she froze because it wasn't only her face looking back at her this time.

Joan.

23

NAN

Nan blinked against the darkness—a reminder that summer was fading and nighttime came much more quickly now. Because the marina was only a short walk from the hotel, she and Wyatt decided to leave the cars in the lot.

Wyatt's phone buzzed with an incoming text. "Smeaton's been busy. Says the yacht's registration was transferred a week ago from an LLC to your name. He's trying to find out about this LLC."

Nan frowned. "What if the yacht is just a decoy? A misdirection of sorts. Everyone is looking for a vessel that has my name on it. But what if Lizzie *isn't* on board? Maybe we should start thinking about where else she might be." She sighed. "Maybe I should go to Greenwich and finally have it out with Catherine."

Wyatt chuckled. "I'd pay to see that. But that wouldn't help Lizzie right now; in fact, it might hurt her."

She had to agree.

"Do you have children?" she asked, curious about this man who seemed to have taken her case to heart and was acting more like a bodyguard than an investigator.

Wyatt hesitated a moment before shaking his head. "No."

"Ever been married?"

He smiled. "This isn't about me, *Ms. Savoy.*" He emphasized her adopted name.

"Then I'm going to assume you *have* been married and perhaps it didn't end well," she said.

Wyatt's brow furrowed slightly. She could tell he was weighing how much to say. Finally, he spoke:

"*There is written, her fair neck round about: / Noli me tangere, for Caesar's I am, / And wild for to hold, though I seem tame.*" His voice was smooth, as though he had practiced the delivery often.

"Who wrote that? It's beautiful."

"I did."

She stopped walking, surprised. "You're a poet?"

He kept walking as he laughed. "It doesn't pay the bills."

"It's about a woman—" Nan quickened her step to catch up to him.

"Let's just say she was unattainable." Wyatt looked straight ahead, and she couldn't see his expression in the shadows. She wondered what he was hiding but had to respect his privacy. It wasn't as though she was telling him everything, either.

They grew silent as they followed a wooden walkway that ran alongside a waterfront restaurant and bar, and the sounds of laughter and chatter drifted across the still air. A waitress hurried out from inside, menus in her hand, and looked at them expectantly. "Table for two?" she asked.

"Just heading out to the water," Nan said. "Thank you."

The waitress's gaze settled on Nan a little too long, long enough to make her uncomfortable. She looked away, picked up her step.

When they were out of earshot, Wyatt asked, "You don't know her, do you?"

Nan shook her head. "No."

"She was looking at you like she knew who you were but couldn't place you."

Nan had felt the same way but brushed it aside. "I've been gone a long time. Out of the public eye. She's young enough so maybe she thinks I'm someone famous, but she wouldn't guess Nan Tudor."

As they approached the marina docks, the shadows of the boats rose up in the distance, the light of the moon piercing the sky.

A small beach dotted with Adirondack chairs was to the left of the entrance to one of the docks. A couple was sitting side by side, hand in hand, their feet in the sand. Nan wasn't sure she'd want to go in the water here, since the boats were so close, but to each their own.

Lights shone from some of the boats, but most of them were dark, their owners most likely having dinner or drinks either here or elsewhere on the island.

Wyatt dropped behind now, allowing her to go on without him.

Nan did a quick assessment of the docks that jutted out into the water. She had no idea which one had housed the *Perseverance*; if Wyatt had gotten that information from the dockmaster, he hadn't shared it, and she hadn't thought to ask. It had been enough to know the yacht was no longer there.

Nan didn't want to stop walking, feeling that if she did, she'd be a standing target, yet she was hesitant to go out onto the dock. While she'd joked with Wyatt that Catherine would throw her into the water to drown her, she wasn't sure that wasn't the plan. There seemed to be no other reason for her to be here. Still, she chose the dock that was right in front of her and ventured out, telling herself that Wyatt was keeping an eye on her, even if she couldn't see him.

She stared at the boats that were a reminder of just how far from her life with Hank she'd gone, and how she wouldn't want it back for anything. She no longer craved the glamour of being in the spotlight or of being on the arm of one of the richest men in the world. She was a completely different person now—or was she? Her priorities had changed, yet deep down she supposed she still had the ambition of her younger self, striving to do her best, to make a success out of the life she'd created. And then there was

Harry—and Lizzie. There was a time when she hadn't thought about being a mother—and then suddenly that was all she thought about. Devoting herself fully to Harry was, in a way, convincing herself that she *was* a good mother—even though she'd left her daughter behind.

Catherine would see it as ironic if she were truly holding Nan's daughter on a yacht named after a character she once played. Nan had seen what could happen at the hands of Catherine Tudor. Would Catherine take out her feelings about Nan on Lizzie? Nan could only hope that Catherine would see Lizzie for the innocent she was. Nan wasn't a part of her daughter's life, and it struck her now that she had no idea how Lizzie would react in her current situation. What if Lizzie had inherited her defiance—and the recklessness that sometimes went along with it? She could make matters worse for herself. Just as Nan had made matters worse for herself, all those years ago.

Nan began to walk more quickly back the way she came. The boat wasn't here, so this was futile.

A sound behind her made her twirl around, and a sudden urge to join Wyatt overcame her. But she didn't see him anywhere. Where had he gone? Something didn't feel right. Nan listened carefully for any other suspicious sounds, but all she heard was the water lapping against the boat hulls. Yet she still had a strong feeling that she was being watched.

And she was, she realized. Someone on the upper deck of the restaurant was leaning against the railing, watching her. Lights from inside illuminated the figure's silhouette, but before Nan could discern whether it was a man or a woman, the figure stepped back into the shadows.

She took a few steps forward before she stopped again. The figure held up a hand, as though in a wave, but not at Nan—at something behind her.

Nan whirled around, and in the corner of her eye, she caught a glint of something in the dim dock lights.

Panic rose in her chest; instinct told her to run. As she turned, the knife sliced through the air, the blade cold against her neck.

PART II

24
KATE

Kate wanted nothing more than to go for an early morning walk on the beach. She stood on the back patio with her decaf coffee, the ocean spread out in front of her, glistening under the sun. This had been Nan Tudor's favorite place, and she could see why. But a walk by herself would be out of the question, what with all the security on the property. Ironic that such a beautiful setting could be a prison.

Because that's what it was. While they had all gathered in Greenwich at Anna's inn earlier this summer after Caitlyn's murder, they could come and go as they pleased. Not so now, since Hank was so concerned about their safety.

Her husband had arrived last night, but he hadn't come to her room. She wasn't sure exactly where he'd stayed—this was a big house.

She certainly hadn't slept much. She kept expecting Hank to slide into bed beside her. When he didn't, she slipped into a fitful sleep, only to be awakened by the crashing of waves on the beach, gulls squawking overhead, the occasional sound of voices. Anna had sleeping pills to help her, but Kate was concerned that it wouldn't be good for the baby if she medicated.

"You're up early." Anna stepped onto the patio beside her, her own cup cradled in her hands.

Kate gave her a small smile. "Hard time sleeping."

Anna nodded. "Understandable."

They stood, looking over the water, drinking their coffee in companionable silence for a few moments. It was one of the reasons why Kate liked Anna: they were comfortable with each other even when they weren't speaking. But now she sensed something in Anna, a nervous energy that didn't seem related to their new circumstance.

"What's wrong?" she asked.

Anna took a deep breath. "I thought I saw her last night."

"Joan?"

"I was looking out the kitchen window, and she was there, plain as day. And then she was gone." Anna gave a high-pitched chuckle. "I know it's crazy."

Kate worried about Anna. It had been two months now, and while she understood the other woman's grief, she also hoped that she could eventually move on. Funny, coming from her, since her marriage was in limbo.

She reached over and touched the other woman's arm. "It's okay," she said softly. "It's not crazy."

Anna's expression told her that she wasn't quite convincing. Maybe because she wasn't completely convinced herself.

"Kate?"

Turning, she saw Hank coming through the sliding door. He wore a pair of khakis and a white button-down shirt, no tie. His clothes were rumpled, as though he'd slept in them. His hair was tousled, and he had a five-o'clock shadow. Kate had never seen him disheveled like this, except in those days right after their wedding at the penthouse. She felt a flush crawl across her face, remembering.

"Anna, do you mind going inside?" he asked, although it was more an order than a request.

"I'll start a new pot of coffee," Anna said, disappearing into the house.

As Hank approached, Kate peered around him, looking for the ubiquitous Cromwell, and fortunately he didn't seem to be close by.

"He's inside," Hank said, reading her mind. "You know, Cromwell's not the enemy."

Kate couldn't help but chuckle. "Could have fooled me."

"Yes, I know his tactics are less than desirable sometimes—"

"Sometimes?"

Hank held her gaze. "He does his job."

Kate didn't like what Cromwell's "job" was most of the time, but she kept her mouth shut.

"He's been vital in helping with all the logistics," he said, as though compelled by her silence to explain, his tone now that of the man she'd worked for rather than the man who was her husband.

"For the ransom money?" she asked, slipping easily into her former role of assistant.

"Yes, that and other details."

Not for the first time she wondered whether she should have said no when he asked her to marry him, keeping their relationship on a professional level only. It had been a good job; they worked well together. She'd been able to anticipate all his needs, and he appreciated her dedication and loyalty. He'd said so frequently, and he richly compensated her for it.

"Did you find anything out about that boat? Nan's boat?" Kate asked.

"It left the Vineyard yesterday before we could get there."

Kate could hear the frustration in his voice. "Is there a way to track it?" she asked.

"That's not for you to worry about," he said. "I've got people on top of it."

His tone told her she should let the matter drop, but she couldn't. "Do you think Nan's the one who has taken Lizzie, like Tommy Seymour said?" she pressed.

Hank shoved his hands in his pockets and stared out over the water, not looking at her now. "It would be in character for her."

Kate let that settle between them for a moment before asking, "Why?"

He frowned. "Why, what?"

"Why would she do this? I mean, she's been gone eight years. Why now?"

Hank's eyes grew darker. "Nan has always been volatile."

Kate didn't want to speculate what might happen to Nan Tudor if Hank found her. If she *had* taken Lizzie, she'd have to face consequences, and while Kate hoped Hank would leave it to the authorities, she was more than aware that he would mete out his own punishment.

Still, she couldn't figure out what Nan's motives might be. Maybe she had financial troubles, that could be a reason for a ransom demand. But to kidnap her own daughter? It seemed far-fetched, especially after what Nan had written in her journal. She had been a devoted mother.

That brought her to another place: Nan's baby. Her child would be eight years old now. Did the child exist? And if so, where was the child? Neither Hank nor Cromwell had indicated Nan had company coming through customs.

She could say none of this to Hank without revealing that she had seen Nan's diary. As far as she knew, Hank wasn't even aware that Nan had been pregnant when she left.

Kate wanted to play devil's advocate. If Nan hadn't taken Lizzie, then who had? Most likely someone far more dangerous. Someone who knew Hank would pay handsomely for the return of his daughter—yet still might harm her anyway, if that photograph of the girl was any indication. Did Hank really think a mother could do that to her daughter?

The question was on the tip of her tongue when Hank ran a hand across the stubble on his face. "I didn't want to bother you last night," he said suddenly, surprising her with the change of subject and confirming that he'd finished discussing Nan with her.

"I wouldn't have minded," Kate said, although that was easy to say in the light of day. She twisted the wedding ring on her finger, noticing her movement caught his eye. A glance at his hand told her he still wore his ring, too.

Their eyes met, and she was overcome with an intense sadness, as though what had happened between them was insurmountable.

"How are you feeling?" Hank asked.

He was asking about the pregnancy. Kate couldn't lie to him now; it was time to face facts. "I should have told you. I just need to get used to the idea. Children were never part of my life plan."

"I know," he said, and it took her by surprise. They'd never talked about children, whether he wanted more or whether she wanted any. It was shortsighted of them—wasn't that something any couple discussed before they married? It was too late now, though.

"You didn't want Caitlyn's baby," she said flatly, remembering how he'd set up "an appointment" for his ex-wife.

Hank stared out at the water for a moment before turning back to face her. "Caitlyn would not have been a good mother."

"But you should have let *her* make that decision. It was *her* life. She was no longer your wife." Kate held his gaze.

"But it was also my responsibility."

"That doesn't mean you make all the decisions."

"So then why do you think *you* can make all the decisions? The last I knew, we are still married. I'm still your husband."

He'd turned it around on her, and she had to admit he was right. But before she could respond, he continued.

"Right now, however, your safety is my number one concern."

Kate nodded. "I understand. That's why I didn't fight Cromwell when he said you wanted me to come here." She forced a smile.

But he didn't smile back. "I'm not sure I *can* keep you safe. Because what I'm about to ask may put you at risk."

She was confused. "What are you talking about?" An odd sense of foreboding settled over her.

"I told you about the ransom. How they want some in cash." He paused.

Kate had never seen him so hesitant about anything, and her anxiety grew.

"We've gotten another request."

"They want more money?"

Hank's eyes locked with hers. "They want *you* to deliver it."

25

Kate kept waiting for Hank to say that she could say no if she wanted. But he didn't. Instead, he told her that he'd have people watching her the whole time; he'd make sure she'd be safe.

"I see you have to get used to the idea," he said. "But we don't have much time. The drop is set for this afternoon."

The drop. He was using jargon she'd only heard before in the movies and on television. She reminded herself that she would be doing this for Lizzie, to get her back. But those same movies and television shows didn't always have happy endings. At least not until there was a shootout or two with the kidnappers, who were always angry to find out that the police were involved. In this case, Hank hadn't told the police, but he had "people," which could be just as perilous.

Her husband also didn't seem to take into consideration that she still had nightmares about the night she'd been shot. This was a much bigger ask than Hank acknowledged. Kate absently touched the scar on her forehead, tracing her finger around to the back of her head where she had a matching one. It was a miracle she hadn't died.

Kate had done a lot of things for Hank Tudor in the past three years but delivering a million dollars in ransom to a kidnapper would be a first. And while she had no problem running interference with the media, business rivals, and the occasional inconvenient wife, this was the first time she wanted to say no.

Instead, she heard herself saying, "Of course I'll do it." She had to. It was about Lizzie, not Hank. And if it were her child, she'd want to know that everyone was doing what they could to get her back safely.

Hank put his hand on her cheek and nodded. "Thank you." As though she really had a choice.

"What about Nan? *Do* you think she's the one asking for the money? I mean, the boat . . ."

"If it *is* Nan," Hank said, "at least we know what we're facing. I know her, I know how her mind works."

Kate shivered as she recognized the ruthlessness in his tone, something he generally reserved for business, not rogue wives. But Nan—and Caitlyn, she realized now—had sparked his anger in ways that she hoped she'd never see herself.

He was saying something about talking to the investigator, preparing her for what she had to do. His tone was matter-of-fact and businesslike. Easy for him, since he wasn't the one who had to make "the drop."

Her husband was looking at her with an expectant expression, and she realized he'd asked her a question.

"I'm sorry," she said softly. "What was that?"

"Come on inside," Hank said, holding out his hand. She hesitated only a moment before taking it. The warmth of his hand did nothing to alleviate her nerves.

A man was waiting for them just inside the sliding glass doors.

"Kate, this is Steve Gardiner," Hank said by way of introduction. "Steve, my wife, Kate."

Gardiner was tall, even taller than Hank, with a long face and long nose and inquisitive eyes. Eyes that she now realized were studying her as closely as she was studying him. He held out his hand, and she took it, his hand closing over hers in a firm grip.

"So, you are the Kate I've been hearing about," he said in a jovial tone, taking her aback, as though they were at a cocktail party and not about to embark on a mission to deliver a million dollars to a kidnapper.

Kate carefully slid her hand out from his and tucked it under her elbow. "Can you tell me just what I'm supposed to do?" she asked, directing the question at Hank.

Hank exchanged a look with Gardiner. What was that about? Kate felt as though they were leaving her out of a joke that she was the subject of. It was not a comfortable position. She had to regain some control; otherwise, she was going to lose her mind—not to mention her resolve. Yes, she was doing this for Lizzie, but Hank knew her well enough to know that she could not be in the dark on any part of it.

Kate heard footsteps, interrupting them.

"What's going on?" Maril asked, her voice echoing against the walls.

Hank waved his hand dismissively. "Nothing for you to worry about." He turned to Kate and Gardiner. "Let's join Cromwell in the den."

Maril's expression changed, and Kate could see her fury. Kate wasn't the only one who didn't like being in the dark. As she began to follow her husband, she noticed Gardiner giving Maril a nod, as though reassuring her. It struck her as odd, but as she thought about it, she realized they must have met already. Gardiner was helping Hank with the investigation, so he would have interviewed Maril about the day Lizzie went missing.

While Gardiner and Maril may have initiated a friendly acquaintance, when Kate entered the den, where Cromwell was sitting at the desk, his laptop open in front of him, she sensed a definite chill in the air, and it had nothing to do with the room temperature. Kate caught what she could only call intense dislike in Cromwell's expression when he saw Gardiner come in through the door. Even though she didn't know Gardiner at all, it wasn't difficult to see that the feeling was mutual.

Cromwell was a fixture in Hank's world, so Gardiner should watch out. Hank didn't tolerate any dissension on his team, but the fact that Gardiner was still here meant he must be very good.

Kate certainly hoped so. The way Hank had talked about "risk," it meant her life—as well as Lizzie's—might be on the line. She wasn't thrilled about putting herself in Gardiner's hands, especially since she didn't have a good first impression of him. It was that rare moment when she agreed with Cromwell on something.

"I understand you're wondering how this is going to work."

That was an understatement. But what struck Kate was, it wasn't Hank who spoke but Gardiner. She looked at her husband out of the corner of her eye. Hank usually wouldn't let anyone else take charge in a meeting. But he was uncharacteristically silent, leaning against the bookshelf, watching everyone.

Gardiner's presence had changed the dynamics, and Kate didn't like it. It didn't feel right.

"When you get there—" Gardiner began, and Kate put up her hand.

"Get where?"

He frowned.

"I don't know where I'm going."

Gardiner grinned. "Why, to the carousel, of course."

Kate counted to ten before asking, "What carousel? The one here on the island?"

Gardiner looked at Hank. "I thought you told her." Anyone else who spoke to Hank in that accusatory way would be sent packing, but Hank merely shrugged.

"The instructions are that you go to the carousel and put the bag with the money under one of the chariots, not a horse." Gardiner leveled his gaze at her. "There will be a lot of people at the carousel since the season's not over yet, and whoever set this up must know that. The location is more a subterfuge for whoever's picking up the backpack. You should be able to get on and off without a problem." He chuckled. "Unless, of course, you decide to take the backpack yourself."

She appreciated that he was trying to inject a bit of levity into the situation, but she was still anxious.

"Don't worry," he added as though sensing her hesitation, "we'll be watching you."

And the bag of money, Kate thought.

She was about to ask just exactly when all of this would take place—"this afternoon" seemed a bit vague—when Hank's phone buzzed. He held up his hand, indicating that the conversation should pause while he took the call, a gesture Kate was more than familiar with. Gardiner, too, was unfazed and fiddled with his own phone. Cromwell, Kate noticed, was watching the other man closely. She could feel the tension in the room rise even more when Hank stepped out, his murmurings unintelligible.

The longer he was gone, the more Kate wondered what was going on. The three of them kept stealing glances at the door, so she wasn't the only one wondering.

Finally, Hank came back, shutting the door behind him. His face was drawn, serious, as he looked from Gardiner to Cromwell and finally to Kate. He began to shake his head, his expression puzzled.

"That was the police. It seems a body has been recovered from the water at the marina near where the *Perseverance* was docked yesterday."

Kate caught her breath. "It's not Lizzie, is it?" she asked, suddenly feeling dizzy. She hadn't even had the chance to deliver the ransom money.

Hank shook his head, relief in his eyes. "No, thank God."

She closed her eyes and took a deep breath in and out, steadying herself. When she looked at Hank again, though, a question popped into her head. "Then why did they call you?" she asked. "I mean, if it's not Lizzie?"

He gave a short snort. "It seems I may have a reputation around here. They wanted to know if anyone in my entourage was missing. Because it was a woman. With no head."

26
CATHERINE

It had been risky, having her killed like the others. But it was the only way. The only way to make sure it stood out, that fingers would be pointed in Hank Tudor's direction. He had a history with women who were decapitated, and since one of them had already been found on Martha's Vineyard, the police would naturally gravitate toward him. Questions would be asked; speculation would be unbounded. That reporter's instincts would be piqued; he needed to be redeemed. What better than another woman found without her head? He was so desperate that crumbs could be strewn, leading him in any direction she chose. Not necessarily to the truth, but he'd get a story one way or another.

The new wife would wonder if she'd be next, that was certain. She would have every right to be concerned, too. There had already been an attempt on her life; she had to be thinking about that. She might even be persuaded that her husband was pulling the strings. It wasn't as though he were completely innocent in this. He'd started everything. If he'd only stayed with her, all of this would have been avoided.

Catherine had accepted her husband's infidelity. They'd had a mutual understanding. Of course, she'd never had any desire to step outside the bounds of her marriage. Sometimes she wondered, though, if she *had* taken a lover, would Hank have turned a blind eye as she had? Perhaps he would have been overcome with jealousy, a natural aphrodisiac. Perhaps he would have resisted those women.

Tossing her laptop aside onto the sofa cushion, Catherine rose and went to the fireplace, her fingers caressing the frame of a photograph on the mantel: her in her wedding gown, Hank looking at her with so much love and desire and, yes, need. When had that disappeared?

Not with the first couple of women, she knew that for sure. He'd come back to her, to their bed, and it had been better than before. As though he'd realized what he'd been missing, how much he truly loved her. He was a powerful man, and he needed a powerful woman at his side.

But then there was That Woman.

And he didn't come back.

Catherine's fingers curled around the photograph, and she took it off the mantel, staring at it as though it would tell her what had gone wrong. What was it about That Woman that had bewitched him enough so she would end up here, alone?

She'd been right to have it done the same way this time. She had to make sure that *he* was alone this time. Who would love him—marry him—after so many wives, so many deaths?

If this was what it took to bring him back to her, Catherine would do it. Would keep doing it.

He was her destiny. It was the only thing in her life that she knew for sure.

27
KATE

It was déjà vu.

Kate's head was spinning with the memory of Caitlyn Howard's decapitated body—not to mention the headless body discovered here eight years ago.

Two might be called a coincidence. Three meant something far more sinister. And Hank was right. Who else on the Vineyard had connections to headless bodies?

"They haven't identified her?" she asked, almost afraid to find out who'd met her demise this time. Anna and Maril were alive and well, so at least it wasn't either of them. But then she remembered. Nan Tudor was back. Had she finally met her fate?

"Not yet," Hank said.

Her husband had had such a visceral reaction to Nan's return—and the possibility that she had abducted her daughter and was demanding a ransom. Kate had been unable to shake her fears that Hank had something to do with Caitlyn's murder. What would he have done to Nan if he'd found her? Had he found her, after all?

"I still don't understand why they called you, regardless of your history," Kate said.

"It was the location," Hank explained. "We were out there yesterday looking for Lizzie, so there's yet another connection, albeit tenuous." He cocked his head toward the door. "Can you excuse us?" he said.

It was not a request.

While Kate understood that he wanted to confer with Cromwell and Gardiner, she did not like being dismissed. She'd been asked to deliver the ransom, but that was now overshadowed by something she wasn't privy to—and did not reassure her doubts about her safety.

Trying to be as quiet as possible, Kate made her way down the hall and through the great room, letting herself through the French doors out onto the porch and further to the patio. She didn't want to talk to anyone right now. She just wanted to be alone and sort out her thoughts.

She again longed for a walk along the water and started across the lawn and down toward the path that led to the beach. She wondered how far she'd make it before someone stopped her.

It didn't take long. Kate heard an urgent shout from somewhere on the beach. But it didn't seem to be about her. Three men appeared over the dunes, two of them flanking the third, who was saying something that Kate couldn't make out because the wind was carrying his voice.

What she *could* make out, though, was who it was.

Tommy Seymour had followed them here, as promised.

He saw her and raised his hand. "Can you call these guys off?" he demanded.

With an exasperated breath, Kate made her way toward them, farther on the sandy path. She quickly glanced back at the house but didn't see anyone. It was a good thing Hank was in conference with Cromwell and Gardiner. She could take care of this herself before anyone else found out about it—and before Tommy made a real scene.

"Hi, Kate," he said casually when she reached him. He looked out of place on the beach, dressed in a pair of khaki chinos, blue button-down shirt, and sneakers, his reporter's notebook shoved in his back pocket. He wasn't here to take a swim, but to do his job.

Kate took a deep breath. "It's okay," she told the two men, one of whom gripped Tommy's arm. They were part of Hank's security detail. "You can let him go. I know him," she said as she swung around to face Tommy.

"What the hell are you doing?" she hissed at him when the men backed off, although not fast enough so they didn't hear. They paused, waiting to make sure she would be all right. She nodded at them. "He won't hurt me." Not physically, anyway, she thought, remembering her broken heart and the days she spent crying in her room. She shrugged that aside.

Despite her assurances, the two security guards didn't move.

"Thanks, Kate," Tommy said as he watched them out of the corner of his eye. "I thought I was going to be swimming with the fishes."

"Don't be an ass," she said. He was casing the property, trying to see how close he could get. Well, he found out, didn't he? "This isn't exactly the best way to get access."

"But it worked." He didn't even try to dispute her.

"Did it?" she asked sarcastically.

When he realized she wasn't leading him to the house, he shrugged. "Worth a try."

"This isn't a competition, you know. A girl is missing," Kate reminded him.

"It's more than that now," he said. The Cheshire cat grin appeared. Damn. He knew about the body at the marina. That news traveled fast. She should have known he'd find out about it, lurking around the Vineyard.

Hank had given her permission to talk to Tommy, but her instincts told her she couldn't. Especially now.

"You know better than to pull something like this," she said, waving her hand toward the beach. "Did you really think you wouldn't be stopped?"

He studied her face, those blue eyes flashing. "You've changed, Kate."

She didn't look away. "I wish I could say the same about you."

Tommy shrugged. "At least I didn't sell out, become a flack."

It hurt more than she expected—and that was exactly what he intended.

Kate cocked her head toward the two guards. "Escort Mr. Seymour off the property."

Tommy held up his hand as though to stop them from coming closer. "Okay, Kate, tit for tat."

"Ma'am?" one of the guards asked.

Kate could see in Tommy's expression that he still might have a card to play, and she was curious just what he may have discovered.

"Give us a minute," she said.

The guards exchanged a look and then backed away, but not too far, still keeping an eye on them.

"I'll decide whether your information is helpful," Kate told Tommy.

"Fair enough." He paused for effect, then continued. "I've got on record that the cops were out at the Vineyard Haven marina yesterday looking for a girl on a yacht. I assume that was your stepdaughter?"

He had already gotten this from the police. He was just looking for confirmation, and she wasn't about to give it to him. She folded her arms across her chest and stared stonily at him.

He chuckled. "I'll take that as a yes, off the record. But there's something else. Last night, I went to the bar at the marina restaurant for a drink and chatted up one of the waitresses."

Of course he'd find a woman to talk to. Women always talked to Tommy.

"I don't want to know what some gossipy waitress told you," Kate said, although that was exactly what she did want to know—and he knew it.

He acted as though she hadn't spoken. "There was a woman who'd been there earlier." He leaned over then, close enough to her that she caught the scent of sunscreen. "Kate, the waitress recognized her."

"Recognized who?"

"Nan Tudor."

Kate was quiet, and Tommy took her silence as permission to continue.

"If what that waitress said is true, then my source was right. Nan Tudor did come back from the dead. And she was seen at the marina where another decapitated body was found just hours later, the same marina where the police were looking for her daughter earlier in the day. Those things have to be connected." He paused a moment. "What do you think? Did something go wrong with the kidnapping? Did someone really kill her this time?"

There was no trace of her old college friend—or former lover—in his tone. He was asking as a journalist, a reporter who was going to write about this. Who was going to put out Hank Tudor's dirty laundry for the whole world to see. She couldn't let that happen.

"I can't comment on that," she said.

"Can you at least confirm that there was a ransom request? I heard it was five million."

Kate struggled not to react. How on earth had he found out about that? "You know better than to ask," she chided gently, her tone belying the panic that was pounding in her chest.

"Come on, we had a deal."

"No, we didn't."

"You can't give me anything?" he asked, still probing, hoping she'd break.

It had been too long, though, since they had been allies. And since then, Kate had protected Hank and his circle—which now seemed to include his second wife, indirectly—in her capacity as Hank's assistant. She'd also signed the nondisclosure agreement. Tommy had to have known that was part of the deal.

He leveled his gaze at her. "I thought we were friends, Kate."

"A lifetime ago, Tommy," she said, truly feeling sad that their encounter was not chance at all, but a reporter wanting to save his career. But then again, would she have wanted to share dumplings in Chinatown with him again, possibly bringing back old feelings that were better left buried in the past? No, it was best this way.

"You have to go through the proper channels," Kate told him. "If you don't have the contact information for the public relations office, I can get that for you."

"I get the message. But you have to know I'm going to connect all the dots, one way or another." He hesitated. "I've just got one more question: Where was your husband last night?"

28

The doubts about Hank crept back into Kate's head. If a waitress had seen Nan, it wasn't as though the woman was hiding. It might have been easy for Hank to track her down. Again, she wondered: How far would he go if he had?

Hank hadn't come to her bed last night. She didn't know where he'd been.

Kate couldn't let Tommy see her hesitation. Even after all this time, he'd know something was off. He knew her too well.

She turned to the security guards, who stood at the ready. "Please escort Mr. Seymour off the property now," she instructed.

Tommy gave her a nod, turned, and waved off the guards. "I can get to the beach on my own." He glanced back once and flashed a grin at her. "Don't underestimate me, Kate. You know I'm good at my job." He winked. "You'll be seeing me again soon."

She was afraid of that.

Lizzie's kidnapping and the body had to be connected. It was too convenient that the body was found where the yacht had been docked—a yacht owned by Nan Tudor. Tommy was right. Should she be sorry that she'd let him go before getting any more information out of him? He may well know more than he'd let on. No, she did the right thing. He was going to be as closemouthed with her as she was with him, both of them unwilling to give anything up without knowing they'd get something in return. And she certainly couldn't give him anything.

Kate made her way back up to the house. Tommy's presence on the beach wouldn't have gone unreported by the security detail, and she braced herself against defending her decision to handle the situation herself. She'd barely stepped inside when Gardiner called her back into the den, acting as though it was business as usual with no mention of the journalist who'd almost infiltrated the property barrier. She glanced around the room, but Hank and Cromwell were conspicuously absent. Perhaps Gardiner's only role was to deal with the ransom drop-off, whereas, as Hank's lawyer, Cromwell was more suited to dealing with the authorities' questions about dead bodies.

She was off the hook—at least for now.

"Mrs. Tudor?"

Gardiner's voice interrupted her thoughts.

"You have to stay focused," he warned.

Easy for him to say. She couldn't stop thinking about the dead woman.

"Do you think it's Nan Tudor?" she asked him. "The body, I mean."

Gardiner pulled a face. "Nan always lived on the edge. She pissed off a lot of people during the time that I knew her."

It wasn't exactly an answer.

"But say that body is her. If she was the one who kidnapped Lizzie, then where is Lizzie?" Her thoughts were pinballing around in her head. "Maybe someone was after both of them." As she spoke, Kate pondered her own words. Who would want to endanger both of them? Nan had been gone a long time. Despite "pissing off a lot of people," Nan hadn't done that for years. She hadn't seen her daughter. But could she have taken her daughter to protect her from someone?

Gardiner was looking at her with an amused expression. "You're a regular Nancy Drew, aren't you?"

She didn't like his tone. He wasn't taking her seriously.

He realized his mistake. "We have no idea who the dead woman is, so we are going to proceed as though it has no bearing on Lizzie's kidnapping," he said, his expression growing serious. "It could have been a boating accident. It's not like amputations haven't happened at the hand of a boat propeller."

Kate cringed, but he was right. Her imagination was running away with her. The memory of Caitlyn Howard's body earlier in the summer was spooking her, and she'd allowed Tommy Seymour to get into her head. It was possible, too, that whoever the woman was, she'd been killed days or even weeks ago and was just now discovered. That thought slowed her heartbeat. She had to be sensible about this.

"Okay, say it's not Nan, and that she does have Lizzie. Do you think once the ransom is paid, she'll let Lizzie go?" she asked. Nan had already successfully vanished; imagine how much deeper she could go with five million dollars—but what if she decided to take Lizzie with her this time?

"Just a little word of advice, Mrs. Tudor," Gardiner said, lowering his voice as though expecting someone to eavesdrop. "I've known your husband a lot longer than you have. He doesn't like it when his wives ask too many questions." One of his eyebrows rose higher than the other.

Was that some sort of warning? Even though he was right about asking questions, Kate wasn't willing to admit it. And despite his suggestion that she didn't know her husband well, it was telling that in the three years she'd worked with Hank, she'd never even heard Gardiner's name.

"Have we gone over everything we need to?" she asked, unwilling to take the bait.

He eyed her curiously. "One more time."

Kate resisted the urge to roll her eyes. "You drop me off a couple blocks from the carousel. I take the backpack. I get a ticket and take a seat in one of the chariots. I leave the backpack." It was pretty simple, when it came down to it. But anxiety gripped her. "You'll have someone there, right? Watching me?"

Gardiner's expression softened as he nodded.

She wondered about the other four million requested. "Have you already sent the rest by wire transfer?" She still wondered why the kidnapper didn't want all the money that way. It really would be easier, more twenty-first century.

"Don't worry your pretty head about that. Leave it to the professionals," he said condescendingly. It was as though he hadn't quite figured out how to relate to her. Was she a friend or a foe? Competition? Kate considered the latter—and Cromwell's reaction to him. She wondered just what his role had been with Hank in the past.

"It's ten A.M. now," he said, checking his wristwatch. "The drop-off is at one. Be ready at noon. We'll meet out front." His phone buzzed, and he picked it up off Hank's desk. He looked at the screen, then up at Kate. "We're done for now," he said.

Dismissed, Kate flung the door open to see Teddy standing there, his hands folded, worry lines around his eyes. How much had he heard? She took a deep breath, trying to relax a little. She couldn't let him see her anxiety—or her fear.

"Hello, Ted," she said softly, but her words sounded wooden. She forced a smile as she moved him away from the den, away from Gardiner.

He didn't respond, and she remembered how he hadn't spoken since Lizzie went missing. "We're all doing everything we can to bring Lizzie home," she told him.

The boy's expression was skeptical as his gaze settled on Kate's face. She didn't blame him. If she were in his shoes, she would probably be doubtful, too. And then she realized something else: His stepmother Caitlyn Howard had been missing and found dead, then Anna's wife, Joan, had vanished. Now his sister was gone. Was Ted wondering who would be next? His father? Anna? Kate?

She reached over and put her arms around the boy, feeling him squeeze her back. He might not be speaking with words, but he was communicating in his own way.

"Come on, Ted." Kate heard Anna's voice behind her. The boy wiggled out of her embrace. "Why don't you go get into your swim trunks and we can go to the pool?" Anna asked him, giving Kate a knowing nod, but she could see tension in the other woman's expression.

Ted obediently headed for his room to get changed, no questions, no arguments. She met Anna's eyes.

"Do you think he'll be okay?" she asked.

Anna shrugged. "Will any of us?" She hesitated, as though she had something else to say.

"What is it?" Kate prodded.

"Who was that out on the beach? I saw you out there talking to someone. A man. Was he trespassing?"

Kate figured someone had seen them; she was glad it was only Anna. "A reporter. And yes, he was trespassing," she said. "His name is Tommy Seymour. I know him from school, years ago. He thought he'd get a direct line, some good quotes. I shot him down." She hoped she didn't sound too defensive.

Ted saved her from having to explain further by coming down the hall dressed in orange swim trunks and a T-shirt sporting a large, cheerful SpongeBob, which belied the solemnity of his expression. Anna pursed her lips and gave Kate a short nod as she guided Ted down the stairs, leaving her alone. Maybe she should join them at the pool. A quick swim might be good for her as well as for Teddy. But then she remembered she hadn't brought her suit. That was an oversight, considering she was heading to a beach house. She and Anna weren't the same size, so she couldn't borrow one from her. Maril might have one that would fit her. Since Maril had been here all summer, Kate couldn't imagine that she didn't have at least one bathing suit.

Kate made her way down the hall to Maril's room, where she could hear the other woman talking. Probably on the phone and probably working. Kate didn't want to interrupt, but as she started to step away from the door, she couldn't help but hear what Maril was saying.

"Kate's the one who's going to deliver the ransom."

29
ANNA

Anna wrapped Ted in a towel and settled him with one of his books in one of the chaise longues at the poolside. He'd only spent a short time in the water, floating on a noodle. Without his sister, Ted was unmoored. He was not used to having to entertain himself, always having had Lizzie as a companion—even when they were fighting. She'd been surprised to see Kate giving him a hug; the other woman wasn't usually that demonstrative with the children. Yet Kate hadn't protested when she led Ted away, and Anna sensed a bit of relief on the other woman's part. Kate hadn't wanted to talk about the reporter; Anna suspected there was more history there than Kate had let on. She knew about Kate's two previous marriages, but little about any other relationships, again underscoring the fact that perhaps they weren't as close as Anna had thought.

There had been a lot of closed doors around here this morning, a lot of secrets brewing. Anna wasn't in on any of them, and the longer she was here, the less she felt useful. She wanted to talk to Hank about Ted, how the boy wasn't speaking and nothing she said or did seemed to get through, but he was busy with trying to find Lizzie and she couldn't bother him with anything else right now. Since her marriage to Hank, the children had been her responsibility anyway, and he depended on her. Not that she was complaining. It was just that sometimes she wished he'd play a bigger role in the day-to-day.

Anna wondered what her role in the family would be going forward. Joan's disappearance and Kate's marriage to Hank had changed everything. Once Lizzie came back—and Anna had to stay optimistic that she *would* be back—she and her brother would be going off to their respective boarding schools. But where would they go on their holidays? They'd been with Anna and Joan for the past three years, and Hank had joined them with Caitlyn, until the divorce. Now, though, Kate was in the picture, and she was pregnant. Lizzie and Ted would have another sibling. Anna was sure Kate would go back to Hank and try to make things work. What was Anna's place in that circle? Would the children call her "auntie" and she'd show up with presents at Christmas and maybe spend a few weekends with them in the summers?

Anna forced herself not to imagine what the future might hold for her. It wasn't doing her any good except to make her sad and anxious. Maybe she could talk Hank into letting her take Ted back to Greenwich with her. This wasn't the best place for the boy right now, that was clear. When they found Lizzie, she could join them until they had to go to school. Kate and Hank could patch things up. Maril could go back to the city and to her work.

She was realistic enough to know it wasn't going to be that easy. But Anna was always happier when her life was a known quantity, when she could organize and sweep up after a mess. She had to start moving forward instead of back.

"I'm going to go inside and get some lemonade, okay?" she asked Ted, who glanced up from his book and gave a short nod. She took that as a win and gave him a smile. "I'll be right back."

Maril had been in her room earlier, but now was sitting at the kitchen island, her laptop open in front of her. She didn't usually work downstairs, but when Anna peeked at the screen, she saw *The New York Times* article about a hedge fund takeover of a newspaper.

Maril noticed her. "Homework," she said simply.

It was none of Anna's business. She busied herself with taking down a couple of glasses and putting them and a pitcher of lemonade on a tray.

"Kate's going to deliver the ransom," Maril said, startling her.

So that's what was going on. Anna wanted Kate to say no, that she wouldn't participate. Hank should negotiate, because Kate shouldn't be asked to take any risks. She was expecting a baby, and Anna could still see the trauma of being shot two months ago in the other woman's eyes. But no one ever said no to Hank—and Anna knew better than to interfere.

She should be happy that she wasn't the one who would have to drop off the ransom money. Now Anna realized that it *could* have been her. She was another wife, the one who cared for Hank's children. It had been more than four years since they'd been married, though, and sometimes she forgot that they had been married at all. Joan had taken up her whole life once they'd met; Hank was easily forgotten—at least as a spouse. If it weren't for him and his settlement money, she wouldn't have had her business at all.

She'd let the inn go because she couldn't let go of her memories of Joan—and now she was having hallucinations, seeing her wife outside windows.

"I'm surprised Daddy's letting her do it, you know, especially now," Maril said. This was supposed to be Anna's cue to chime in, but she wasn't going to take the bait.

Anna didn't like talking about Kate with Maril, who was upset that Hank married Kate—and very happy about their estrangement—so it was best to stay out of any conversation that involved Kate. Maril had tried a few times, but Anna quickly shut her down by changing the subject or telling her she had things to attend to. But she was worried that Maril wasn't going to let it go this time.

"We have to focus on Lizzie," Anna said, hoping to remind her that this was bigger than a petty rivalry with Hank's wife. "This is all about her and trying to get her back safe."

The longer the girl was gone, well, Anna didn't even want to think about it. She remembered the messages she'd found in that hidden phone. If Lizzie was with her mother, she couldn't imagine she'd be hurt. But that brought her to a new place, something she hadn't thought about before. If Lizzie was with her mother, would she even want to come back? Was she old enough to tell Hank she wanted to be with her mother rather than with him—and, by extension, Anna?

Anna wasn't knowledgeable about custody laws, but the girl was going to be twelve soon. She might legally have a say in what she wanted. Hank couldn't control her forever, and Lizzie had a strong will and a stubborn streak.

"She's just like her mother." The moment Anna spoke, she realized the Pandora's box she was opening. She hadn't meant to say that out loud.

"Yes." Maril's tone was short, angry, but she quickly composed herself. "But she's like Daddy, too."

Maril was kind to her half sister, even though Hank had left her and Catherine and created a new family with Nan. Anna had often thought it was a good thing that Lizzie was so much younger. She could already see that the younger girl's intelligence and intuition might someday outshine that of her sister. But the age difference kept it at bay—for now.

"Do you think they'll get back together?" Maril was asking, pivoting to her previous topic of Kate. So much for Anna's attempt to turn the conversation around.

"I don't know," Anna said, and it was the truth.

Maril snorted. "Maybe something will happen to Kate, too. I mean, Daddy's got a track record."

Her statement took Anna aback. Was Maril alluding to Caitlyn's murder? There had already been an attempt on Kate's life. Anna struggled with how to respond—should she respond?

Anna reminded herself that they were all on edge. That even under better circumstances, Maril could be harsh. She wondered if Maril felt the same way about her as she did about Kate. After all, Anna had married her father, too.

It was best not to engage, Anna told herself as she picked up the tray and slipped out the back door. She rounded the corner on the stone walkway and glanced at the kitchen window—the same one where she'd seen Joan the night before. Of course it hadn't been her, but a figment of her imagination.

Yet she had seemed so real.

Anna had a clear view of Maril through the window as she worked on her laptop, but the woman's back was to her, so she didn't see Anna lurking.

What was she doing? She needed to get this lemonade out to Ted. She'd already been gone too long.

Instead, she leaned over and put the tray on the ground, studying the flower garden under the window, looking for—what, exactly? Hallucinations don't leave footprints. Still, she stooped down and ran her hand along the edge of the garden, pushing aside the foliage, peering underneath.

Nothing. What was she expecting to find? She was being ridiculous. Next thing she knew, she'd be holding séances or using a Ouija board. She'd be one of those crazy widows in a gothic novel, living in the attic and scaring the neighborhood children.

Anna straightened up, turning her back on the window and looking out toward the horizon, the water shimmering under the early-morning sun. She closed her eyes, the briny scent of the ocean filling her nose as she took a deep breath.

"Did you find what you were looking for?" Cromwell's voice caused her to stiffen.

His tone was accusatory, as though she *did* find something.

"Why do you think I was looking for something?" she asked, aware that she was being confrontational. She never would have been like that with Hank, but Cromwell always got under her skin, and she was tired of it. She hadn't answered his question, but in her estimation, she didn't have to. Cromwell was the help, just like those security guards out there. He may have not thought himself disposable, but he had to know everyone in Hank's world was—with the exception of his children.

"You found Lizzie's hiding place, where she put that phone," he reminded her.

"That was an accident," Anna started to argue, but Cromwell put his hand up and she stopped.

"Poking around out here is not an accident," he said.

It was almost as though he knew she'd seen Joan last night and was trying to trip her up in some way, so she'd admit to it.

"I wasn't looking for anything," she insisted.

Cromwell leaned closer to her.

"Maybe you were hiding something, instead," he said, then lowered his voice to a whisper. "Girls have hiding places. Is this yours?"

30
LIZZIE

Anna has a hiding place. She puts her things in shoeboxes on the top shelf of her closet, things like her passport and birth certificate and love letters from a woman named Susanna that are tied up with a purple ribbon. Joan thought she was the one great love of Anna's life, but I know different.

I've got secrets, too. I guess that's what got me into this mess, because now I see how dangerous it is to want something so bad, to wish for something that might be a lie.

I don't know what's the truth and what's a lie anymore.

All I know is, I was so desperate to meet my mother that I didn't even think that it might be a trap.

The messages first started coming not long after Joan went missing, and we were already here on the Vineyard. Of course I have my own phone. I've had it since I was ten. I wanted a phone before that—everyone else had one—but Dad said that kids didn't need them. He didn't get how hard it was when everyone was texting each other all the time and I couldn't. They'd give me the side-eye and call me the "poor little rich girl," and when I said, "Oh, the old Shirley Temple movie," they laughed at me because they didn't have a clue. Anna eventually talked Dad into buying me a phone. Said I'd be safer or something, they could keep an eye on me. Yeah, I know about the tracking app. But it wasn't that. She knew how much I wanted it, wanted to be included.

Having a phone didn't do much for my popularity, though. But at least I had one. I downloaded one of those language apps and started learning Finnish. I mean, no one speaks Finnish except the Finns, but why not? Someday I might go to Finland.

When I got the first message from her, I figured it was a joke. Someone was playing tricks on me. One of those girls who hated me. I heard their whispers. It wasn't just about not having a phone. It was about not having a mother. Not that they all have perfect families. There are a lot of kids whose parents are divorced, and they've got stepparents, like me and Teddy. Absent dads and absent moms. We're all sent away to school for a reason; otherwise, we'd stay home and go public and live normal lives.

But there is something even more different about me. About my mother. Because she completely disappeared, and moms usually don't do that unless they're dead—and there's also that. Is my mom dead? No one knows for sure. But we do know there was a woman who had her head cut off—like Caitlyn—and some people think it was my mother and some people don't.

I played along with the messages at first, answering questions about how I was, school, Dad's new wife. I didn't give long answers, and I didn't want to talk about Kate, since I don't really know her.

But then she started talking about me, when I was little, things no one would know except for her and my dad. Stories about her speaking French to me, and then we started texting in French. It was like texting in another language meant I could say things I'd never said before, and suddenly I just knew I was texting with my mother. She never said where she was or what happened, but it was her.

She had to be my mother.

I hate it when I'm wrong.

31
KATE

Kate slung the backpack over her shoulder and shifted its weight. She hadn't been to the gym in two months, and she was regretting that now. At least the intense heat of summer had passed, and a cool breeze was coming across the water.

She was sure that she'd overheard a conversation between Maril and her mother. Maril always kept Catherine apprised of what was going on in Hank's households—at least when she was present. But to tell Catherine that Kate was supposed to deliver the ransom was a bit too much. Kate debated whether to tell Hank but decided against it. He didn't need the distraction, and she didn't need it, either. It didn't do any good to worry about Maril gossiping when she had to deliver a million dollars to a kidnapper.

Anna had been distracted and oddly evasive, too, and Kate didn't have the energy to pursue it. She decided she'd talk to Anna and find out what was bothering her when she got back, abandoning her plan to take a swim and instead trying unsuccessfully to relax by taking a hot bath. She spent too much time carefully applying her makeup and choosing what to wear. What did one wear to a ransom drop-off, anyway? She hadn't packed much, so she ended up in jeans and a pink V-necked T-shirt. Easy for the kidnapper to spot her.

Did the kidnapper have her in his sight line now? Her eyes shifted from right to left, scanning the tourists along Circuit Avenue, where Gardiner had dropped her off, promising that he'd keep an eye on her. She didn't see him anywhere, but she supposed that was the point. His job was to be invisible.

Hank had not been happy that Gardiner didn't want him along, and the two had disappeared for a short while. Kate assumed Hank would win that argument, but surprisingly, he came back and told her that Gardiner would take her. She had the sense that he wanted her to back out, say she wouldn't do it. Instead, as he tucked her into the car with Gardiner, he gave her a kiss on the cheek and whispered, "I'll see you when you get home."

This must be killing him, not being in charge. It certainly didn't give her much confidence.

When she'd told Hank that Tommy knew about the ransom request and that the waitress recognized Nan, he'd given her a curious look and merely said, "Thank you for letting me know. I'll take care of it." While it was likely his security team had told him about the encounter on the beach, he hadn't asked for any details. Something was amiss, as though Gardiner's presence had changed all the dynamics.

Now, though, she put that aside to think about later. She had to concentrate on the matter at hand.

A young man with a man bun and wearing a Black Dog T-shirt brushed past her, jostling the backpack. It slipped a little, and she hoisted it back up. It wouldn't do to lose the bag in the middle of the sidewalk before she even got to the carousel.

She tried not to think about the fact that she had a million dollars on her back.

The small, red wooden building was up ahead. Kate hadn't realized that the carousel would be enclosed, but then it would be good for tourism if people could still ride the horses even if it were raining. She remembered riding the carousel at Disney World when she was a kid, a plastic poncho covering her to protect her from the downpour that was not uncommon in Florida. The trip had been an indulgence her parents had given her; they preferred more educational traveling to Europe or Asia. But she'd desperately wanted to go and wore them down, agreeing to only three days. They were the best three days of her young life.

Kate pushed the memories away as she came closer to the building. A line had formed and was spilling outside onto the steps. Who knew there would be this many tourists wanting to ride the carousel? She took her place behind a family of four, the little girl in blonde pigtails and holding a stuffed horse. If anyone wondered why a grown woman with a backpack was waiting to ride the Flying Horses, they didn't indicate it.

Music wafted out overhead, but she was no longer nostalgic. She just wanted to get this over with.

Put the bag on the floor under one of the chariots.

Looking at the line of people, she began to wonder if there would even be room.

The scent of popcorn joined the music in the air, and as she stepped inside the building, she saw the small concession stand and just beyond that, the ticket booth. She pulled a few dollar bills out of her pocket and handed them over.

Kate wasn't even aware of the weight of the bag now. She was focused on getting in and out. But when it was finally her turn to ride and she stepped up onto the carousel's wooden platform, she realized she couldn't just leave the bag and get off. She was going to have to stay on the ride until it was over.

Would the kidnapper be on the carousel with her? It would be easier that way, wouldn't it? He could pick up the bag the moment she stepped away from the chariot.

Scenarios ran through her head as she made her way to one of the chariots. Everyone was jostling for a horse, so she didn't have any competition for her chosen seat. She stuffed the bag down at her feet and sat back, trying not to be obvious as she watched parents hoist toddlers up, teenagers straddling the wooden horses.

"You can't get the brass ring from there," came a voice from behind her.

Kate swung around to see a young woman barely out of her teens, her hair up in a ponytail and a tattoo of a rose trailing along her bicep. Since getting a brass ring wasn't a priority for her, she merely shrugged, but the young woman's attention had already moved on.

A woman slid into the seat next to her, forcing her to move over. Kate had hoped to sit alone, but it seemed that all the horses had been taken, and the chariot seats were the only ones left. She used her feet to move the bag with her as she shifted, not looking at the woman so as to avoid eye contact. She didn't need to be making small talk with anyone. Not that she felt she'd be able to. Her throat was dry, and she folded her hands tightly in her lap to keep them from trembling.

She was relieved when the carousel began moving, the traditional music filling her ears. The horses didn't go up and down, she noticed now, and the manes looked like real horsehair. She wished she had her phone to search whether it was, but Gardiner had taken it, telling her that it would be best if she didn't have it. In case the kidnapper saw it as a threat.

She felt naked and exposed without it.

As the carousel turned, Kate surreptitiously studied the other riders. No one looked like a kidnapper, but then again, what did she know? It didn't have to be like the movies or on television: a large, sinister man dressed in black. Maybe this kidnapper was that father over there, standing close to his child to make sure the child didn't fall off the horse. Or maybe it was that woman grabbing a brass ring and grinning at her boyfriend, who was clearly only doing this for her, based on the bored look on his face.

Kate became a little more aware of the people standing in line, too, waiting for their turn. Was one of them the kidnapper? She could be completely wrong about the kidnapper already being on the ride.

On the first pass past the line of people waiting to ride, Kate spotted Gardiner in the background, his arms crossed over his chest, studying her. She was puzzled. Shouldn't he be scanning the other riders, as she was? Why was he watching *her*?

She chided herself. Maybe she wasn't the only one he was watching, and it was most likely that Gardiner wasn't the only one of Hank's people scoping out the carousel as they waited for the kidnapper to take the bag. Gardiner probably had a team of undercover investigators there, but he was the only one she'd recognize.

As the ride continued to turn, he was now out of sight. Kate felt a moment of panic. She didn't like the man, but she was reliant on him for her safety. What if he couldn't see her anymore, either? When the carousel came around again, she scanned the crowd, but Gardiner was no longer there.

She caught her breath, though, when she saw who was: Tommy Seymour, peering over the heads of the people waiting in line.

It would be too much of a coincidence to think that he'd randomly decided to take a ride on the carousel while on the island. No, he had to know something was going down—but how had he found out about this? Someone was feeding him information, someone on the inside of Hank's organization. How much did he know, though? Kate again regretted the loss of her professional role, since she would have made sure nothing had leaked to anyone—especially Tommy.

Kate's heart was beating too fast. She took a few deep breaths, wondering how long this ride would last. She couldn't wait to get off, to leave this bag and escape the building. Her job would be done then. It wasn't her responsibility to catch the kidnapper as he took the backpack.

Children were shouting about the brass rings they'd caught, how many they had. One little girl was screaming with joy because she'd caught the gold one, which meant she'd be able to ride again. Kate wondered absently if they'd make the girl get off and wait in the line again or if she could just stay on the horse she was riding.

Kate glanced down at the backpack, then up at the woman seated next to her.

The woman was wearing a white T-shirt and jeans, a blue scarf around her neck. Her hair was pulled into a ponytail underneath a blue ball cap with *Martha's Vineyard* stitched in pink on the front, the bill pulled down over her forehead, obscuring her face from this angle. Something was familiar about her, but Kate couldn't put her finger on it.

The woman caught her eye and held her gaze.

And in that instant, she recognized her.

It was Nan Tudor.

PART III

32

NAN

It had all happened in slow motion. As she spun around, away from her attacker and the knife, Nan saw Wyatt running toward her. He came too close as he rushed past her, his gun in his hand, and she felt herself topple to the ground. But by then the figure had disappeared over the side of the dock, and the sound of a boat motor revving filled her ears. She rolled over and lifted herself onto an elbow, seeing the wake of the small motorboat as it sped away.

Wyatt came back to her, the gun returned to its holster—he hadn't even fired it, at least she didn't think so, her head was reeling—and reached down, holding out his hand to help her get up.

"Are you okay?" he asked.

Nan stood, a little wobbly, and nodded.

"They were too fast for me," he said apologetically. "I didn't even get a good look. Did you?"

"No." Nan touched her neck where the blade had nicked her. Wyatt reached over and moved her hand away.

"It's bleeding, but it doesn't look like more than a scratch," he noted. "Let's go to the restaurant and see if someone has a bandage."

Nan stared at the smear of blood on the palm of her hand, black as the night. "I thought she'd drown me, not try to take off my head," she said, attempting a laugh but it came out as a choked cough instead. "Although I guess she tried it before, so why not again?"

She shook off Wyatt's offer of his arm. "I'm fine," she said, although in her effort to prove it, she stumbled on an uneven board and fell, her knees slamming against the wooden dock. She held up her hand and said, "I'm fine," again.

Wyatt stepped back slightly, giving her space.

"We can't go back to the restaurant," she said. "That waitress . . ." Her voice trailed off, remembering as she stood. "Someone was watching from the deck."'

"Anyone you recognized?"

"No." She looked over at the restaurant deck but no longer saw the person at the railing. Maybe she'd imagined the wave. Maybe the person had merely been looking at the yachts and the ocean. Those anonymous texts and now this attack were making her paranoid. She said as much to Wyatt.

"Let's think about this a moment," Wyatt said, interrupting her. "Someone texted you to be here. They knew you'd show up. You were attacked here on the dock, and if he really wanted to hurt you—or kill you—he could have." He let his words settle a moment.

"You think he was just trying to scare me?" Nan turned this over in her head and wrapped her arms around her torso and shivered. Catherine was playing with her. Where was it going to end? How would it end?

"Come on," Wyatt said, his hand under her elbow. "We have to get you a bandage."

Nan was grateful for the scant streetlights that allowed the darkness to envelope them as she stepped up her pace. While her attacker had escaped on the motorboat, she had no guarantee there wasn't someone else lying in wait.

"No one's following us," Wyatt whispered, but she couldn't—wouldn't—stop until they were safely back at the motel. But that wasn't right, either. She wasn't safe—hadn't been since she'd boarded that plane and wouldn't be until she was home with Harry.

Nan brushed off Wyatt's concerns about her wound—"It's not even bleeding anymore"—and left him outside her motel room. It wasn't more than a cat scratch, not too deep, so she washed it, patting it dry with a towel, nervously listening for any sounds outside her door. She spent the next couple of hours peering out from behind the window blinds, her nerves on edge, her bag packed on the bed, ready to make a quick escape.

Her phone alarm made her jump. Glancing at the time, she recalled that she'd set it so she could talk to Harry before he left for school—especially since she wasn't sure just when she'd have the chance to call again. She took a few deep breaths to force herself to relax. He couldn't know how anxious she was. As far as her son was concerned, Nan was on a short holiday in Spain. He'd initially been upset that he wasn't going with her, but when he'd found out he was going to stay with Gabriel and his family, he'd cheered up.

"Bonjour, Mama!"

Nan sighed with relief. She'd had no idea until she saw Harry's face on the video call just how concerned she'd been about him. If someone could take Lizzie, they could also take Harry. But all was well. He was exuberant as he told her about the soccer match the day before, how he'd gotten the first goal. His face was lit up with the excitement of it, and she wished she'd been there. He demanded to know when she'd be back.

"I told you, in a few days." She hated lying to him, since she had no idea.

"I miss you," he said to her in English.

"Not as much as I miss you." She struggled to keep her emotions out of her voice, to keep her expression as bright and happy as his; she didn't want him to worry.

After talking for a few more minutes about his schoolwork and then a short conversation with Gabriel's mother, Marie, Nan reluctantly ended the call. She missed Harry so much. They'd never been separated like this before. She wanted to put her arms around him and hold him tight. And, she realized now, she wished desperately that he could meet his sister. That she could have both her children together with her.

Hank would never allow that. She'd have to take him to court. But a judge might not look too kindly on a woman who'd abandoned her daughter.

Nan leaned back against the pillows on the bed, a headache forming behind her eyes. Her phone, which was upside down on the bedside table, buzzed with an incoming text.

She froze, hesitating a second before turning it over.

It wasn't from the kidnapper, but Wyatt.

Found the boat. It's at a marina in Essex CT.

Nan had heard of the town on the Connecticut River but couldn't remember ever being there. A quick look on the internet told her that it had a historic district with houses dating back to the 1700s and something called the Connecticut River Museum—not to mention a place to dock a 103-foot yacht.

Before she could respond, however, another text came through. This one was not from Wyatt.

The Flying Horses. 1pm. A woman will leave a black backpack on one of the chariots. Take it.

33

What the text hadn't told her was that the woman on the carousel would be her ex-husband's new wife. Nan recognized her immediately. She had seen pictures of her from the wedding at City Hall, a surprisingly low-key affair for a billionaire.

Nan brazenly sat down next to her in the chariot, but the woman wouldn't even look at her. Nan saw her hands clenched in her lap, the backpack between her legs underneath the seat, hardly looking like a tourist merely enjoying the ride.

As the carousel began to turn, Nan recalled her own wedding day, how she'd imagined a long, happy marriage to a man for whom she'd waited for years. When she closed her eyes, she could still feel how the intricately beaded strapless bodice of the fairy tale white gown hugged her torso above the full skirt rippling out in layers of chiffon—no one except Hank knew she was two months pregnant. She'd wanted to look like a princess, and when she saw Hank in his elegant black tuxedo, she knew she'd found her prince. They were so happy that day, so full of joy and passion for each other. They'd gone to Paris and Nice for their honeymoon, Hank indulging her love of France. He indulged her in everything back then.

This wife, though, the one whose eyes were darting around like a scared rabbit, had had her honeymoon interrupted by the discovery of the headless body of Hank's previous wife.

Nan snorted. That alone should have been a warning to the woman.

She studied the other woman's profile. Hank was sixty now; the wives were getting younger, although this one was older than Caitlyn Howard, who'd been barely out of her teens.

Nan had been in her twenties when she met Hank all those years ago. She'd been young and impressionable, Catherine's assistant. This woman, though, had been Hank's assistant, which meant she was not naïve. She would know all about Hank, his secrets—at least the ones he wanted her to be privy to. Kate would also have known about Nan, about how she may or may not have been that body on the beach—and that Hank had been divorcing her at the time. Nan had stayed away, the mystery of what had happened to his second wife shrouding Hank Tudor—yet four women had married him anyway.

Why would Kate Parker marry him? Could she actually love him?

As Nan asked herself that question, she realized Kate might. This woman might love the man who'd switched out wives in quick succession over the past few years. Nan had been in love with him, too, all those years ago. It was easy to love Hank, when he wanted to be loved. Which meant that Kate Parker was in a lot of trouble.

As much trouble as Nan had been in when she'd fallen in love with him.

And as much trouble as she was in now, because while she was aware she was most likely being watched—*take the backpack*—this was a twist she didn't see coming.

Nan finally caught the woman's eye and saw recognition in her expression.

"Look straight ahead," Nan said in a low voice, leaning slightly toward her, trying not to be obvious. She was aware she didn't have a lot of time.

Perhaps it was because she was caught off guard that Kate Parker did as she was told, but after a second, she said, "Hank knows about you. He knows you kidnapped her, that you're holding her for ransom."

Everything she said verified Nan's suspicions about those texts luring her to the Vineyard, to the marina, and now to the carousel. The backpack held ransom money. If she took it, she would be walking into a trap. She was expected to be caught. The police could be outside right now, ready to arrest her—or worse, Hank and his people would be waiting for her.

"Listen, I'm only trying to find my daughter. Keep her safe—and alive. That's all," Nan said.

Kate Parker frowned, dubious.

"I get why I'm here," Nan continued, "but why are *you* here?"

Confusion crossed Kate's face. "Hank said that I was supposed to be the one to drop off the money," she said softly, her tone indicating that she was turning this over in her head as well. "He said there had been a request, and I had to do it. Gardiner went over all of it with me."

Nan caught her breath. "Steve Gardiner?" she asked, wanting to make sure she'd heard right over the carousel music.

"Of course. He's Hank's—"

"Investigator," Nan finished for her. "Yes, I'm familiar with the man."

Gardiner had been working under the radar for Hank for years. He'd first come on board when Hank wanted to divorce Catherine. Nan and Steve had been allies then, because they were on the same side, both with the same goal: get Catherine out of the picture so Hank could marry Nan. Was she proud of that now? No. Especially with what happened later, when she was the one being targeted, after Hank had met Jeanne and Gardiner used some of the same methods to try to build a case against *her*. She was more than aware of what Gardiner was like. The man changed loyalties as easily as someone would change their clothes—as long as the price was right. And Hank had plenty to pay for that loyalty.

Nan should have figured Hank would bring Gardiner in when Lizzie went missing. But was it more than that? Nan tried to puzzle it out. Why had both wives been sent to this same place, one to drop off the money and one to pick it up? Was Kate being set up, too, for some reason? She wondered if Hank had already tired of his sixth wife, even though they'd been married only a couple of months. If he had, then why not send her out with bundles of cash and manipulate the situation by having the ex-wife involved? They could make it look like Kate was in on it and that would give Hank ammunition in a divorce—or worse. Granted, the idea was a stretch, but Nan wouldn't put anything past Gardiner.

"I had nothing to do with Lizzie's kidnapping," Nan said, eager to claim her innocence and show this woman that something bigger was at play. "I got an anonymous text telling me to come here, to take that backpack, or they'd kill her. If I can get out of here without anyone recognizing me, I might be able to find out who's behind this. Can you help me?" She paused a moment and took a breath. "I need to find her. Make sure she's okay."

It was risky to ask Kate Parker to trust her, and the woman might not hesitate to tell anyone waiting outside about this encounter, so she added, "You and I both being here? I don't think it's a coincidence. I think it's a setup. Be careful."

"Be careful of who?"

Nan was surprised by the honesty of the question, so she decided to be truthful. "Everyone. Gardiner, Cromwell, even your husband." She hesitated a moment, then added, "Catherine. Watch out for Catherine. She's a killer."

34
KATE

Someone had once told Kate to talk to Catherine if she wanted answers, but the only thing she'd found out was that Hank's first wife had Nan Tudor's diary in her possession—and she discovered that by accident. What Nan Tudor was suggesting now was far more sinister.

Kate had a million questions, but the carousel had slowed to a stop and Nan was done talking. The other woman pulled the ball cap bill even farther over her forehead as she stood, keeping her head down as she swiftly made her way around the wooden platform to the exit.

Nan had denied being the kidnapper, and while she claimed she was supposed to take the backpack—or Lizzie would be killed—she didn't. The backpack still sat on the floor where Kate had put it. Why wouldn't Nan have taken it if her daughter's life was threatened? Or was she lying?

Even though she was close on Nan's heels, by the time Kate reached the exit—the backpack still tucked underneath the chariot—Nan had vanished. There was no telltale ball cap or blue scarf in sight.

It was possible Nan had an accomplice, someone else who was on the carousel and took the backpack after they'd gotten off. Kate turned and stood on her tiptoes, trying to see if the backpack was still there, but from where she stood, she wasn't able to see the chariot where she'd been sitting.

Her instructions were to leave the building as soon as she got off the carousel.

"The car will be out front," Gardiner had told her.

But she lingered near the exit. No one was carrying the black backpack out. Maybe it *was* still on the carousel. She shivered at the thought of a million dollars possibly ending up in lost and found. Maybe she made a mistake leaving it behind.

Nan had seemed genuinely perplexed that Kate had been the one with the backpack. Since the kidnapper was the one who'd made that request, her presence shouldn't have surprised Nan if, in fact, she *was* the kidnapper. The more she thought about their brief conversation, Kate became convinced that Nan didn't have anything to do with Lizzie's kidnapping—and maybe she was right that it was some sort of setup.

So, she believed Nan Tudor? That Nan had not kidnapped her own daughter to extort five million dollars from her ex-husband and that someone was framing her? It seemed that she did. She'd seen the truth in Nan's eyes, heard it in the tone of her voice.

Kate was good at reading people; her entire career had been spent doing damage control for people who were both innocent and guilty. She could tell the difference.

Why could she be so sure about Nan Tudor, but she continued to question her own husband?

Caitlyn Howard's murder had planted too many doubts.

Would she honor Nan's request and not tell anyone she'd seen her? Give her a chance to get away? Maybe she should. This was, after all, about Lizzie.

At the very least, she now knew that the headless body discovered at the marina wasn't Nan Tudor. Kate hated to admit it, but Gardiner had been right: that body could be anyone, and it wasn't as though boating accidents didn't happen.

Speaking of Gardiner, she didn't see him anywhere. Nan's reaction when she'd mentioned Gardiner was akin to her own, and it made Kate even more curious about his history with Hank—and with Nan. Kate had read only parts of Nan's diary. Not once did she see a mention of Gardiner, but it was possible that he was in the sections she hadn't seen. She wished she could turn back the clock and press Nan for more information.

People were starting to move through the entry to the carousel, climbing onto the horses, chattering and laughing. Was one of them going to take the backpack when they got off the ride?

"Fancy meeting you here."

Kate started as Tommy Seymour sidled up next to her, but she really shouldn't have been surprised. She'd seen him here earlier, of course he'd stick around. "Let me guess. You got a tip," she said. Where was he getting his information? Who was leaking it?

He gave a short chuckle. "Yeah." He grabbed her hand. "Come on," he said, and suddenly they were cutting the line, moving through the entry gate and onto the carousel.

"What are you doing?" she hissed at him.

"Same thing as you. Riding the carousel."

He hadn't let go of her, tugging her along after him. As they passed the chariot where Kate had sat, she realized something: the backpack was gone. She hardly had time to process that, however, when she heard a shout.

"You there!" A young man wearing a T-shirt with the carousel logo on the front pocket strode toward her and Tommy. "You can't cut the line!"

Tommy raised his hand in acknowledgment and shouted, "Sorry!" as he pulled Kate down off the platform and through the exit.

"What was that all about?" Kate asked as Tommy led her into the arcade, the sounds of pinball machines ringing in her ears and the scent of popcorn hanging heavy around them.

"Who took the backpack?" he asked her, his eyes studying her face. "It's not there, so someone had to take it."

How did *he* know about the backpack?

"What are you talking about?" she asked as innocently as she could, pulling her hand out of his.

"Come on, Kate. I saw you go in there with the backpack. You're not carrying it anymore. You left it. Did you see who took it?"

"No." How on earth did someone manage to take it out of there without being seen? She'd been at the exit, watching everyone who got off the ride. It wasn't as though it was a small bag; it had to be large enough to hold a million dollars, and it was heavy. She would have noticed if someone was carrying it. Was there another way out?

"It was supposed to be Nan Tudor," Tommy said.

Who was feeding him all this information? And how on earth would someone know Nan Tudor would be there? "What are you talking about?" she asked, playing dumb.

"My source said it would be Nan Tudor. That's who I was supposed to see get off the carousel with a backpack full of ransom money." But just as he said it, realization dawned. "You were sitting with someone, a woman. You were talking to her. It *was* Nan Tudor, wasn't it? Sitting next to you."

He'd always had good instincts, but she wasn't going to be his ticket to a story. Kate shook her head. "You're desperate. It's not a good look, Tommy. Anyway, I thought that body they fished out of the water was Nan Tudor. Did she come back from the dead just to pick up a backpack?"

The more she thought about it, it would be easier for Nan if everyone thought she was dead.

Tommy studied her face, and she felt herself flush beneath his gaze. He stepped closer to her, and as he traced her jaw with his finger, an electric current ran through her.

"Help a guy out, Kate," he said softly. "Tell me about her. Where did she go?"

"I don't know what you're talking about," she whispered, acutely aware of his touch.

Someone cleared his throat loudly behind her, and she jumped back, away from Tommy.

"Kate."

She swung around. Hank's eyes were dark as he took in the scene in front of him. The optics were definitely against her.

She didn't have time to say anything before Tommy took out his notebook and pen and went into full reporter mode. "Can I get a comment from you about your daughter's kidnapping and the ransom request?"

Hank glared at him. "No comment." He took Kate's elbow and began to steer her toward the exit. But it wasn't fast enough.

"Do you know your wife had a conversation with your ex-wife on the carousel?"

Tommy's words cut through her, and Hank dropped her arm as though he'd been lit on fire.

35
NAN

The plan was to head straight to the ferry. Wyatt would meet her there.

Nan had gone back and forth on whether she should tell Wyatt about the text instructing her to go to the carousel and get the backpack. In the end, she decided she still might need him.

She didn't want to admit to herself that she felt safer with him. She hated that she was skittish, looking over her shoulder constantly, ever since she'd been attacked. She worried that she'd have some sort of post-traumatic stress reaction whenever she saw a knife—that wouldn't be good, in her business. People in the kitchen were constantly wielding large, sharp knives.

Nan had to shake off her fear, take that energy and refocus it on finding Lizzie.

She hoped Kate Parker would keep her secret just long enough for her to get off the Vineyard. Granted, whoever had tried to kill her knew she was alive—but *someone* was dead. And just like she had eight years ago, Nan was going to use a decapitated body as a misdirection.

Wyatt had found out about the dead woman that morning. He'd gone back to the marina to see if he could find any more clues as to who'd attacked her and saw the police presence, heard the gossip, the speculation.

That waitress had recognized Nan, after all, and she'd already talked to at least one reporter. So, while the person who did try to kill her would know that the reports of Nan's death were premature, no one else would be looking for her—for the moment.

Nan moved swiftly between the people exiting the carousel, leaving Kate Parker behind. She ducked into the restroom and tossed her ball cap into the trash bin before retrieving a plastic bag that was tucked behind it. To anyone else, it would have looked like garbage. She took it into a stall and pulled out a white sundress. Shedding her T-shirt and jeans, she slipped the dress over her head, adjusting it around her figure. It was a little wrinkled, but that was no matter, and the white canvas slip-on sneakers were stylish. She stuck her hand into the bag again and took out a pair of sunglasses, sliding them onto her face. She stuffed her own clothes—and the blue scarf—into the bag. As she came out of the stall, she removed the ponytail holder and let her hair fall around her shoulders.

While she'd second-guessed Wyatt's insistence on the costume change, when she stepped out of the carousel building and spotted Steve Gardiner, she was happy she'd complied. If he noticed her, he might not draw a line between her and the woman who sat with Kate Parker.

She put her hand over her face as though shielding her eyes from the sun as she made her way down Oak Bluffs Avenue, carrying the plastic bag with her clothes in it. It looked like she'd been shopping on a day trip to the island.

The ferry building was a short walk away. Through the internet, she'd already bought a one-way, walk-on ticket to the mainland. The ferry was just pulling into the dock; cars were lined up, waiting to board. Nan ducked into the ladies' room. She didn't want to be seen milling around with the other waiting passengers. She took some time to redo her ponytail, taking the scarf out of the bag to cover up the cut on her neck. She tied it differently than the way she'd worn it on the carousel.

She hoped Wyatt would make the ferry, but they'd agreed if he didn't, they'd meet up in Falmouth and head to Essex—and the *Perseverance*.

While she'd gotten no further text instructions since the one about the carousel, she was convinced that Lizzie was being held on the yacht—especially since someone had gone to so much trouble to make it look as though she was connected to it. Lizzie had to be there. Call it maternal instinct—there had to be something to that, even though she hadn't been a mother to her daughter in such a long time.

She acknowledged it was more than likely that Hank also knew the *Perseverance*'s whereabouts. That marine tracking app wasn't exclusive to Wyatt and Smeaton, and Hank may have already sent someone out to the yacht. Still, she had to see it for herself.

An announcement came over the loudspeaker that the ferry was boarding. Nan hurried out and joined the other day-trippers, showing the QR code on her phone screen to the attendant, who waved her on without a second glance. It was just as easy as when she went through customs at the airport, but she was far more anxious here.

Nan went up to the top deck and looked out over the cars pulling onto the ferry. The line seemed never-ending. She tried to spot Wyatt's car but didn't see it. It was more than possible he would have to take the next one—and, as she stood there, she began to wonder if maybe they'd taken too much of a risk. There was no way anyone would have known who the man sitting behind her on the carousel was, but what if Wyatt had run into trouble?

It had been her idea for him to take the backpack. Wyatt had scoped out the carousel earlier and with a few well-placed questions found out that anything left behind would be brought immediately to lost and found—which happened to be located in the back of the building with an exit into a small alleyway.

Once he had the backpack, Wyatt would head back to the motel. He had suggested leaving her rental car in the parking lot—and putting the backpack in the trunk. It would delay him, but this way when the kidnapper contacted her, she could say where the money was, that she'd done what was asked. Granted, Hank and his people—Gardiner, especially—might discover the car first, but by leaving it, it would play into the idea that she was dead, since it was in her name. They could puzzle it out how the backpack got into her car.

Was it a perfect plan? Maybe. Maybe not. But it was the only one they had.

The ferry began to move. Nan stood at the railing, looking out at the water. She didn't want to look back at the island. She no longer felt the nostalgia that had wrapped itself around her yesterday. She only wanted to escape—again.

Her scarf had slipped, and as she reached up to straighten it, Nan's fingernail caught the raised edge of the cut on the side of her neck. When she took her hand away, she saw blood on her fingers.

"Here, let me."

Wyatt was holding a tissue. He dabbed it against Nan's neck. "Hold that there," he instructed.

A wave of relief at seeing him washed over her as she did as she was told, feeling her pulse quicken under her fingertips.

He took in the dress, his eyebrows rising slightly with approval. Nan felt herself flush under his gaze, noticing now that his eyes were a deep brown with a touch of hazel.

"How did it go?" she asked brusquely, wanting to get back to business. She didn't have time to think about Wyatt in any other way except professionally.

"No problems." He paused. "Did you get anything out of the wife?"

Nan nodded. "She told me they thought I was the one who asked for the ransom. But I got the sense that my presence was unexpected. At least for her."

"The way I see it," Wyatt said, "they want to pin this on you."

"I agree. When I saw the wife sitting there, that was a huge red flag. I didn't expect that. She said the kidnapper asked for her to be the one to deliver the money. I think we're both being set up. It's not just about me anymore, but I can't figure out why her."

"Have you gotten another text since the carousel?" he asked.

Nan checked her phone and shook her head. "No."

Wyatt held out his hand, and she put the phone in his palm. The last message from the kidnapper was on the screen.

"Time to go on the offensive," he said, tapping out a response.

The money is in the rental car.

"Now there's no question that you didn't do what was asked of you," Wyatt said, handing the phone back to her. "What do you know about Steve Gardiner?"

"You know him?" she asked, not answering the question.

"He's your ex-husband's investigator."

"There's no love lost between me and Gardiner," she admitted, quickly telling him about their history.

Wyatt was quiet a moment. Finally, "He was there, at the carousel."

Nan snorted. "Of course he was there. Hank's money was in that backpack. He certainly wasn't going to let Kate Parker go it alone."

"No, of course not. But I saw him talking to a reporter—and not just any reporter. A reporter who was romantically involved with Kate Parker at one time."

Her first thought was how that wouldn't make Hank happy. Not at all. But then she thought about the implication of Gardiner talking to this particular journalist. Again, Nan believed that Kate Parker might be some sort of target.

"It has to be Catherine," she said. "She's not just going after revenge on me. She wants to see if she can split up Hank and his new wife." She was a little puzzled, though, about the connection between Catherine and Gardiner, who had come into Hank's inner circle *after* Hank had left his first wife—and pushed her out of his business. Had they developed a relationship since she'd been gone? It was possible, but Hank had split so definitively from Catherine that it was unlikely he would be aware of the relationship—which could be the point, come to think of it.

Gardiner as a free agent was worrisome, and she said as much to Wyatt.

Wyatt cocked his head and looked at Nan out of the corner of his eye. "So, this is what I'm suggesting: When we get off the ferry, I'll take you to Boston, to the airport. You can go home to your son. I'll pick up Smeaton and we can go out to Essex and find that boat. We'll make sure your daughter is safe."

Nan stood up straighter and gave him a small smile. "I might fire you for that suggestion, Mr. Wyatt." Her tone was that of the old Nan, the one who'd been a tough businesswoman, who'd been confident of her place next to Hank Tudor for so long. Wyatt was underestimating her.

He shrugged. "It was just an idea."

She wondered why he'd give up so easily, unless he'd merely been trying it on for size, knowing she wouldn't go along with it. She sighed. All she wanted was her daughter. She didn't care who got the money, as long as she and her daughter stayed alive—and maybe they could start over. Maybe she could finally be a mother to the daughter whose absence she'd felt every day since she'd left her behind.

36
KATE

Tommy didn't care if he blew up her marriage—not that he knew it was on tenterhooks already. He just needed a story, but two could play this game.

"I have no idea what he's talking about," Kate told Hank with as innocent an expression as she could conjure. "A woman sat next to me on the carousel, but I don't know who she was. And she didn't take the backpack, so she couldn't have been the kidnapper." Her tone was calm, matter-of-fact, but at the same time she realized she was talking too much, giving him too much information too quickly. It made her look guilty of something. She used to know how to talk to Hank, how to calm him down. That was her superpower, he used to tell her.

Tommy Seymour seemed to be her kryptonite.

But she had to stick to her story right now; she couldn't let Tommy know about Nan. It didn't escape her that by telling this tall tale, she was lying to her husband, too—at least until she could get him alone.

Hank looked from Kate to Tommy, then back at his wife again. His rage was palpable. This was exactly the kind of encounter she'd always protected him from, and now she was thrusting him right into the middle of it—and *she* was right in the middle of it.

Not to mention that he'd caught them in a moment. It didn't matter that it was innocent on her part and manipulative on Tommy's. That's not what Hank saw. She was going to have to dance as fast as she could to divert his anger—and hope that he'd understand once she told him the truth.

Kate tugged on her husband's arm. "Come on, Hank. Let's go," she said.

"I have more questions," Tommy tried, but Kate glared at him.

"No comment. I already told you that," she said sharply.

Hank was watching their exchange, and she could see he was trying to decide if she meant it or if she was putting on a performance for his benefit. He had never looked at her like he was looking at her now. She forced herself not to show her fear.

Because for the first time, Kate was afraid of her husband. She'd seen him turn his wrath on others, but he'd never directed it at her like this before.

Was it merely jealousy? Or was it more than that?

Abruptly, Hank turned and began walking away.

"Kate?" she heard Tommy say, but she'd already begun following her husband, leaving Tommy behind.

The sunlight hit her eyes, and she squinted against its brightness as she stepped outside and skipped down the steps after Hank, who was heading for the black car idling at the curb. She should have known he'd be nearby. He wouldn't have let Gardiner keep him away if he wanted to be here, no matter who Gardiner was to him and his business.

Hank opened the door and stepped back, waiting for her.

"Hank—" she started, but he held up his hand, cutting her words off.

"You'll go back to the house and stay there," he ordered. He didn't even wait for her to get into the car. He was already across the street, his long strides taking him further away from her.

Kate glanced back at the carousel building. Tommy had come out and was watching her from the steps. She gave him a short shake of her head before climbing into the back seat of the car.

The rift with Hank was even wider now. Kate remembered Nan's words in her diary, how the second Mrs. Tudor was afraid her husband would kill her. Someone had killed his fifth wife. And someone had tried to kill *her.* Violence seemed to follow Hank Tudor around when it came to his wives—and now his daughter had been taken. Would all of his children become targets—including hers? Would everyone close to Hank be at risk?

Despite the sense of dread and uncertainty, Kate's anger at her husband began to rise. She'd done what was asked of her. She'd delivered the ransom. While she now knew Nan Tudor was supposed to pick it up, she hadn't known that going in, and she'd faced that particular threat in order to help keep Lizzie safe. Considering her own brush with death, Hank should be more appreciative and understanding instead of treating her like a child—*go home and stay there*. He didn't even know she'd lied, because he hadn't given her the opportunity to tell him about Nan.

It didn't escape her that this meant she was doing what Nan had asked: give her time to get away.

As the car moved slowly along the tourist-congested streets, her thoughts turned from Hank to Nan and what the other woman had said on the carousel. Was she right that Lizzie's kidnapper had arranged for the two of them to be in the same place at the same time with a million dollars between them? What would that mean?

Nan's warning about Catherine crept into her head, but it seemed a little over the top. Catherine, a killer? Yes, Catherine was delusional, in that she still thought of Hank as her husband and was unwilling to accept the divorce—even after so long and so many subsequent wives. Catherine was also agoraphobic. Granted, when Nan knew her, she hadn't yet quarantined herself in her house, but still. This might be more about Nan's history with Hank's first wife and perhaps should not be taken literally.

The car hit a pothole, and Kate glanced up to see the driver's eyes in the rearview mirror, glancing back at her and then at the road in front of him. She was sure he'd be reporting back to Hank—or even Gardiner. This was not the life she envisioned for herself when she married Hank. She'd seen herself as more of an equal to the powerful Hank Tudor, at least in part because of how they'd been able to work together in the past. But he hadn't had that type of relationship with any wife besides Catherine and Nan, and she'd been foolish to think that would change. She was the steady, sensible, practical wife after the trainwreck that had been Caitlyn Howard—and that would be the extent of it.

Kate's thoughts were interrupted by the muffled sound of an incoming text notification. Had Hank brought her phone and neglected to tell her it was in the car? Since he'd been so angry with her, it was likely the last thing on his mind. Kate reached into the compartment between the seats and pulled out a cell phone. But it wasn't hers. It couldn't be Hank's, either. He would never have left his phone in the car. He always had it in his pocket.

The text was displayed on the screen:

The money is in the rental car.

What money? Her fingers hovered over the screen, her curiosity piqued. But then she chided herself. This was not her phone. She had no business reading someone else's messages. But as she read the text again, she couldn't help herself. She touched the bubble on the screen, and to her surprise, the message app opened without a prompt for a passcode.

This wasn't the only text, but it was one of just two—and it was a response to the first:

The Flying Horses. 1pm. A woman will leave a black backpack on one of the chariots. Take it.

Nan Tudor had said she'd gotten an anonymous text, telling her to take the backpack. Was this the message she'd received? If so, then this phone could belong to the kidnapper. But what was this about the money in a rental car? Had Nan managed to retrieve the backpack? Then why leave it behind and tell the kidnapper where it was?

Kate gripped the mystery phone in her palm as another thought struck her. If this really was the kidnapper's phone, as she suspected, what was it doing in Hank's car? Did Hank have something to do with Lizzie's kidnapping?

No, there was no way he could be involved. It was his daughter. She was a child. But even as she tried to convince herself, this phone could be telling a different story. Hank knew exactly when Nan came through customs. He had people on it, he'd said. As though he'd been expecting her.

Kate took a deep breath. But to what end? Nan was years ago. Hank had moved on—several times. Unless there was something he wanted from Nan, something that was worth orchestrating a kidnapping of his own daughter.

Would Hank use his own daughter as a pawn?

Her thoughts were pinballing between not being able to believe her husband capable of such a thing and knowing he absolutely was capable of it.

Kate's fingers worried the phone in her hand. If Nan was on the other side of this conversation, maybe she could get some answers from her. It was worth a try.

How did you get the backpack out of the carousel? And what rental car? she texted before she could stop herself.

37

CATHERINE

Nothing was going the way it was supposed to. That Woman was defying her at every turn. She was like a cat with nine lives. How could it be that she'd escaped once again with her life?

Catherine hadn't approved of the plan—it had been tricky at best—but if it had worked, she would have been rid of at least one obstacle. That was why she didn't object too strenuously, although she had expressed her concerns.

"If the attempt is made, it must be successful," she'd warned.

"It will be" came the promise.

Yet it was not.

It was bad enough that she didn't bleed out on that dock, but she didn't take the money, either. Who wouldn't take a backpack full of cash? Wouldn't she need it? She was a lowly restaurant cook, living like a pauper with her boy. Didn't she want a better life for him? For herself?

Of course, that would assume she'd survive to even get back to her little life in France.

Failure was a part of life, and that lesson had to be learned. But it didn't make the situation any less problematic. Because now the woman would be on alert—and more careful.

Catherine didn't want to harm the girl, but she would if she had to. Threats are only good if they're followed up on.

Catherine pushed aside the anxiety that had settled under her skin. It wouldn't do to start harboring second thoughts based solely on her affliction. There were prescription drugs that would take care of that quite nicely and allow her to do what needed to be done. She could not be seen as weak, especially now.

Catherine surveyed the contents of her closet and carefully chose a pair of beige linen slacks and a light blue tank top. She completed the outfit with a short white jacket and a chunky necklace made of pink stones. A pair of strappy sandals on her feet. She had brushed out her hair, which she now pulled back into a loose knot on the nape of her neck. She admired her reflection in the full-length mirror and relished how stylish she looked, how much she resembled who she'd been in those heady days with Hank.

It was all the exercising, finally leaving the house, moving past her grief. Now only the anger simmered below the surface, but she was able to conceal it, control it.

Catherine's overnight bag sat on the bed, and she surveyed its contents. It would be enough for one, two nights at most. It shouldn't take longer than that to get the job done properly. She closed the bag and zipped it up, carrying it downstairs and setting it by the door that led to the garage.

She checked her phone. She'd installed the app from which she was able to turn on and off the house lights to indicate someone was home. She could also monitor the security cameras.

She wished it had been as easy to get rid of Lourdes. Well, not permanently, but at least long enough so she could do what she had to without anyone noticing. She had suggested that since Lourdes had not had any time off recently, perhaps she should go visit her sister in Pennsylvania.

Catherine wasn't usually so magnanimous with her offers of time off, and Lourdes had been suspicious. Catherine had made a mistake, even though she really didn't have to explain. Lourdes may have been her companion, but she was still just the help. She was paid handsomely to cook and clean and keep her mouth shut. She couldn't have the audacity to think she was anything more than that.

Realizing her error, Catherine had decided to use Maril as an excuse. "Maril said she'd like to come and stay for several days. A girls' visit, you know, mother-daughter time." No matter that it was a lie. Catherine always said if a lie is said with conviction, everyone will believe it. Also, she didn't say when Maril would come, just that she'd like to. That itself was not a lie.

When Lourdes's face had relaxed into a wide smile, Catherine knew that had been the right thing to say.

"It would be good to have Maril stay," Lourdes had agreed. "And yes, I have missed my sister and her children."

"Then perhaps you want to finish up and start your holiday tomorrow. Of course it's with full pay," Catherine had added.

Lourdes's smile had become even wider, and for a second, Catherine had regretted the ruse. Lourdes had been loyal for a long time, and it was a risk to send her away. Yet no one would be able to prove that Catherine had duped her companion into leaving her alone. Sometimes plans go awry at the last moment: *Maril had to stay on the Vineyard. Isn't that a shame?*

Anyway, she didn't have time to second-guess any decisions. Now it was time to get to work.

Catherine wasn't afraid of getting her hands dirty, if it came down to that. Nothing would be traced back to her. She wasn't going to leave any witnesses behind.

38
NAN

Nan wanted to respond immediately to the text. Whoever had sent it was not the kidnapper—she was willing to bet on that—and Wyatt agreed. But he told her they needed to be careful.

"We don't know who it is, exactly. It could be a trick," he warned.

"It's someone who knows I didn't take the backpack but doesn't know about the rental car. My money's on the wife." She hesitated a moment before adding, "If she's got the phone, then the kidnapper doesn't know where the money is."

"If she's got the phone, you have to wonder how she got her hands on it," Wyatt pointed out. "She might not be as innocent as you think."

Nan hadn't thought Kate Parker had anything to do with the kidnapping—but if she had the phone, then she must, right? Was she more involved in this than Nan had suspected? Maybe Kate Parker wasn't being set up, after all. Maybe it had all been a ploy to catch her.

"Let's just get to Essex," Wyatt said. "All of this might be moot anyway, once we get there."

Nan truly hoped it would be, but she couldn't stop thinking about the text and her suspicion that Kate Parker had sent it. The more she tried to sort it out, the more her curiosity grew. She glanced at Wyatt, who was concentrating on his phone.

"I'm a little chilly out here," she told him. "I'm going inside."

He looked at her out of the corner of his eye, as though he knew she was up to something. After a long moment, he nodded and went back to whatever was on his small screen. While Nan didn't need his permission, she interpreted his reaction as just that, and she bit down irritation. Who was paying whom, anyway?

Nan reminded herself that Wyatt had come to her defense and was invested in helping her find Lizzie—not just as a hired investigator, either. He'd immediately dropped everything when she mentioned Maggie—and why Maggie had hired him all those years ago. Nan sensed that this wasn't just another job to him, although she still hadn't figured out his ulterior motive. Did it matter, so long as they found Lizzie?

Nan found her way through the heavy metal door into the warmth of the cabin. Rows of seats filled the middle of the space, with tables and chairs against the windows on the sides. She chose a seat in the back with a clear view of the door. If Wyatt came in, she'd see him, but he might not spot her right away.

She was still holding her phone, and she entered the number that the texts had come from. Her finger hovered over the SEND button for a moment; she took a deep breath and then hit it, holding the phone to her ear.

"Yes?" The voice that answered the call was female.

"You sent me a text," Nan said instead of introducing herself. She had to get confirmation as to whom she was speaking before she'd admit who she was. "I'll tell you what you want to know, but first you have to tell me who you are."

The person on the other end didn't even hesitate. "We met earlier. On the carousel. You told me to be careful."

It was the wife, as she'd thought. Interesting that she wasn't willing to put her name out there, either.

"Are you still on the Vineyard?" the woman asked.

This seemed most definitely to be a trick. She was trying to find out where Nan was—although Nan gave her credit for coming right out and asking. It made her seem more trustworthy, somehow. But Nan had no intention of giving anything away. She should just end the call now, but decided she'd play into it—on the off chance she could get some information.

"No." The moment she said it, she regretted it. She should have said yes. Thrown everyone off her trail.

"Have you found the yacht? Do you think that's where Lizzie might be?"

The question took Nan aback. If she knew about the yacht, maybe she really *was* involved.

"What do you know about it?" Nan asked, not answering her question.

"Nothing, except that it's registered to you."

If Wyatt and Smeaton had found out about it, why not Hank and his minions? What if they'd gotten there first? What if they were rescuing Lizzie right now? Her hopes for a reunion with her daughter would be for naught—and once she arrived in Essex, it would be as though she had a target on her back.

"That's why Hank thinks you kidnapped her yourself." Kate's statement confirmed her suspicions. "A reporter saw you on the carousel and recognized you."

So, the dead woman wasn't as much of a misdirection as Nan had hoped.

But Kate's next words made her take pause.

"I lied and told him it wasn't you."

Even though Nan had asked her to buy her time, she was genuinely surprised that the woman did so. Maybe that was why it was so easy for her to get to the ferry without being stopped.

"I appreciate that," she said.

"I haven't told Hank yet. That I saw you, I mean."

While the implication was that she *would* tell him, Nan was curious as to why she hadn't already. And maybe the delay meant that Hank's people might not be waiting for her at the yacht after all. "I don't think I have to tell you that there may be serious repercussions for lying to your husband—even for a little while."

"Let me worry about that."

If Kate Parker thought she could handle Hank, all power to her.

"You know, that phone was my only connection to the kidnapper and now you have it." Nan hesitated. "Where *did* you get it, anyway?" She might as well try to get as much out of her as possible before she hung up.

"Hank's car. He doesn't know I found it." Her voice broke slightly, betraying her confidence—and revealing something akin to fear. "I don't think I have to tell you that this needs to stay between you and me."

Any doubts Nan had about Kate Parker vanished. She couldn't explain why she believed her, but she did. She was trying to make sense of this. The phone was in Hank's car? Was it his phone? Could Hank have taken Lizzie himself? Maybe Catherine had nothing to do with it. But why would he want to bring her back? They had nothing to settle between them. Once he'd fallen out of love with her, he'd moved past her quickly and very thoroughly. Unless he had found out about Harry.

The thought made her catch her breath, but then she shook the idea away, unwilling to let it distract her. "He thought I kidnapped my own daughter, and yet he had the phone? The one the kidnapper used to text me?" she asked.

Nan's words settled between them for a moment before Kate spoke again. "I don't know what it means, either. I'm trying to figure it out. You warned me to be careful, but I have to extend the same warning to you."

Nan knew what it was like to be on the wrong end of Hank's wrath, and if he ever found out they were communicating, he'd have both their heads.

"I really hope you can find Lizzie," Kate said then. "We all love her. She's a wonderful girl. We want her to come home safe."

Nan felt a lump rise in her throat, but she didn't have time to ruminate on what Kate Parker had said, since she spotted Wyatt push his way into the cabin, his head swiveling as he looked for her. She had to get off the phone.

"I have to go," she said quickly. "If you find yourself in a jam, there's a million dollars in a backpack in the trunk of a rental at the Vineyard Motel near the marina. I don't know who wanted it, but it's up for grabs. Keys are under the rear wheel well."

Nan didn't wait for a response before she ended the call. Maybe in another lifetime, she and Kate Parker would've been friends. It was a nice idea, even if completely unrealistic.

39

KATE

Kate stared at the cell phone in her hand. That had been unexpected. Nan Tudor calling her on the kidnapper's phone.

It didn't have to belong to Hank, did it? As it were, the phone could belong to anyone: Cromwell, Gardiner, even the driver. Gardiner was a good possibility. He'd been in the car, too, come to think of it, and she couldn't shake her initial distrust of the man. But was that just wishful thinking? She didn't want to believe her husband had any part of Lizzie's kidnapping. She didn't want to jump to conclusions.

If Hank ever found out about her conversation with Nan, it could irreparably damage her relationship with him. She had to make sure that he never found out. Nan certainly wouldn't tell him; she was sure of that. And Kate had made sure to keep an eye on the driver as she'd spoken to Nan. The glass shield was up; she knew he couldn't have overheard her. Hank always secured his cars for privacy, considering how many sensitive discussions he had while doing business on the road.

She looked up as the car took a sharp turn. Kate had been concentrating so intently on the phone call that she hadn't been paying attention to the drive. They must be almost back by now. But instead of the familiar house, she saw boats up on blocks, masts rising toward the sky. What were they doing in a boatyard?

They came to a stop behind two large boats. The driver got out, and Kate quickly shoved the cell phone into her pocket before the door opened. The driver held out his hand, as though to help her out, but she didn't take it.

"What are we doing here?" she demanded. "We were supposed to go back to the house."

His hat was low over his forehead, and she couldn't really see his face—not that she'd recognize him anyway. All of Hank's employees were strangers here, hired for their protective skills, even the drivers. When Kate worked for Hank, she'd gotten to know his regular drivers and security details, since they traveled together. She'd had a casual, relaxed relationship with some of them. That changed, though, once it was clear she and Hank would be getting married. Suddenly, everyone was very formal with her, calling her "Ms. Parker" instead of "Kate." Now she was "Mrs. Tudor," and there was no going back.

"Just after we left the carousel, Mr. Tudor asked that I reroute you here," the driver explained.

"Why?"

He gave her a small smirk and shrugged. "It's not my job to ask questions."

She shouldn't even have asked. It was just like Hank to change plans at the last moment, like when he'd changed his mind suddenly yesterday about going to the penthouse instead of taking the jet out of Teterboro. Still, it would have been nice to get more of a heads-up.

The driver, sensing her hesitation, held out a cell phone. "Would you like to see?"

Yes, she would most definitely like to see, especially since Hank couldn't communicate with her himself. She wished Hank had given her back her phone before tucking her into the car, but it was possible he didn't even know that Gardiner had taken it. She hadn't put up a fight when he insisted. It had made sense at the time.

Kate took the driver's phone and saw the text:

Please take Mrs. Tudor to the Edgartown boatyard instead of the house.

It was from Hank's number. Kate thanked him and handed the phone back to him as she spotted a man in jeans coming toward them. He wore a light jacket over a T-shirt, and she could see a bulge underneath, a gun peeking out from under his arm.

"Mrs. Tudor?" he asked as he approached. "I'm with your husband's security detail. Can you come with me?"

She again wished she had her phone so she could call Hank and ask what was going on, but all she had was the mysterious phone from the car—and she did not want to call him using that since she still didn't know who the phone belonged to.

"What's going on?" she asked. "Where are we going?"

The man in jeans nodded at the driver, who got back into the vehicle. Something was afoot, if this security guard didn't want the driver to hear their destination. She stepped out of the car.

"You'll be joining Mr. Tudor on the yacht."

Kate immediately thought of the yacht where Lizzie was supposed to meet up with Nan. But it couldn't be the same one.

"I don't understand," Kate said. "My husband doesn't own a yacht."

The man gave a short chuckle. "When someone as rich as your husband wants something, he can get it, you know that?"

He was being cheeky, but he was right. If Hank wanted a yacht for some reason, he'd get one. Maybe he'd found Nan's and the only way to get to it was by water.

"Okay, where to?" she asked.

"This way." He started walking, and she followed, his long legs allowing him to move more quickly and she had to step up her pace to keep up.

They rounded the building and came to a dock with small dinghies tied up. She didn't see a yacht anywhere.

"Where's the boat?" she asked.

He pointed in the direction of the water, where she saw a large yacht moored. "We have to take a dinghy to get out there."

He led her to one and helped her on board, settling her in before untying the ropes that had anchored it to the dock. "It's just a short way," he said, expertly starting the engine and steering the dinghy away from the dock and into the open water.

Kate hadn't spent any time on boats. She gripped the sides of the dinghy and hoped he didn't see how uncomfortable she was. He hadn't given her a life jacket, but she was a strong swimmer, so there was that.

The closer they came to the yacht, the larger it seemed. Kate had seen vessels like this in movies and on television but had never dreamed she'd be on one. Of course, only the best for Hank Tudor. She wondered now why Hank didn't have a yacht. He had several private jets; it would make sense for him to have a glamorous mega-yacht.

The dinghy was slowing down, and the security guard pulled up next to the back of the vessel. Kate took note of the name—*The Aragon*, written in script on the back. She scanned the swim deck and the deck above but didn't see anyone. Hank must be inside, and she wouldn't be surprised if Cromwell was here as well.

For a moment, she wondered where Gardiner had gone. Was he here, too? She hadn't seen him when she left the carousel, although in retrospect that shouldn't surprise her since she'd been too focused on Hank and his anger. That's right. Hank was angry with her. But he must have gotten over it, if he'd arranged for her to meet him here. At the very least, he was thinking of her safety. For some reason, he hadn't wanted her to go back to the house.

Maybe the house was no longer safe. She wondered about Anna and Maril—and Ted. Would they show up here? All of them sailing off, away from any danger?

Except for Lizzie, whose whereabouts were still unknown. At least as far as she knew. Nan wasn't the kidnapper; so then, who was? Kate felt a chill run down her spine, and it wasn't only because she'd become anxious about climbing up off this wobbly dinghy onto the platform.

The security guard—he hadn't told her his name, and she hadn't asked—jumped out of the dinghy and onto the platform, tying it securely. He held out his hand to help Kate climb aboard the yacht. She sighed with relief once her feet hit the platform.

Kate heard the security guard chuckle. "Safe and sound," he said. There was something in his tone that made her take pause. For a moment, she recalled Will Stafford, head of Anna and Joan's security detail at their inn—the man who'd killed Caitlyn Howard and who'd tried to kill her. Will had seemed trustworthy, and she'd even liked him.

As her eyes strayed to the man's jacket, which hid his gun, Kate struggled to breathe, panic rising in her chest.

"Are you okay, Mrs. Tudor?" he asked, peering into her face, concerned.

How could she explain about her PTSD? About how the anxiety came out of nowhere as the flashbacks played like a movie in her head?

"I'll be okay," she whispered, then cleared her throat and pushed the panic down. "Where is my husband?" she asked loudly in a tone that elicited much more authority than she felt.

The guard cocked his head toward the stairs. She didn't wait for him to answer, took the stairs two at a time. No one was on the deck, and she wove her way around a table and chairs and a full bar before reaching a set of sliding glass doors. She pulled on the handle and the door slid open to reveal a luxurious salon with a white leather sofa, plump chairs, and a large glass coffee table. Colorful artwork lined the paneled walls.

But what stood out was that no one was in the room. She turned around to see the security guard standing behind her.

"Where is my husband?" she demanded, but the fear again crept up through her chest. Something wasn't right. She'd made a big mistake.

Kate started toward the door, but he grabbed her arm. "I'm sorry, Mrs. Tudor, but where do you think you're going?"

40

ANNA

A hush had fallen over the house ever since everyone had left. Gardiner had taken Kate to drop off the ransom money; Hank and Cromwell had left only moments after. Anna was certain Hank didn't trust Gardiner and wanted to keep an eye on him. There was bad blood between Gardiner and Cromwell. That was obvious, too.

A loud knock at the front door startled her just as she'd settled Ted in with some cheese and crackers. Even though he wasn't speaking, his appetite seemed to be relatively intact. It was something, anyway.

"I'm just going to see who it is," Anna told him. "Stay here."

A police officer stood on the front stoop, flanked by two of Hank's security team. Anna stiffened. The last time she'd had close contact with the police was when Caitlyn Howard's body had been found—and her own wife had gone missing. She did not equate the police with good news—although maybe this was about Lizzie?

"Ma'am? This officer has asked to speak to Mr. Tudor," one of the security guards said.

The officer tipped his hat, and Anna held the door open further to let him in. He slipped between the security guards and stepped inside. "I'm with the state police, Trooper Walsingham."

"Do you have word of Lizzie?" she asked eagerly.

His eyes darted around the foyer, landing on the small watercolor painting of a beach scene. It had been one of Nan's acquisitions that Lizzie had pounced on when she arrived, choosing its space carefully.

Anna took his hesitation as a no to her question, and her spirits immediately deflated. But he was here for a reason, and while she wanted to invite him in further, she worried that Ted might overhear the conversation. She held her finger to her lips. "We need to be quiet. Mr. Tudor's son is in the kitchen, and he's been very distressed. I'm trying to ease his trauma."

Walsingham gave her a nod. "Not to worry," he said. "Is Mr. Tudor at home?"

Since the police knew nothing of the ransom request, Anna assumed that this officer was ignorant of what was happening just a few miles away at the island carousel. "He's not available at the moment."

He shifted his feet slightly. He was nervous. Anna wondered what this was about and realized that he probably thought she was merely the help, a babysitter perhaps. "I'm Mr. Tudor's ex-wife, Anna Klein," she said. "Can I help with anything?"

His expression darkened. "You're the one whose wife . . ."

"Went missing," Anna finished for him. "Yes." When they married, she hadn't been fully aware of what being Mrs. Hank Tudor would entail for her private life—or that she might not have a private life at all. That notoriety meant it wasn't unexpected that Walsingham was aware of what had happened with Joan.

She could tell he was debating with himself over what to say next. She decided to save him the trouble.

"Unless you have news of Lizzie, I can let Mr. Tudor know you wanted to speak with him and he can reach out to you," Anna said. "Do you have a card?"

"It's not about the girl," he said then. "It's about her mother."

Anna frowned. "What about her?" Did the police find out that Nan Tudor had come back after all these years? It hadn't sounded like it was common knowledge when Hank told her. "She's been gone a long time."

"Maybe not that long," he said, and she could tell from his expression he'd spoken before thinking—and verifying that he did know Nan had come back.

"Perhaps you should just tell me what this is about," Anna suggested. "I can relay any message to Mr. Tudor."

He pulled a card out of his shirt pocket and handed it to her. "Just have Mr. Tudor call me as soon as he can," he said. "I appreciate it."

Anna walked him to the door and watched as he went out to his cruiser in the driveway, the security guards also keeping an eye on him. She worried the corner of the card he'd given her, wishing she'd done more to convince him to tell her why he'd come before sticking it on the refrigerator with a magnet. Teddy had finished his crackers and stared at her with wide eyes.

"Is there anything you'd like to do now?" she asked. "Take a swim?"

He nodded slowly.

"Then go up and get your trunks on. I'll meet you outside."

Just a few days ago, the boy would have bounded upstairs with a shout, but now he walked with leaden steps as though he were an elderly man trying to navigate without the help of a walker.

Anna sighed as she began to clean up his plate. He hadn't used his napkin, so she pulled open the drawer in the island to put it away. Kate's phone lay nestled in the corner. Gardiner had given it to her "for safekeeping" until Kate returned, and she'd stuck it in here—and now it was lit up with notifications, text messages from a phone number she didn't recognize.

I didn't mean for it to get out of control like that.

It's just the job. You know that.

He can't really think there's anything going on between us anymore.

Anna stared at the last message, which had just come in. These must be from that reporter, the one who'd been on the beach, the one who had a history with Kate. What had happened between them? And why would he think Hank was upset about it?

Anna hadn't pressed Kate about her marriage and estrangement from Hank. She figured Kate would tell her in her own time. Although the fact that Kate hadn't told her about the pregnancy made her wonder if Kate would ever tell her anything. If she was somehow involved with this reporter, even peripherally, Kate would be even more closemouthed. Not that Anna would blame her. But she hoped that Kate could settle her feelings about Hank, not only for the baby's sake. She did believe that Hank loved his wife, and Kate was good for him. And it was a bit selfish, too, since Anna liked Kate and if Kate left Hank, he'd undoubtedly find himself yet another wife whom Anna and the children would have to get used to.

As Anna started to put the phone back in the drawer—she had no business looking at Kate's messages—the phone began to buzz with an incoming call. The phone number was the same one on the texts.

While she didn't want to overstep, Anna couldn't keep her curiosity at bay. She swiped the screen to accept the call. "Hello?"

"Kate?"

"No, I'm sorry, she's not available. May I ask who's calling?"

"It's Tom. Tom Seymour. Okay, I know she's pissed at me. But can you tell her I really need to talk to her?"

There was a desperation in his voice that was unmistakable. He was assuming, too, that Kate was there and didn't want to take his call.

"She's not home."

He was quiet a moment. "I saw her an hour ago. Her husband put her in the car. She should be home by now." She could hear the concern in his voice, but it seemed misplaced.

"Well, she's not here." If Hank was with her, Kate would be fine.

"When she gets home, give her this message, okay? It seems that the dead woman at the marina *does* have a connection to her husband," he said. "She needs to know that. She needs to be careful."

The visit from that police trooper suddenly made a lot more sense, and a chill settled into Anna's bones and made her shiver.

"What's the connection?" she asked, knowing that she should just leave it alone. Hank wouldn't like it that she was talking to this reporter, but he seemed to be genuinely concerned about Kate, and if she asked Hank, she most likely wouldn't get a straight answer.

"She was wearing a ring. A ring that belonged to his second wife and vanished the same night she disappeared."

41
LIZZIE

My wrists are still bound, and I've still got this blindfold on. I read somewhere that if you lose a sense, you make up for it with the others. But I'm not sure that's true. I try to ignore the hum of the engine in the background and listen carefully for any possible sound outside. I can't even hear seagulls anymore, but maybe seagulls stay close to land. If they do, that means we might be way out in the ocean, and I may never get back.

I think about Teddy, how we've been at the house all summer, feeling like prisoners. Funny, because now I really am one.

I've been counting the days til I can go back to school. Usually, my breaks are spent at the inn with Anna and Joan, but this one was different because Caitlyn was killed and Joan disappeared and Anna's been sad. We were sent to the Vineyard with Maril.

I know I'm supposed to love my sister, but she's only my half sister. She makes a big show out of babysitting me and Ted, but I'm too old for a babysitter now, and Ted's better off with me. Maril spends most of her days working—or talking to her mother. I've never met Catherine. I guess she never leaves her house. I don't understand that, but I guess if my husband left me for another woman, I'd go to extremes, too. Especially since he left Catherine for my mother, and everyone tells me my mother was the love of his life. No disrespect to Kate—or Ted's mother, Jeanne. I don't know what happened between my parents. How can you go from someone being the love of your life to hating them? Because I know my dad hates my mother. I hear what he says to Cromwell about her when he thinks I'm not around. I've gotten really good at eavesdropping.

That's how I found out about the ring.

They were talking about it one day, a ring that my dad gave my mother when I was born. He said he was pretty sure she took it when she left, and that made him really mad. I think it was because it was expensive. But then he said something about how maybe it was better that she had it, because if she left it behind it would just be a constant reminder of her.

That was exactly why I wanted it. I wanted a constant reminder. Because I had nothing else.

It became kind of an obsession, and I started imagining that maybe my mother didn't take it with her, after all. I mean, my dad didn't know for sure. When we got to the Vineyard house this summer, I figured if it was anywhere, it might be here since this was the last place she was—and it was her house. No one else has been here since she left. The house is exactly the way it was then. Anna told me dad didn't want to deal with it, so he just closed it up and then he left. All the furniture was my mother's; Anna said she'd redesigned the whole house herself.

I've had a lot of time alone, so I started a search. It gave me something to do when I got bored—which was most of the time, since I was here with Maril and Ted. Every once in a while, I could see Blanche at the beach, but Maril can be stingy with letting me have a life. Maybe it's because she's stuck here, too, with two kids, but sometimes I think she likes being miserable. Like her mother.

Anyway, we were here only two weeks when I found it. There's a secret compartment in one of the dressers in storage in the attic. There were letters in there, too. Letters from my dad to my mom from when he loved her—and, wow, did he love her. His letters are like they're from a totally different person. I don't know what happened to make him hate her. Whatever it was, it wasn't in the letters. I left them where I found them after I read them, but I couldn't help myself and took the ring and hid it in my room.

I still can't believe how beautiful it is. All those rubies set in gold. And the locket, with our pictures, one of her and one of me as a baby. I know it's me because I've seen another picture that looks like it.

When I started getting the texts, I couldn't believe it. It was almost like that ring was magic, like it brought her back to me. Of course, now I know that was stupid. To believe my mother was really texting me. But I guess because I wanted to believe, it was easy to. That's the way magic works, right?

I wore the ring when I went to meet her. To show her how much it meant to me.

Now it's gone. I was twisting it around on my finger when I walked up to the boat. When I started up the gangway, it fell off. I looked for it but couldn't find it. It must have fallen in the water. It feels like I've lost her all over again.

I'm feeling sorry for myself when I hear the door open. I wonder if I should start screaming again—it feels really good to scream—but decide against it.

Someone pulls at the blindfold, and suddenly I can see. I blink a few times to focus. I'm in a bedroom with a lot of wood and gold. Maybe it's supposed to look nautical or something, but it looks like a regular bedroom, like in a hotel.

And the only other person in the room is a kid, like me, wearing a white T-shirt and board shorts with palm trees all over them. His hair is blond, like he's been in the sun, and his nose is sunburned.

This is not who I was expecting.

"Hey," he says, like we're just hanging out and I haven't been kidnapped and tied up for who knows how long. "You okay?" He takes out a pocketknife and cuts through the ties on my wrists.

I rub them and wiggle my fingers as I climb off the bed and stand up straight. "I am not okay."

He raises his eyebrows and shrugs. "Yeah, I guess not." He glances at the door. "We gotta go."

"Go where?" I don't like the idea of going anywhere with this kid. I don't trust him. I mean, why would I? I have no clue who he is.

But he's already started across the room. When he sees I'm still standing in one spot, he comes back, grabs my hand, and tugs me along after him. "Come on," he hisses.

"Who are you?" I ask. "I'm not going with you unless I know who you are."

He rolls his eyes at me. "Okay, fine. Robert Dudley, at your service." And then he gives me a short bow, like I'm the queen or something.

42
ANNA

When Hank and Cromwell got back to the house, Anna was surprised that Kate wasn't with them. The reporter had told her that Hank "put Kate in the car," and she'd assumed that Hank was with her.

"Where's Kate?" she asked.

Hank's expression darkened. "She's not here?" He and Cromwell exchanged a look that Anna couldn't read, but it was enough to tell her that something was very wrong.

"No," she said, shaking her head. "She didn't come back. Maybe she's with Gardiner? He's not here, either."

Another look exchanged, but neither of them seemed inclined to share their thoughts with her. "The police were here earlier," she said, expecting to catch them off guard. "Someone named Walsingham. But it wasn't about Kate. It was about Nan."

Hank nodded. "We've just been with the police." The implication being that he was already aware of what Walsingham had come here for, and she didn't need to worry herself about it anymore.

But she couldn't let it go. Especially not after what that reporter had said.

Hank might not take it well that Tom Seymour had called his wife—especially considering what his texts had said and that he had felt compelled to warn Kate about her husband. She decided to let them think it was Walsingham who had spoken out of turn. "Something was found on that body. The one that was decapitated at the marina. It was a ring. It belonged to Nan."

"Those cops need to keep their mouths shut," Cromwell muttered.

"How did the police even know about the ring, I mean, that it was Nan's?" she asked, ignoring Cromwell.

Cromwell had moved to the corner of the kitchen and was tapping away on his cell phone. Anna wouldn't allow herself to get distracted by him.

Hank sighed. "The ring went missing at the same time Nan did. I reported it, and the police have been very thorough in their investigation. Since they initially thought of me when they found that dead woman's body, due to the nature of the crime, someone dug out the old missing person report from their files, which included the description of the ring."

That did seem quite thorough. Had Walsingham's superiors really thought Hank had had something to do with the dead woman? And if so . . .

"Do the police think that body is Nan, then?" She might as well ask straight out. Dancing around it wouldn't get her any answers.

Hank shook his head. "They don't know. They're checking the DNA against their records, but it will take a couple of days to determine whether it's her or not."

Anna was a little taken aback that he was answering her questions so easily. This wasn't like him, but his daughter had been kidnapped, and his life had been turned upside down. Of course he would be more forthcoming—less like himself.

Cromwell, on the other hand, was still the same.

The lawyer rejoined them at the kitchen island and waved his phone at Hank. "I don't know where Gardiner is. I've tried every way possible to reach him, and nothing." He seemed slightly gleeful at this report, his disdain for Gardiner obvious.

"And Kate?" Hank asked.

Cromwell glanced at Anna quickly, then back at Hank. "Perhaps you should reach out yourself." His tone was guarded; Anna again wondered what had happened with Kate and that reporter. Hank had seen something between them, although she was certain it was nothing—at least on Kate's part.

Hank took out his phone and hit the screen. In a second, they heard a buzzing sound.

Anna swung around and pulled open the drawer where Kate's phone lay. She took it out and handed it to Hank. "Gardiner took it from her and left it here," she explained.

"She doesn't have her phone? Where the hell is she?" His words were tinged with irritation. He turned to Cromwell. "See if you can find that damn reporter. If she's with him—"

"She's not," Anna said, interrupting his order.

Both Hank and Cromwell stared at her.

"How do you know that?" Hank asked.

Anna couldn't lie now. "He called her phone. I answered. He was looking for her. So, she can't be with him."

"Where's the car?" Hank barked at Cromwell. "Who was the driver? We have to find him." His anger had been replaced with concern. He paused a moment and added, "Find Gardiner, too."

Anna tried to think of where Kate could be but was hard-pressed to come up with anything. Kate had nowhere to go on this island. She didn't know anyone except the people standing here in this room.

"What's going on?"

The three of them turned at the sound of Maril's voice. She stood in the doorway, holding Ted's hand. Ted's face was white, his eyes wide as he stared first at his father and then at Anna, who forced a smile. "Nothing,"

Anna said. "Why don't you take Ted outside until dinner?" She nodded at Maril, as if to convey to her telepathically that the boy couldn't be part of this conversation. If she were honest, she didn't want Maril knowing what was going on, either, but it was more than possible she'd already eavesdropped. Well, that would make it easier later—she wouldn't have to explain everything.

Maril and Ted were barely out the door, the glass sliding shut, when Cromwell's phone buzzed. He held it to his ear, and after a few moments ended the call.

He kept his eyes lowered for a moment before looking at Hank. "That was Gardiner," he said. "The police found your car at the Edgartown boatyard. The driver's throat was slit. He's dead."

"What about Kate?" Anna asked.

Cromwell shook his head. "Nowhere to be seen."

PART IV

43
NAN

Nan couldn't help but think that once you saw one marina, you've pretty much seen them all. This one, in Essex, was not too different from the one in Vineyard Haven, with the exception being that it was on a river and not the ocean. It wasn't even a particularly wide river. If she had binoculars, she might be able to see into the windows of some of the houses that dotted the shore on the opposite side.

The other difference between the two marinas was that while this one was also on a small island, it was only a two-minute ferry ride.

"Really?" Nan mused as they climbed on board, not bothering to lower her voice. Wyatt gave her a frown, cocking his head slightly toward the older man who'd taken the wheel. Wyatt had said they couldn't draw attention to themselves, and a sarcastic comment from a stranger might elicit curiosity.

Sometimes it was difficult tamping down her personality.

Essex itself was charming, its Main Street lined with shops and restaurants and historic homes boasting gardens full of hydrangeas bursting with color. In a way, it reminded her a little of the Vineyard on a much smaller scale and with fewer tourists—but no beach. For that alone, she crossed it off the mental list of places she might someday want to visit with Harry. An eight-year-old boy needed more entertainment.

They stepped off the ferry onto the dock within moments, Wyatt thanking the older man, Nan barely acknowledging him. She was too tired and frustrated and eager to find the *Perseverance*—and Lizzie.

The sun still shone bright in the sky, although it was starting to lower as the day was stretching to an end. People were enjoying cocktails outside at a small restaurant, their chatter wafting in the breeze off the water.

Nan pointed out the sign saying that only members were allowed any further. "What about that?" she asked.

"If we look like we belong, no one will pay any mind," Wyatt said softly.

She slipped her hand around Wyatt's arm. "Where to, then?"

Nan saw Wyatt's mouth twitch, like he wanted to smile but kept it at bay as he glanced down at her hand before he covered it with his own. It was warm and a little calloused. "This way," he said. "It's a big yacht and a small marina. I doubt we'll miss it."

They strolled companionably along the dock, eyeing the boats bobbing in the water. All of them seemed far too small. None matched a description of a 103-foot yacht, even though several were impressive. Nan was beginning to wonder if there had been a way for the *Perseverance* to trick the phone app into showing that the yacht was here—and yet it wasn't.

They were nearing the end of the dock. Nan might have looked relaxed and casual, but she was covering up the anxiety that had risen with each step she took. She was frightened that the only clue she had to her daughter's whereabouts and safety might be a mere pipe dream. She was about to say they should turn back and regroup when Wyatt stopped abruptly, pointing at the last boat at the end of the dock.

Nan could see the lettering on the back of the yacht: *Perseverance*, written in script with a gold crown over the top of it.

The boat looked very similar to the one Hank had owned, and, if Nan remembered correctly, it had had several staterooms and cabins for the crew and captain. It was a reminder of just how far from that life she'd come, and how she wouldn't want it back for anything. Nan tried to recall those days on Hank's yacht, but they were too far away, and she was too caught up in this moment.

"It doesn't look like anyone's on board," she mused softly to herself, her eyes scanning the decks, hoping to see *something* that would indicate Lizzie was here—or at least had been. But there was a stillness about it, like a ghost ship, that made her shiver. Nan Tudor was supposed to be dead. Was this boat, registered in her name, a symbol of that?

A gangway led up to the small swim platform on the back of the yacht, flanked by two stairways. Nan pulled her hand out of Wyatt's, glancing around to see if anyone was watching, and swiftly went aboard, heading up the stairs. Just as she reached the covered patio, decked out with a sleek teak table and cushioned chairs, the glass door to the inside cabin slid open, startling her. A tall young man with a mop of blond hair stepped out.

"Oh, sorry," Nan started to say, backing up.

"It's Smeaton," Wyatt said behind her. "Did you find her?" he asked the young man as he brushed past Nan as though she wasn't even there.

They both disappeared inside the cabin, and she caught the end of Smeaton's response as she burst through the door.

"—no sign of her," Smeaton was saying.

Nan's heart skipped a beat. Not here? That was impossible. She'd found the yacht. It existed. Lizzie had to be here. She ignored Wyatt and Smeaton as she rushed through the salon. It was as though her brain was on autopilot, remembering the floor plans of Hank's yacht all those years ago—these yachts all had to be relatively the same, didn't they?—as she found her way down the small stairwell to the staterooms below. She was barely aware of Wyatt on her heels as she took in the three rooms. She was like Goldilocks, starting with the smallest with twin beds, then a larger one with a queen-size bed, and finally what could only be the owner's suite with a king-size bed and a luxury marble en suite.

Each room had been made up perfectly. There were no signs that anyone had been here at all.

She sank down on the bed in the owner's suite, her head in her hands. Wyatt settled in next to her, his arm around her as she rested her head on his chest, hearing his heartbeat.

"Why isn't she here?" she whispered.

"I don't know. I thought we'd find her here, too," Wyatt said.

"But there *is* something."

Nan pulled away from Wyatt and looked up at the sound of Smeaton's voice. He curled his index finger, indicating they should follow him back up the stairs and into the salon. Smeaton pointed at the wall behind the large leather sofa where a bright silver sword hung.

"It's just like the emoji, the one in the text," Nan whispered, absently touching the wound on her neck as Wyatt studied the weapon. Smeaton had his phone out, the flashlight app on and illuminating the blade. Wyatt moved closer, studying the sword under the small light. Nan noticed he was concentrating on small red specks along the blade's edge.

"Is that blood?" she asked.

44

Wyatt leaned in to study the sword. "It's dried, whatever it is," he said. He took out his own phone and snapped a couple of photos before producing a pocketknife.

"Hold this," Wyatt said, handing Nan his phone. Smeaton's light was still on. "Point it here," he directed, indicating a spot on the sword, then took a small piece of paper from his shirt pocket. He deftly scraped the blade, flicking the specks of red onto the paper before folding it tight.

Once he had both the paper and the knife back in his shirt pocket, Wyatt stood up straight and scanned the room. "Say it is blood, for all intents and purposes. If something happened here, we might see signs of it, even if not at first glance." He cocked his head at Smeaton. "Why don't we start here and work our way to the back?"

"Not so fast."

Nan twirled around to see a man standing in the doorway. They'd been concentrating so much on the sword that they hadn't heard him come up the stairs and across the patio deck.

"You're not allowed on board," the man said loudly, as though volume would make more of a point. Nan noticed he was wearing a uniform of sorts: white polo shirt with the marina logo on the breast pocket, khakis, white sneakers. His name tag indicated his name was Craig.

Nan stepped forward and threw her hair back as she stood up straighter, channeling her former self. "I am certainly allowed on board," she said haughtily. "It's my yacht." It wasn't a lie. According to the registration—if Craig chose to check her story—Nan Tudor owned the *Perseverance*. And since she was Nan Tudor, she might as well own this moment.

Her intimidation tactic worked. Craig took a step backward and lowered his chin in deference. If this was the marina's idea of security—and if she actually had a vested interest—she might have a talk with management. "I didn't realize you'd arrived. We weren't expecting you until tomorrow," he said.

Nan tried not to react. They were expecting her? What was that about?

Craig's eyes wandered from Nan to Wyatt to Smeaton, staring at the younger man for a few seconds longer than seemed necessary. "I've seen *you* around. Don't you play guitar with the band that was here last night?"

Smeaton gave him a small salute. "Guilty as charged."

Nan, still in character, grinned at Smeaton. "You're holding out on us, Mark. I didn't realize that's why you wanted to come on ahead."

Smeaton flashed a wink at her that indicated a familiarity even though they had only just met. "It was one night only, but I'm sure I could arrange a private performance if you're interested."

Cheeky, but Nan decided to play along. She swatted playfully at him and said coquettishly, "I bet you perform for all the girls."

She felt Wyatt's arm slip around her waist as he pulled her close to him. "Darling, you know we're supposed to meet Mary and Charles for drinks." He made a show of looking at his wristwatch. "If we don't leave now, we'll be late."

She stiffened for a moment at his touch but forced herself to relax. It was all a performance. "Certainly," Nan said. "Let me freshen up." She threw a look back at Craig. "Thank you for your diligence. I'll talk to the manager about what a good job you're doing." She didn't stop again until she pushed open the door and stepped inside the small bathroom on the other side of the bar.

Nan slumped against the vanity, taking a deep breath. It took a lot of energy to be Nan Tudor. How had she done it all those years ago—and all the time? She struggled against the sob that rose in her chest. It wouldn't do to admit defeat yet. Just because the yacht was abandoned and the specks on the sword *might* be blood didn't mean that Lizzie had come to harm. Nan still believed that this was more about her than her daughter, hoping that the kidnapper would be lenient on the girl even if she wasn't following all the rules.

Nan blinked back her tears and disappointment as she looked up at her reflection in the mirror, fluffing her hair, splashing some water on her face, and pinching her cheeks to give herself a little more color. She was paler than she'd ever been. Would Hank even recognize her these days?

Nan admonished herself. Hank and his approval no longer mattered. What mattered was Lizzie—and where she might be. The yacht must be a misdirection. She hired Wyatt—and Smeaton—to help her, and they'd gotten this far. If they put their heads together, she was sure they'd manage to figure out where her daughter was.

She had to be sure—to keep herself from falling apart.

When she opened the door, Wyatt was standing on the other side. "You okay?" he asked.

She nodded. "I'm fine." Although she felt anything but.

"We think we found something else."

The spot on the floor of the stateroom was tiny, no larger than a quarter. It could be blood, or it could be grease or oil or even spilled food. Nan eyed it dubiously.

"This doesn't exactly prove anything," she said, noticing now that Wyatt held a brown bottle in his hand. Where did he find hydrogen peroxide—and why was he dribbling it on the spot on the floor? She watched as the liquid foamed, like it did when she would pour it on a fresh cut to clean it.

Wyatt and Smeaton exchanged a glance.

"What?" she asked, impatient to find out what exactly they thought they were doing.

"Blood," Smeaton said softly. "It's blood."

"And you can tell that from pouring hydrogen peroxide on it? What are you, MacGyver?" Nan asked Wyatt, chuckling, belying the dread that had begun to spread through her.

"I'm not going to get into the science of it," Wyatt said, "but yes, I can tell from this."

"But is there a way to tell *whose* blood it is?" she asked, even though she really wasn't sure she wanted to know. If Lizzie had been on the yacht and there was definite evidence of blood, what did that mean? Nan pushed the thought aside. It was possible that the blood wasn't Lizzie's. A woman's body had been found near where the yacht had been docked on the Vineyard. This might be *her* blood instead.

"Unfortunately, there's no way of telling outside of a lab," Wyatt said. He then took the folded paper out of his pocket and opened it, revealing the remnants of the substance he'd scraped off the sword. A drop of hydrogen peroxide confirmed that, too, was blood.

While it wasn't very much blood, it was enough to send chills down her back. What had happened on the *Perseverance*?

Wyatt was curiously quiet, staring at the spot on the floor, then scanning the room looking for—what, exactly? "Wish I had gloves," he said and, covering his hand with his sleeve, flipped over the pillows on the bed. Dark red, almost black smears on the pillowcase seemed to taunt them.

Wyatt checked the rest of the bed, but there didn't seem to be any more stains.

"Shouldn't we call the police?" she asked. "I mean, this is blood, and my daughter may have been here. There might be other evidence, too, that we're not seeing."

Wyatt nodded thoughtfully. "I'd bet that there is, and you're right." He handed her his phone. "Do you want to call?"

It felt like a dare.

He took back the phone after seeing her hesitation. "Thought so. Once we get off the yacht and are far enough away, we'll let them know what we've found. Anonymously, of course. But Craig has already seen us—and he knows your name. Your real name. This yacht is registered to you, and it came from Martha's Vineyard, where your daughter went missing. It won't take much for them to think they've put two and two together."

While Nan felt strongly that this needed to be investigated by the authorities, the risk to herself was real. Whoever had planned all this had planted enough evidence against her so that even if she could eventually prove she had nothing to do with Lizzie's kidnapping, it might take a long time. She had to think about Harry. She had to get home to him.

Nan had made a choice between her children eight years ago, leaving Lizzie behind. She'd struggled with that decision ever since, regretting that she hadn't been strong enough to stand up to Hank. It was easy in retrospect to think that she could have made *that* choice instead, when in reality, Hank's power and money would have meant she would have lost both of them.

She now had the opportunity to turn a wrong into a right. A chance to redeem herself, to save her daughter just as she'd saved her son. She had to stop thinking about herself. Her daughter's life was on the line.

"I should have taken that backpack," she said. "I think that was a miscalculation, not taking it. They would have let her go."

"Not necessarily. There was no guarantee that Lizzie would have been released. And if you had taken the backpack, your ex-husband would have had you arrested." Wyatt was making sense, but he didn't understand. He wasn't a parent. And she was ready to take a risk.

"Whoever has done this wants me, not her, I'm sure of it," she said, her voice growing stronger with a new conviction. "I have to give myself up to whoever it is. It's the only way."

45

You're proposing that we use you as bait to secure your daughter's release," Wyatt said slowly, as if to give her a chance to change her mind.

"You sure about that?" Smeaton asked. "They already tried to kill you."

Nan shrugged as nonchalantly as she could. "But they didn't."

Wyatt was quiet while he mulled over what Nan was saying. As he hesitated, Nan began to have a twinge of doubt as well. Not about giving herself up, but the logistics of it. She hadn't gotten any more texts or instructions. She hadn't been sent here, to this marina, to the *Perseverance*. She was only here because Wyatt had found the yacht on that app.

The first texts had come from different numbers. Had the kidnapper left the phone in Hank's car because he'd already gotten a new one? That would mean he was someone connected to Hank. And now Kate Parker had the phone.

It was then she realized that she still hadn't told Wyatt about her conversation with Kate Parker. She'd known ever since she'd ended that call that she should tell him, but she'd kept mum for the rest of the ferry ride and during the long car ride to Essex, procrastinating, trying to figure out how to explain why she'd made the call in the first place. Because she really didn't know why. It had been an impulse, and she had a strong feeling that he wouldn't approve.

Nan stepped back, wringing her hands together, uncertain how to tell him, and finally decided to just come out with it. "I've got a confession to make," she said. "I called her. I called the wife."

Wyatt's expression didn't change, but his eyes narrowed slightly.

"She didn't tell me much, except that she had the phone. The kidnapper's phone. And she found it in Hank's car." Nan let herself take a breath.

"Did she tell you anything else?" Wyatt's tone was low, and she heard a tinge of annoyance for the first time.

Nan shook her head. "No." She stood up a little straighter, reminding herself that he worked for her. It wasn't the other way around.

"Do you think your ex-husband had anything to do with your daughter's kidnapping?" He was serious. It was a serious question.

She'd wondered the same thing, but until Kate told her the phone had been in Hank's car, she couldn't really believe it. Now, though, maybe it wasn't out of the realm of possibility. "I don't know," she admitted.

If Wyatt had found the yacht through that app, then Hank's people certainly would have found it as well, and they most likely would have been here first. Hank had access to a plane on the Vineyard and there was a small airport in Chester, the next town over. But there had been no indication from Craig that anyone else had been at the marina. If Hank hadn't had anything to do with the kidnapping, why wasn't he already here looking for his daughter? Or at least his people? Nan said as much to Wyatt.

"But what about Catherine Tudor? You've suspected her all along," Wyatt reminded her, playing devil's advocate so she could sort out her thoughts.

"I'm still leaning toward her, rather than Hank," Nan conceded. She paused a moment, then said, "Anyway, the biggest problem will be getting in touch with whoever was texting me and took Lizzie because neither of them has the phone I got those last messages from."

"*That's* the biggest problem?" Wyatt asked, incredulous.

"You could try texting the earlier number, see if those messages actually came from a different phone. But there are apps that will allow someone to text or call using a different number, so there might be only one phone," Smeaton mused. She'd almost forgotten he was there, he'd been so quiet, listening to her confession.

"Or you could wait and see if you get more instructions," Wyatt suggested.

It was odd that she hadn't gotten any more. Why not? Until the carousel, all of her movements had been orchestrated. She said as much, but then something else dawned on her. "I'm supposed to be here, at the *Perseverance*," she said, "even though the kidnapper didn't send me. Not yet, anyway."

Wyatt and Smeaton both frowned.

"Craig said that I wasn't expected until tomorrow. They're expecting me." She let that sink in for a moment before adding, "The question now is, do I wait for instructions or go on the offense and reach out myself?"

"We need to be strategic and formulate a plan. Something that will keep you and your daughter safe—and allow you to get home to your son." Wyatt's concern was obvious, yet he seemed willing to go along with what might be called a crazy idea. "Let's go to the house and put our heads together. Mark can pick up some food and meet us there."

Smeaton had managed to book a house rental not far from the marina, a yellow Colonial on a side street with a redbrick walkway and a magnificent garden full of blue and white hydrangeas. Their three-bedroom rental meant it had plenty of room, but it was still too crowded for Nan's taste. She wanted to be alone—both physically and with her own thoughts, despite Wyatt's proposal to "put our heads together." She had to psych herself up, give herself a pep talk, so to speak. She was aware of Wyatt watching her as she paced the worn hardwood floors, finally sinking down onto a plush armchair.

He had mixed martinis when he discovered a fully stocked bar tucked away in a cupboard in the pantry off the kitchen, handing her a cocktail without asking if she wanted one. He sat across from her now and looked as though he were in his natural habitat as he sipped his drink. Even though Nan had noticed his good looks when they first met at the restaurant in Providence, she hadn't had time to pay attention to them again until now.

Nan found herself drawn to him. There was something soothing about his demeanor. He was quiet and thoughtful, carefully weighing the situation. The total opposite of her. She had always been quick to come to conclusions and eager to take action. Granted, when she'd met Hank, she strung him along for a long time, allowing her intuition about him to slow her down. She hadn't wanted to break up a marriage, and she had to make sure that it was already over before she allowed a relationship to develop. Drawing out the romance meant that she had all the control, and it drove Hank crazy with desire for her. She soon learned the longer she held him off, the more he wanted her.

Nan wondered if that would work with a man like Wyatt.

Who was the woman who'd been unattainable? She found it curious that any woman might not be interested in him.

"Ms. Savoy?"

He'd caught her staring at him, and Nan felt herself blush.

Wyatt smiled at her. "You've been going nonstop for two days. It's okay to take a rest. I have a feeling tomorrow will be another long day." He was misinterpreting her body language, and she was glad of it.

Wyatt leaned forward, his elbows on his knees as he stared at her. "We'll find her, Nan."

It was the first time he'd said her name, and she liked how it sounded. God, what was wrong with her? She pushed the martini glass aside and stood, a little shakily because of said martini.

"I need some air," she said, going through the kitchen and out through a sliding glass door onto a patio.

The anxiety from the past two days bubbled up in her chest. Tears slipped down over her cheeks. This day was supposed to have gone so differently.

That carousel should have been the last stop; her daughter should have been released.

Fumbling with her phone, Nan scrolled through to the original text message she'd received just a couple of days ago.

We have your daughter.

It was possible that the kidnapper still had access to this number. This could be her direct line to the person who'd taken her daughter. She didn't stop to think; she knew what had to be done.

Bring my daughter to the Perseverance tomorrow at noon. When I see that she's safe and free, I will turn myself over to you. But only then.

It wouldn't hurt to also send this message to the number she'd called Kate Parker on, so she added that one as well. Covering all her bases.

And then she hit SEND.

46
CATHERINE

Catherine pulled the car over at the rest stop, her heart pounding in her chest as her hands gripped the steering wheel, her knuckles white. She had forgotten how stressful it was, driving on the highway, the tractor trailers looming large, blocking her line of sight as they slid past and around her white Mercedes, too close for comfort.

Catherine pushed open the door and stepped out onto the pavement, drinking in deep breaths of air, attempting to ease the panic that always came when away from the comfortable confines of her home.

The building drew her like a magnet, a safe space where she imagined the walls pressing against her like a hug. Once inside, strangers pushed around her, and she had to nimbly step from side to side to keep from having any physical contact. She drew her arms in close, clutching her bag in front of her torso. Was she proud of this? Certainly not. She'd believed she was ready, carefully venturing out for longer and longer periods of time. But she'd had little exposure to large numbers of people, and it was more claustrophobic than she'd expected.

Shutting the door to the cubicle in the ladies' room, Catherine leaned against the door, unable to release the tension that stretched across her back and down through her arms and legs.

Catherine reached into her bag and felt around until her fingers closed over the familiar pill bottle. It didn't matter that she'd left her water bottle in the car; she stuck two pills in her mouth, managing to produce enough saliva to swallow them whole. Experience told her it would take a few minutes before the anxiety eased, so she closed her eyes and drew deep breaths into her nose and out through her mouth.

Slowly, her muscles relaxed. Finally, Catherine slid the lock on the door and stepped back out. Two women stood at the sinks; she bypassed them, keeping her gaze averted. She no longer thought anyone would recognize her, but she didn't want to take any chances.

Catherine hadn't had fast food since before she'd begun sequestering herself in her home, but she found herself having a craving. She took her bag back to the car and settled in behind the wheel, setting her soda in the cup holder next to her. As she ate, she wondered why she'd never asked Lourdes to make french fries. She could get one of those air fryers and pretend it was healthy.

Once the Xanax was at full strength, her nerves calm, and her appetite satisfied, Catherine pointed the car back to the highway. She still had about half an hour or so before she got to her destination, according to the GPS, so long as there were no traffic delays.

She told herself that she wasn't in a hurry. There was no need to rush. She'd waited too long for this and would not make a mistake just because of impatience.

She'd been back on the road only about five minutes when she received an incoming call. She pressed the button on the steering wheel that allowed her to answer. While she would normally prefer to get a text, this was easier while driving, although she'd rather not have any distractions at all.

"Yes?" she asked, the number on the display familiar.

"She was at the marina."

Catherine didn't like surprises. That Woman wasn't supposed to be at the marina yet, not until tomorrow; Catherine was supposed to be there first. As it was, she'd left later than she'd wanted, but she'd had to make sure Lourdes was long gone and would not return unexpectedly for anything. Now look what that delay had meant.

Her caller didn't wait for a response before speaking again. "She was with two men."

Catherine frowned. "Are you sure it was her?" she asked. "She should be alone."

"Well, she's not. And yes, it was her. She told one of the marina employees who she was, and he found her picture online. He said it was definitely her."

Catherine pondered this new information. "And who were the two men?"

"One of the men was a musician. He plays with a band that performed at a bar."

"What's his name?"

Silence on the other end.

"You didn't get his name," Catherine said, her tone flat and disapproving. "Find out who he is and get rid of him. The other one, too."

She was well aware of what she was asking, but That Woman could not have allies. She could not have anyone helping her. She had to be alone when Catherine confronted her. It was between the two of them, no one else.

47

ANNA

The house had become a flurry of activity with Hank's security team, investigators, and police officers. Anna recognized Walsingham from the upstairs window as he climbed out of his cruiser and approached the front door. He'd been looking into the death of an unidentified woman and was now pulled into a search for a woman who'd been very much alive only hours ago. Anna suspected he'd gotten this assignment because he'd already been here, already looking into Hank Tudor's ties to the dead woman.

Something went wrong at the carousel. Lizzie was still missing, and now, so was Kate.

What had happened? Anna didn't want to say "I told you so," but she'd worried about Kate and the ransom drop-off, which was no longer a secret from the police. She wondered how Walsingham would handle that with Hank, could imagine the police trooper admonishing the billionaire for allowing his pregnant wife to leave a backpack with a million dollars on a carousel. *Why would you feel you could handle that yourself?* she imagined the trooper asking in a stern tone. And just as sternly, Hank would stare him down and remind him of who he was, as though that would keep his family safe when it obviously had no bearing now that his wife and daughter were both gone.

Anna kept an eye on Ted, who was playing a solitary game on his tablet. His focus was mostly on the screen, but she could see him occasionally glance at the closed door as though wondering whether it would hold if someone were to come in and try to take him, too.

He was right to be worried. Anna was also worried. None of them were safe. It had all started with Caitlyn's murder—and then Joan's disappearance. It was like playing a game of dominoes with wives—too many wives—and a daughter caught in the middle. Had Lizzie's kidnapper decided to take Kate as collateral? She'd heard Hank and Cromwell talking about that backpack full of cash—it was left where directed and no longer there, so they assumed the kidnapper had gotten what he'd asked for. The rules had obviously changed somewhere along the line, unbeknownst to them.

Anna felt claustrophobic in here with Ted. As when Joan went missing in June, Anna wanted to be on the front lines. She felt the same way now, eager to be assisting in the search for Kate and Lizzie. Instead, she and Ted had been relegated to this bedroom, with a view of the front drive, a lookout of sorts. She would have a bird's-eye view of anyone arriving—or departing.

That's how she saw Maril furtively skipping down the front steps and sidestepping the vehicles that had parked haphazardly on the stone pavement and along the side yard. *What is she up to?* Anna wondered as she stared out the window. As far as she knew, Maril had been relegated to *her* bedroom after telling Hank that she had an important work meeting she needed to join remotely, regardless of Kate's disappearance. Anna had thought it cold but not out of character. Hank had been too distracted to notice—or care.

Yet now, Maril was heading to the gate and letting someone in.

It was that reporter. Tom Seymour, the one who called about Kate. She recognized him from when Kate met with him on the beach. Hank would not be happy about Maril letting him on the property.

Anna watched as Maril had what looked like an animated discussion with the reporter, who'd taken out a notebook and was taking notes. What *was* Maril thinking?

"I'll be right back," she promised Ted, who looked up briefly before she stepped out into the hallway. He'd be fine alone for a few moments, she told herself as she gently closed the door behind her. This house was the safest place he could be, with police and investigators and the security team right downstairs.

The only place that might not be so secure was the gate where Maril had let in a reporter.

If Maril could get outside without being noticed, then Anna certainly could, too. She tiptoed to the front door, opened and then gently closed it behind her without a sound.

Maril and the reporter were still talking, but he spotted her as she approached. Maril turned around, hands on her hips, her lips pursed in obvious displeasure at the interruption. Anna didn't care if she was angry.

"What on earth are you doing?" Anna hissed as she approached. She frowned at the reporter. "You need to get off the property."

"He's my guest," Maril declared.

"He's a reporter," Anna stated flatly. "And you know how your father is about reporters."

"You're Anna Klein." His eyes locked with hers. His gaze was unnerving, as though he could see right into her soul. In that moment, she understood how Kate might have fallen for him.

Maril chuckled. "Your charms aren't going to work on her, you know," she warned him.

"Oh, I'm well aware," he said lightly. "But she and I have history." He made it sound clandestine, flashing a grin at Anna. "We spoke on the phone earlier."

Maril's expression grew curious.

"He was just looking for Kate, like the rest of us," Anna explained. But then something dawned on her. The familiarity between the two of them was not that of people who had only just met. "You two know each other?" she asked Maril. "How?"

Maril tossed her hair back and shrugged. "Oh, here and there, you know how it is."

Anna most certainly did not *know how it is*. "Are you feeding him information?" she demanded.

Maril merely stared at her, which Anna took as a yes. She didn't want to get into it with Maril in front of the reporter. Instead, she said, "You need to go into the house. Now."

Maril hesitated, debating whether to obey or not. Anna wasn't anyone she had to answer to—and usually she did not. However, to Anna's surprise, she tossed a look back at Tom Seymour and put her finger to her lips. "To be continued," she said as she moved past Anna back toward the house.

"What exactly has she told you?" Anna asked, even though talking to reporters was more Kate's job than hers. She wasn't sure she had the same finesse to get anything out of him, but she had to try. It wouldn't do to have Hank discover Maril telling tales out of school—and then having those tales end up in the press.

"I asked her about Kate, but all she said was that no one knows where she is," he said.

She could hear the worry in his voice. Maybe he really did care about Kate.

"You saw her at the carousel," she said, trying to keep her tone from being too accusatory. "What happened there?"

He glanced up at the house, as though he expected to see Hank, but no one was there. Even Maril had already gone inside.

"I was sure that Nan Tudor sat next to her on the carousel, but she said it wasn't her. Then Tudor showed up and whisked her to the car. That's the last I saw her."

Anna frowned. "Nan Tudor was at the carousel?"

"Kate said it wasn't her, but it sure looked like her. Although since that dead woman was wearing her ring, it couldn't have been, could it?"

He was trying to get her to confirm it. Anna had once been in the newspaper business; she was more than aware of reporter tactics. Had he been asking Maril the same questions? Or had she interrupted them before he'd had the chance?

"No comment," Anna said. "I think we're done here." She turned to go back to the house, but he reached over and touched her arm, stopping her.

"Wait." He paused a moment. "How about if I give you some information, and in return, you give me something?"

"Is that the deal you had with Maril?"

He chuckled. "More or less. What do you think?"

"Tell me what you know, and I'll make a determination."

Tom Seymour grinned. "Okay. The Vineyard Motel contacted the cops about an abandoned car in their parking lot. The name on the rental agreement is Nan Tudor."

Anna didn't have time to react before he continued.

"The woman driving the car checked in yesterday afternoon and checked out this morning. The name on her ID was Louise Savoy. Does that mean anything to you?"

Anna had never heard that name before. "Should it?"

"What about a man named Wyatt? He's a private investigator from New Haven."

Anna was getting tired of playing twenty questions, and the longer she was out here, the riskier it was that Hank would find out she was talking to a reporter. Still, she was intrigued by what he was telling her. "Get to the point, Mr. Seymour."

For the first time, his expression grew serious, his eyes growing dark. "They found a black backpack in the abandoned car. It had a million dollars in cash inside."

Anna froze. That must be the ransom Kate delivered. As she was trying to piece together what Tom Seymour was telling her, she realized he wasn't finished.

"That wasn't the only thing they found in Nan Tudor's rental," he said. "They also found a woman's head in a bag."

48
KATE

It was the way the man grasped her arm that the realization came to her. She'd been taken—the fear settled like a weight on her chest, and Kate struggled to breathe. Her eyes drifted to the gun under his arm, and her memory exploded with the flashback of Will Stafford firing a bullet into her scalp.

Would this man shoot her, too? Would he drop her body in the ocean, leaving her to vanish, another of Hank Tudor's wives gone without a trace?

This was exactly what Hank had tried to avoid by bringing her to the Vineyard.

Nan Tudor's warning came back to her: Did the kidnapper set her up by sending her to the carousel to meet with Nan? She'd gotten into the car, believing she was heading back to the house. Had this been the plan all along?

Was her husband innocent in this? Hank had told the driver—his driver—where to take her, but then there was the text, telling the driver to take her to the boatyard instead. It came from his phone. She'd made sure to look at the number. But as she thought about it, it was easy these days to make a call or text look like it was coming from a different number, if you knew what you were doing.

She should have been more alert. It was the same ploy that had been used to take Lizzie. While they'd tricked the girl by telling her that her mother was waiting for her, they used Hank as bait for Kate. She had no reason to believe that both she and Lizzie weren't part of the same plan; it was far too similar. Would Hank take his own daughter just to trap his ex-wife? Maybe. But why would he take *her*, too? It couldn't be because of Tommy Seymour. Nothing had happened; he had to know that. Didn't he?

Anyway, there were other ways to get to Nan Tudor, if Hank knew where she was. And if he wanted to get rid of *her*, well, he wasn't a stranger to divorce. Cromwell was more than adept at drawing up the papers and settling everything between parties. He'd done that for four other wives; why would she be any different?

But then her thoughts drifted back to Caitlyn and how the other woman had been pregnant when she was murdered. Kate absently touched her abdomen. Hank had seemed as though he wanted this baby. But what if he didn't? Maybe divorce wouldn't be enough.

The man let Kate go—but not before he discovered the phone in her pocket—and pushed her down on the sofa. Could she try to fight? Where would she go, even if she could get away? They were too far from land to swim—and getting further away. The yacht was moving. She could hear the soft purr of the engine.

Even if the yacht had stayed where it was, she doubted she'd be able to defend herself long enough to get that dinghy going. There was also the baby to think about. Kate didn't want to do anything to jeopardize the little life inside her, if she didn't have to.

"What's this?" he asked, waving the phone around. "I didn't think you had a phone with you."

That was curious. As far as she knew, even Hank wasn't aware she didn't have her phone with her. Had Gardiner confiscated it, knowing that she was going to be taken?

The thought made her take pause. That would mean he was in on it. But how could he be? He was Hank's investigator; he was looking for Lizzie. None of this made any sense.

"Where are you taking me?" she asked.

He was still fiddling with the phone and didn't respond.

"May I at least know your name, if we're going to be traveling together?"

He gave her a slow, ugly smile. "You're full of yourself, aren't you?"

His question reminded her of the way Gardiner had spoken to her this morning when she was speculating about the identity of the decapitated woman. She was aware that there were some men who felt threatened by women, and they responded by trying to belittle them. This man was clearly one of those; she'd have to tread carefully. Kate kept an eye on the gun under his jacket. So far, he hadn't reached for it. She hoped it stayed that way.

"You know who I am, but I don't know you," she insisted.

He gave her a sideways glance, as if assessing how much information he should give her. Finally, "It's Gage."

"Gage what?"

"Just Gage," he said, again studying the phone. "It's a burner. No one can trace it. What are you doing with it?"

"I found it."

He snorted. "Right."

She wasn't going to elaborate, but she didn't have to worry that he'd press her because his attention had already wandered.

"Where's this rental car?" he asked.

Kate realized he'd gotten into the text messages. She remembered the last thing Nan had said to her before she hung up. "The Vineyard Motel. That's where the money is. The million dollars I left on the carousel." She assumed he knew about the ransom drop since he didn't question the mention of "the money" in the text and figured that mentioning "the million dollars" would hit a nerve.

It did. Gage's eyes widened, and she could see the greed in them. Maybe he knew about the money but hadn't been told how much.

"I'm not sure anyone's found it yet," Kate said conspiratorially. "You don't have to tell anyone. You could be a million dollars richer." She hesitated. "In return, you could let me go. I won't tell anyone. I might even be able to get you more money."

His face darkened, but she could see him thinking about her offer.

"I don't know who put you up to this, but do you owe them anything?" Kate was talking too much again, like when she had been with Tommy and Hank at the carousel, but she couldn't seem to make herself stop.

"What do you know about it?" Gage demanded, fiddling with the phone. If he called or texted Nan, what would she think? Maybe she would put two and two together, and she'd realize that Kate was in trouble. But after a moment, Gage threw the phone on the floor. "Damn dead zone."

She hadn't thought about that, that being offshore might mean no cell service. She didn't like the odds: no communication, being held by a man with a gun.

He couldn't be the only one on this yacht, though. Someone was piloting it, and there had to be other crew members. But how many? Kate had no experience on boats of any size, so she couldn't even hazard a guess. Although she was willing to bet that since she'd been abducted, they would want as few witnesses as possible, so the crew might only be as many as they could get away with.

She supposed she should be more frightened—and she surprised herself by realizing her fear had abated. Not that it was gone completely, but thinking things through had helped. Anyway, what good would it do to allow the fear to engulf her? Gage hadn't taken his gun out of its holster; all he'd done was twist her arm. While she couldn't go anywhere, it wasn't uncomfortable sitting here on this plush sofa.

Kate had to keep her head about her. It was the only way she might get out of this. She suspected that Gage was not the brains behind this operation and could perhaps be manipulated.

She tried not to look at the phone, which was just a few feet away from her. If she could get ahold of it, when they got out of the dead zone, she could call for help. But as she had that thought, Gage picked it up and stuffed it into his pocket.

So much for that.

He strode over to her, and she braced herself, uncertain what to expect. He put his hand under her armpit and yanked her up, pulling her through the salon and stopping at the top of a staircase. For the first time, he took out the gun and pointed it at her. "Downstairs," he ordered.

But at the sight of the gun, Kate froze, her fear rushing back.

"Downstairs," he repeated, pushing her.

Kate stumbled, managing to get down the stairs without falling. He waved the gun toward a closed door. "In there," he said.

Kate put her hand on the doorknob and turned it, pushing the door inward. Gage shoved her inside, and as she landed on the floor, the door shut and a loud click indicated she was locked in.

She heard a soft exclamation, and as she got to her feet, Kate came face-to-face with Lizzie.

49

Lizzie was curled up on the king-sized bed in the stateroom, her T-shirt stained with what might be blood, her feet bare and covered in dirt. Lizzie's hair was tangled in knots around her face, which looked as though someone had ripped her skin, leaving it red and raw. But her eyes were wide and alert as she scrambled down off the bed, her long limbs a reminder that the girl was growing into a teenager.

The relief at seeing her was overwhelming.

"Kate!" she exclaimed.

Lizzie was not a hugger, but Kate didn't care. She pulled the girl into her arms and held her tight for a moment before Lizzie gently extricated herself. "Why are you here? Are you rescuing me?" Her voice was full of hope, and Kate hated to dampen her excitement.

"No. It seems that you and I are now in the same boat," she said, realizing the pun after she said it. "You know, everyone's been looking for you, hoping you were safe."

Lizzie gave a short bark. "I got kidnapped!" she exclaimed. "I am *not* safe." But then she seemed to realize something. "And neither are you. Not now."

Kate didn't need to have anyone remind her. She studied the girl's face a little more closely. "Does it hurt?" she asked gently as she ran her finger along Lizzie's cheek, careful not to touch the wound.

Lizzie shook her head. "It did when they pulled the tape off, but not anymore." She hesitated, then asked, "How did you get here? Did Robert Dudley bring you, too?"

"Who?"

"The boy who brought me from the other boat."

Kate frowned. She must be talking about the *Perseverance*. "No, not him. It was another man, named Gage."

"You know about the other boat, right?"

Kate nodded. "Anna found your phone. We saw the messages. Your dad went to the marina, but the boat was gone by the time he got there. Who is Robert Dudley?"

Lizzie shrugged. "Some kid who brought me here. I thought he was rescuing me. Instead, it's just another boat." She snorted with exasperation. "I don't know how to get out of here. I've tried to come up with a plan, but the door locks from the outside and the windows don't open. Not that I want to jump into the ocean. There might be sharks."

There were certainly landsharks on this boat, Kate thought grimly. And they might be as dangerous as the ones in the water. But she didn't want to be too pessimistic with Lizzie. It dawned on her now that the ransom was just a ploy; Lizzie had not been freed. Whoever had masterminded this—and she was sure it wasn't Gage or that car driver—already had the four million that Hank had transferred electronically, even if he didn't have the million in the backpack. Yet the girl remained a captive.

However, she'd always believed the adage that there is safety in numbers, and since there were two of them, perhaps they could figure a way out of this. Lizzie was a smart girl, and she'd been here longer.

"Do you know who else is on this yacht?" Kate asked. "I mean, besides the boy." Maybe she'd even heard them talking so as to give them a clue who they were.

"I don't know," Lizzie admitted. "I don't even know if he's still here." A shadow crossed her face, and Kate wondered what she wasn't saying. She decided not to push it for now; Lizzie had suffered a trauma, even if she was acting like she was fine.

To be honest, Kate was glad to have Lizzie to focus on. It kept her mind off herself, off her own fears. She had to be strong for the two of them now—no, three, if she were to count the baby. Lizzie didn't know about the baby, but that could come later. Once they were off this boat and safely home.

"I really thought it was my mother, you know, who wanted to see me," Lizzie said softly, climbing back up on to the bed and pulling her legs underneath her, as though she was trying to make herself as small as possible. She was still a child, Kate reminded herself as an unexpected emotion formed a knot in her throat so she couldn't speak.

Kate got onto the bed next to the girl, careful to leave some space between them. She wanted to tell Lizzie how she'd seen Nan, that her mother was looking for her, but she also didn't want to give her false hope—and she wasn't sure it was up to her to make this call. While Nan had seemed sincere, she *had* left her daughter all those years ago. What if she abandoned her again? Kate hoped she wouldn't, for Lizzie's sake, but there was no telling.

Of course, any reunion with Nan was ultimately up to them getting off this yacht safely—and then, up to Hank. Kate wasn't optimistic that Hank would be open to the idea. She wondered if she'd have any sway with her husband, if she could convince him to allow Lizzie to get to know her mother.

Lizzie's expression had softened, and Kate could sense that there was a lot going on in the girl's head. But she wasn't sharing, and Kate wasn't going to push.

Lizzie cocked her head and asked, "How much money have they asked for? The kidnappers?"

The question took her aback. Lizzie was more than astute for someone her age. Kate saw no reason to lie. She told her that the ransom had been paid.

"But I'm still here," Lizzie mused. "Weren't they supposed to let me go when they got the money?"

That was the five-million-dollar question, wasn't it? And now Kate was here. She wondered if there was a price on *her* head. If a daughter was worth five million, what was the price tag on a wife? More? Less?

Lizzie had that look on her face again, the one that told Kate she knew something but wasn't sure if she should tell.

"If you know anything that might get us out of here," Kate said, "then you should tell me. We can work together."

Lizzie's lips pursed in a grim line before she finally spoke. "I'm not sure if we will get out of here," she whispered, and Kate now saw her own fear mirrored on the girl's face.

"Why do you say that?"

"Because they already killed someone."

50

NAN

Mark Smeaton should have been here ages ago with the takeout, but he hadn't shown up yet. He hadn't told them where he was going, so they couldn't check to see if he'd even picked up the food. Wyatt tried texting and calling him, but there was no response.

"Maybe he hooked up with his band friends," Nan suggested, although her light tone belied her worry. The blood on that sword and in that stateroom on the yacht—not to mention the attempt on her own life—reminded her that they were facing a dangerous enemy. However, she had a hard time imagining anyone would want to harm Smeaton. It was more likely that he'd gotten distracted. If she could go by first impressions, he seemed the type, despite his obvious skill with the computer.

"That wouldn't be like him," Wyatt said, contradicting her perception of the young man. "Something's wrong."

Nan had found a bag of potato chips in the cupboard that held the cocktail ingredients, and she bit into one, chewing thoughtfully. "Should we go out to that bar at the marina to see if the band's playing tonight? Just to make sure?" she asked. They didn't know the name of the band, so they couldn't do an online search for a website, much less where they might be playing.

Wyatt held out his hand for some chips. She shook out a few, then took another for herself. Now that she'd sent that text, it was as though a weight had been lifted. She was hungry for the first time since she'd left home and thought she might even be able to sleep a little. While she'd heard nothing back yet, she felt more in control.

Wyatt, however, didn't share her feelings.

"I wish you'd talked to me first," Wyatt had scolded when Nan told him what she'd done. He hadn't liked it that she'd set the time and place. "The yacht has to be secure to assure your safety. We don't have a lot of time to set it up."

And now they were missing Smeaton, who would be needed to arrange surveillance. Wyatt pointed out that it would be critical to get to the yacht early enough to install strategically placed cameras and microphones.

"Smeaton is the brains behind all that," Wyatt explained.

Nan chuckled, taking another potato chip. "You're the brawn, then?" She made a show of studying his biceps, gently tracing one with her fingertip. "Impressive, Mr. Wyatt," she said.

He pulled his arm out from under her touch and turned to check his phone, although it wasn't fast enough that she didn't see a faint flush along the neckline of his shirt.

She put the bag of chips on the kitchen table. "Well, then, we need to find Mark, don't we?"

Wyatt shook his head. "No, not you. You should get some rest. I'll go out and see if I can find him."

While Nan had become aware of her exhaustion and need to sleep, she didn't like the idea of being at the house alone.

"I'll make sure the house is secure before I leave," Wyatt said. "Just don't go outside or unlock any doors or windows. Keep the shades drawn and the lights low."

All good ideas, but they didn't make her feel confident that she'd be completely safe here alone. She'd gotten used to Wyatt's company—and the sense of security he gave her. "No, I'll come with you," she insisted.

"Absolutely not," he said, his tone firm. "You'll be safer here."

Wyatt had shed his shoulder holster holding the gun, and it hung over one of the kitchen chairs. He reached over and took the weapon out, handing it to Nan. "Do you know how to use this?"

Nan had once thought about buying a gun, back in the days when she was afraid Hank would come after her. She'd always regretted not doing so; perhaps if she had, she could have had the courage to take Lizzie from him. Yet she knew that, ultimately, she would never have been able to use it against Hank—or anyone. Her fear had been real, but she'd worried that if she had a weapon, she'd use it recklessly, and it was possible Lizzie could have gotten caught in the crosshairs. She'd heard stories of children getting their hands on guns and accidentally shooting themselves. It had been too unsafe to have one in the house, so she'd opted against it.

"I've never even held a gun," she admitted.

Wyatt placed the weapon in her palm. It was cold and hard and heavy, and she could only think of the violence it would cause. She shook her head. "No," she said, pushing it back at him.

He hadn't let go of it, his hand covering both hers and the gun. "Are you sure?" he asked.

She tossed her head back with a show of bravado she didn't feel. "I'll put a knife under my pillow," she promised.

"And that's less dangerous?" he teased.

"I'll have less of a chance of missing my target," she said.

"But you know what they say: Don't bring a knife to a gunfight."

Nan pulled a face. "I can take care of myself. Don't worry about me. I'm rather good at dicing and slicing."

Despite her attempt at levity, Wyatt gave her a concerned look as he slipped the gun back in the holster and slung it over his shoulder, securing it before slipping on his blazer. He checked and locked every window and door. Nan followed him around the house, the wood floors smooth and cool under her bare feet.

At the front door, he stopped and turned. She was close, too close, and she could feel his breath. "Lock it after me," he instructed.

She had a brief, distinct feeling he wanted to kiss her, and she wondered what that would be like. But then the moment passed, and he disappeared into the night.

Nan carefully locked the door and turned out the lights. Her eyes adjusted to the darkness as she moved through to the kitchen. She wished she'd told him to bring back some food; those potato chips were hardly satisfying and there weren't nearly enough of them.

A block on the far counter held six knives, three large and three small. Her hand closed over the handle of the largest one and slid it out. The weight of it was familiar, comfortable in her hand. If she could break down a whole chicken in a matter of minutes, she could certainly use this to protect herself. She touched the blade and hoped it was sharp enough. Who knew if anyone had sharpened them lately.

Wyatt had brought her bag in from the car and upstairs to one of the bedrooms. She plugged her phone into its charger before shedding the white sundress she'd bought this morning and stepping into a hot shower, the knife within reach on the bathroom vanity. It might have been overkill—she was locked in, no one could come in—but she'd promised Wyatt.

The shower invigorated her. Or it might have been nerves, the longer Wyatt was gone. She kept checking her phone to see if he had anything to report, but the screen remained dark. She hadn't heard anything back, either, from the kidnapper about her proposal for tomorrow.

Nan slipped on her leggings and an oversized T-shirt, gauging the time difference between here and home, mentally figuring when she could call Harry. Her son was never far from her mind, and now she felt an even more urgent need to talk to him, to see him, even if it was merely a video call.

Was she being reckless, telling the kidnapper she'd turn herself over? It had seemed like a good idea at the time.

Second-guessing herself was normal, she told herself. She'd already made her decision; she'd put it out there, and there was no taking it back. Unless, of course, her text went nowhere because the earlier number was no longer in use. She wondered about Kate Parker, how she'd react when she saw the text—if, in fact, she still had the phone. She may have handed it over to Hank after their conversation. Nan's cynicism had returned. Could she really trust Kate Parker, after all?

Nan eyed the knife she'd placed on the bed and absently touched her neck. Maybe she should have taken the gun.

The house was quiet—too quiet.

Her phone screen remained dark.

Nan slid under the covers, the knife tucked under the pillow next to hers. She held her phone and scrolled back through the texts, trying to see—what? There were no clues; Wyatt had dissected them all. She opened the internet app and did a news search for "Martha's Vineyard" and "Tudor." Maybe she hadn't heard anything from the kidnapper because Lizzie had been returned after all. Maybe she'd been wrong about the kidnapper's motives. It was worth checking.

But what she found made her sit up in bed. A headline she hadn't expected.

BILLIONAIRE HANK TUDOR'S WIFE MISSING

Nan had just started to read the news story—*Billionaire Hank Tudor's wife Kate Parker's car was discovered abandoned at the Edgartown boatyard, her driver murdered*—when a text notification popped up on her screen.

It's Wyatt. I'm at the back. Let me in.

Nan made her way down the stairs. She peered through the shade to make sure it was really him. He wore an anxious expression as he kept glancing around behind him. Another text: *Let me in.*

Nan swung the door open, and he came inside quickly, shutting and locking the door.

"Get your things. We need to leave. Now."

51

Wyatt didn't elaborate as he scrambled around the house gathering up his laptop and bag. Sensing there was no time to change clothes, Nan slipped on her canvas sneakers before zipping up her carry-on, slinging the Birkin over her forearm, and heading downstairs. Wyatt practically pushed her out the door to the waiting car, cursing the light that had been activated by the motion detector.

"Can you tell me what's going on?" Nan asked as Wyatt maneuvered the car along side streets—although it seemed every street around here was a side street.

"We have to get far away from that house as soon as possible."

It seemed a rather extreme reaction. While the quiet that had settled around the house had been unnerving, she hadn't heard anything or anyone outside—and she'd been paying attention.

Wyatt checked the rearview and side mirrors before pulling over onto the shoulder. There were no streetlights illuminating the road, nor were there any telltale headlights anywhere. Nan supposed this was the type of community that went to bed early.

He shifted in his seat, so he was facing her.

"Smeaton's dead."

Nan struggled to breathe, unable to speak. She felt as though a weight was crushing her chest. Finally, "How? How could he be dead?" she asked, even though she wasn't sure she really wanted to know.

Wyatt pursed his lips and took a deep breath through his nose. "I went to that restaurant at the marina, to start there to look for him. It was possible the band was playing tonight, and I wanted to see if he'd stopped by." He was backing into it, but Nan wasn't going to interrupt. He had to tell the story in his own way. "I was right that he'd gone there, but his band wasn't playing. I talked to the bartender—I guess they'd gotten friendly last night—and he told me Smeaton met someone there."

Wyatt paused again and took another deep breath. "It was Gardiner."

Nan frowned. "Gardiner? Really? Are you sure?"

"I showed him a photo, and he confirmed it. He also told me he overheard some of their conversation. Sounds like our friend Craig at the marina told Gardiner who Smeaton was, at least that Smeaton was with that band. Gardiner managed to get someone in the band to lure Smeaton to the restaurant."

Nan didn't like the sound of this.

Wyatt was still speaking. "Gardiner was demanding he tell him where you were. Smeaton held him off, said he didn't know, but then they left and didn't come back."

A shadow crossed Wyatt's face.

"You know where they went," Nan said. "Did they go to the yacht?"

"I found him there," Wyatt said flatly. "I found his body." He wasn't telling her everything, but that was okay. She didn't need to know details. Smeaton was dead.

Nan reached over and put her hand over Wyatt's, which was resting on the gearshift between them. "What did you do?" she asked softly. "When you found him?"

He met her gaze. "I got the hell out of there. I don't know what Smeaton told Gardiner, maybe nothing. But we have to assume that Gardiner got something out of him."

"What about Gardiner? You didn't see him?"

He shook his head, staring out through the windshield. "No. I thought I'd find him at the house." Nan understood what he was saying—he'd been afraid that Gardiner had gotten to her.

"That house was so quiet, I would have heard a pin drop. I don't think anyone was lurking around. Maybe Smeaton *didn't* tell him where I was." She paused. "Did you call 911?" she asked.

"I stopped back at the restaurant and told them that there was trouble at the yacht, and then I left." His voice broke. Smeaton was his associate, his friend, and he left him there.

Nan tightened her grip on his hand. "It's not your fault," she whispered. "It's mine."

Smeaton was murdered because of her. And if Gardiner had found Smeaton, he most likely knew there was another man who had been with her at the yacht today—and it wouldn't take too much digging to find out that Smeaton worked for Wyatt and that Wyatt was the second man. She was the one Gardiner wanted, but he might not hesitate to kill Wyatt, either, intending to leave her all alone, with no one to come to her aid when he finally came for her.

Who was Gardiner working for? He was technically Hank's investigator, but when she'd found out he was talking to that reporter at the carousel, she'd questioned his alliances.

And then she remembered . . .

"Kate Parker is missing," she told Wyatt, pulling up the news story on her phone and showing it to him.

He seemed glad for the distraction. After he finished reading, he gave her a puzzled look. "First your daughter and now the new wife? I'm having a hard time thinking that a man could kidnap and threaten those who are closest to him."

He didn't know Hank. Kate had found the phone in his car, after all. Still, Gardiner had been at the carousel. He probably had access to the car, too.

It seemed Wyatt was having the same thought. "Your initial instincts could be right. Gardiner might be freelancing. Could the first Mrs. Tudor have hired him to keep everyone off her trail—and point a finger at her ex-husband?"

"I wouldn't put anything past her. Catherine might well want to settle an old score with me and may have found it convenient to get rid of the newest wife at the same time."

The more Nan considered the idea, the more she wondered if that wasn't the case. Catherine was ruthless. Even if she were able to set Hank up as a suspect, Hank had enough power and money to fight it and clear his name—and Catherine could be counting on it. She might feel she was clearing the playing field to set the stage for her return as Hank's wife and partner. Under other circumstances, Nan might have felt a twinge of sympathy for the older woman. Hank had discarded her a long time ago. If he'd wanted her back, he wouldn't have kept marrying other women.

Wyatt handed her back her phone and pulled his own out, tapping the screen.

"What are you doing?"

"The reporter who wrote that story was the same one at the carousel. The one who was involved with Kate Parker. I'm sending him an email and asking that he call. Maybe we can use him, find out what he knows."

It was a good idea. He'd found out about the ransom drop somehow—had Gardiner given him the tip?—so it was possible he had information off the record that he could share. "He might want something in return," Nan said.

Wyatt chuckled. "We can count on that. He's a journalist."

Nan stared out into the darkness. "So where do we go now?"

"We're not exactly in the middle of nowhere," he said. "Even though it might seem like it." A quick internet search turned up a room at a motel not too far away, and a phone call secured a reservation. "It's not going to be fancy," he told Nan.

"I prefer that," she said. "I don't do fancy anymore."

Wyatt cocked his head at her Birkin bag. "I think that begs to differ." He was trying for levity, but it fell flat as they were both thinking of Smeaton and what they were running from.

Wyatt had started to pull the car back into the road when they heard the ping of a notification. Maybe it was the reporter.

But it wasn't Wyatt's phone. It was Nan's. A text had popped up on her screen.

You don't set the rules. Defiance has consequences. Do you want your daughter to end up like your friend Smeaton?

52
LIZZIE

Kate can't stay still. She's been pacing around the room ever since I told her about Joan.

I'm certain it was Joan's voice I heard when they first took me.

"But you were under duress," Kate says. "Could you have imagined it? Just thought it might be her, but it wasn't?"

Kate doesn't want to believe that Joan would kidnap me—or at least be a part of it. I don't really want to believe it, either. I liked Joan. She made Anna happy, and I thought Joan was happy, too. They were always hugging and kissing and smiling at each other. They had no problems with public displays of affection, and it was kind of nice to see it. Dad isn't the touchy-feely type, even when he was with Caitlyn. I saw him kiss Kate once, like, really kiss her, like in-the-movies kissing, but it was only once.

It was awful when Joan went missing. Anna changed overnight into this sad person who cried all the time.

I was pretty sure Joan was already dead.

Until I heard her voice.

"It was her," I say. "I'm sure of it."

I can tell Kate doesn't know what to think of this. Neither do I. Joan was with the kidnappers; she was part of it. But why? Had she been tricked into this, like me and Kate?

After I recognized her voice, I had thought if I could talk to her, she could help me get away. We could both get away, and then Anna didn't have to be so sad anymore and we could be a family again.

So, the next time I heard the door open, I asked, "Joan? Is that you?" It was really annoying not being able to see.

For a second, the person didn't say anything, but then a woman's voice barked at me. "Keep quiet!"

The door slammed shut, but they were right outside; I could still hear them, even though they kept their voices low.

"She's asking for Joan. What are we going to tell her?"

"Nothing."

"But she knows Joan was here."

"She's not anymore. You better be careful what you say. Don't screw up or you'll end up dead, too."

"They didn't have to take off her head."

"She can't be recognized, you know that. Not yet, anyway."

It was just like Caitlyn. I said a little prayer for her. For Joan. For Anna. It was the right thing to do.

Kate listens as I tell her all of this. She's not treating me like a kid but someone who should be taken seriously. I wonder if I should give her more of a chance. I didn't want to get to know her too well because my dad marries women like they're on a conveyor belt—pluck one off now and then after discarding the previous one—but maybe he chose right with Kate.

"Tell me what happened with Robert Dudley," Kate says, changing the subject. I'm grateful, because I don't want to think about what happened to Joan anymore.

"He made it sound like he was rescuing me." He didn't, not really. He never said he was, and I'm embarrassed that I didn't run. "He said he was taking me to my dad on another boat." I trusted him because he was a kid, like me.

Kate is quiet a moment. "That's how Gage got me. I was in the car and thought I was going back to the house, but he told me your father was on a yacht and wanted me to join him. He made it sound like your dad was trying to keep me safe."

"So, whose boat is this, anyway?" I ask.

Kate says she doesn't know. They knew about the other yacht, but not about this one. That can't be good.

We wonder where we are. We can see out the window, and there's a thin line of land but it's not that close. I remember a movie about a woman who swam from Florida to Cuba—so it can be done—but she was surrounded by jellyfish and sharks and had a whole team of people keeping an eye out for her.

Even without the sea creatures and the shorter distance, I don't think I could make it to shore from here. I can swim, but I'm not a great swimmer. I ask Kate if she thinks she could. She says probably not. She doesn't have to mention the man with the gun. We're both thinking about him, too. He is worse than a sea creature.

And as though we've conjured him up just by thinking about him, the door swings open and he comes in, the gun very much pointed at us. He waves it at Kate. "Come on. This reunion is over."

She looks at me, then back at him, but she doesn't move. He comes over and yanks on her arm, pulling her off the bed and to her feet.

"What about Lizzie?" she asks, and I see how worried she is about me. "Can she come, too?"

He doesn't say anything, just pushes her out the door, and I am alone again.

Where is he taking her? I close my eyes and try to concentrate, hoping I can hear something. A shiver of fear rushes through me as I think about Joan. But I don't hear anything. Nothing at all. Is that a good thing? Or are they killing her somewhere far away on this boat so there are no witnesses?

I can't keep the worst scenarios out of my head. They swirl around until my stomach is in knots and I have a hard time breathing.

I don't know how long I lie there; there's no clock in the room. But I doze off, even though I don't want to, and when I wake up, I can see a glimmer of color in the sky. It's almost morning, and I'm still alone.

53

CATHERINE

Catherine hadn't woken up anywhere except in her own bed for years. The sun streamed through the window and splashed across the wall opposite where she lay under a light duvet. The mattress was remarkably comfortable, and her head had barely hit the pillow before she fell into a deep sleep. Funny that she'd had the best rest she'd had in a long time, considering the circumstances—and that she hadn't needed anything to help herself sleep.

Catherine hadn't counted on That Woman finding anyone to help her, much less a private investigator. She was familiar with his work—and that Maggie had hired him all those years ago. He was always willing to fight a losing battle. She wondered how he stayed in business. Well, they'd taken care of his associate—such a silly young man, so eager to try to save himself. Would they suspect that he was more than willing to give her up when faced with the threat of a blade? Catherine felt no guilt about the death of a man who was so weak.

She wasn't concerned that they'd discover her. She'd hidden her tracks well, buried deep in financial documents so obscure that they'd confuse any expert. Her offshore accounts couldn't be traced; the LLC was only one of many. She was playing a shell game, much like with her stock trades. She had no doubt she would continue to come out ahead.

Gardiner was a problem, though. She'd been reluctant to bring him in. She didn't know him; he'd come onto Hank's payroll later, about the time Cromwell also made his debut. Yet he'd been vouched for, assurances made. He was willing to switch loyalties; Hank had not appreciated his skills. Of course he had a price, but Catherine had expected that. His arrogance was problematic. He believed he was smarter than everyone else. However, that made him the perfect fall guy. When she threw him to the wolves, he wouldn't even know what was happening. He was so power hungry that he deserved what he would get.

Catherine answered the knock at her door, pulling the terry cloth robe closer around her body as the breakfast cart rolled into the room. She handed a tip to the steward; not too much, though. As a middle-aged woman, she understood she was invisible, and she couldn't afford to be remembered.

She was tucking into her toast and coffee when her phone buzzed with an incoming call. Catherine frowned. Communication was supposed to be restricted at this point. She'd made it clear that she should not be directly contacted at any stage from now on.

Before she was able to issue a stern reminder about the rules, the caller asked, "What do you want us to do with the woman?"

The question startled her. "What woman?"

"The wife."

"What wife?" Had someone beaten her to it, taken That Woman before she could confront her? They all knew she was off-limits, that they were to leave her for Catherine.

"The new one. You know."

No, she did not know. "What have you done?" she asked.

"We took her to the yacht. Like the girl."

Catherine still didn't understand. Had there been a reunion between the girl and her mother? That definitely wouldn't do. The girl was bait. Without that lure, That Woman wouldn't do her bidding. But then she realized what had been said: *The new one*. "Are you talking about Kate Parker?" she asked, her anger rising because she should not have to ask directly.

"Of course. Just like you wanted."

Who had been giving instructions in her name?

Catherine couldn't let them know that this had caught her by surprise. "She's on the yacht?"

"We haven't hurt her. Not yet."

Catherine needed time to think about this. She'd already cleaned up one mess, and now she had another. But this one was more delicate. While she'd hoped to drive a wedge between the new wife and Hank, taking her was not part of her plan.

Yet clearly it was part of someone's. But whose?

54

ANNA

While Tom Seymour had said he would stay in touch with her, Anna was still surprised when she saw the text from him when she awoke. She'd assumed it had been an empty promise, since he hadn't gotten much information from her.

Heading to Essex, CT. Want to come?

It must be a rhetorical question, almost flirtatious, although Anna did find herself wanting to accompany him. She was frustrated by the confinement and lack of communication on Hank's part, not to mention that Maril was becoming increasingly annoying and not at all helpful with Ted.

Does this have to do with Kate? Do you think she's there?

She'd read his story about how Kate was missing, but he didn't have anything more than what he'd told her. Was he holding something back?

Three bubbles appeared, indicating he was typing.

But then the bubbles disappeared.

She'd been concentrating so intently on the phone that the short knock on the door startled her.

"Anna?"

It was Hank.

She glanced over at the bed, which was still unmade, and was aware that she hadn't changed out of her pajamas. The day had barely begun; the house was only now starting to stir with activity. If she hadn't been distracted by Tom Seymour's texts, she would already be downstairs getting breakfast ready.

Anna pulled on her cotton robe and opened the door to see Hank freshly showered and shaved and dressed in a white button-down shirt and khakis.

"I'll see to breakfast," she said quickly, but when she saw his expression change, she realized that wasn't why he was here. "What is it?" she asked anxiously.

"Cromwell and I are heading to the jet."

He was being far too cryptic, and Anna was tired of being left in the dark. "Does this have to do with Lizzie or Kate or both?" She reminded herself she shouldn't be combative, so she kept her tone merely inquisitive. Anyone would be curious under the circumstances.

Hank sighed and, to her surprise, shut the door behind him and indicated she should sit on the bed. When she did, he pulled over the chair from the corner and sat across from her, his elbows on his knees, hands folded.

"Gardiner found the yacht. It's in Essex, Connecticut. He went out there yesterday."

Anna forced herself not to react by biting the inside of her lip. Tom Seymour was going to Essex. Hank would find that bit out soon enough, but not from her. "Did he find Lizzie?"

"No. But there was a body."

Anna caught her breath. "Not . . ."

Hank shook his head. "It was a private investigator. He was murdered. He'd been seen there with Nan earlier. Gardiner doesn't think she's too far away."

Hadn't Tom Seymour mentioned a private investigator? He hadn't said much about him, and she hadn't pushed. Was it the same one? She couldn't ask Hank without telling him about their conversation.

And then something else struck her. The murdered investigator had been seen with Nan, which meant that body found with the ring was not her, after all.

"Do you think Nan killed him? Is she capable of that?" she asked, keeping her thoughts to herself.

"I think she's desperate," Hank said.

"So, you *do* think she had something to do with Lizzie's kidnapping?"

He didn't answer her, but she could see that he very well did think Nan had something to do with it. But to kill someone? It seemed a little far-fetched.

"What about Kate? Do you think her disappearance is related?" she asked when it was clear Hank was done talking about Nan.

"Has to be. Gardiner's working on it. But that's not why I've come to talk to you."

"I assume you want me to stay here with Ted while you're gone." It made the most sense.

But he was shaking his head. "No, that's not what I want. I'd like you to come with us."

Anna wasn't sure she heard him right. "You're asking me to come with you?" Even when she was married to him, Hank had never included her. Her job was to stay home with the children. She said as much.

"But that's why you have to come," Hank said. "When we find Lizzie, she'll need you. You're the only mother she's ever known."

She blinked back tears. She couldn't cry. By telling her this, he was counting on her to stay strong.

"You're her father," Anna reminded him gently. "She'll need *you*."

When his eyes met hers, she saw the pain etched in them. First his daughter and then his wife. His pregnant wife.

Hank stood, pushing the chair back to where it had been, and opened the door. "Can you be ready in ten minutes? I'm afraid time is of the essence."

"Of course," Anna said. "But what about Ted?"

"Maril will stay with him."

She wondered if Maril had had any choice in the matter and decided that she hadn't. Hank had his mind made up. While Maril wouldn't be happy being left behind, Anna was pleased that she wouldn't be tagging along.

As Anna slipped on a pair of linen slacks and a sleeveless blouse, she glanced down at her phone on the bed. She'd dropped it there, face down, before she'd opened the door to Hank. She gave a sidelong glance at the door, then picked it up.

The moment she touched it, the screen lit up, and she saw a new text from Tom Seymour.

That PI I told you about emailed me. We're meeting this morning.

Wasn't the private investigator dead? Now she had even more questions, but she didn't have time right now.

Anna was relieved that he'd texted her, rather than calling while Hank was here. It was ironic that he'd asked her to come to Essex with him, and then Hank had, too. Now both men would be in the same place at the same time—looking for the same woman.

Anna turned off her phone, grabbed her bag, and went downstairs to join Hank and Cromwell.

55

NAN

Before she opened her eyes, Nan imagined she was home, in her soft bed under the old wooden beams that crisscrossed the ceiling. Harry was in the next room, snoring softly, his small body growing too fast. She would get up and pad into the hallway, waking up her son for school, beating eggs for his breakfast, putting bacon in the skillet, coffee on the stove.

She'd talked to Harry before going to sleep, his eyes wide with excitement because Gabriel's dog had puppies—*Could we have one, please, please?* She wanted to say yes. She wanted to make him happy, come home to him and a puppy and resume the life she'd made for herself.

But when she opened her eyes, reality hit, and she realized that life as she'd known it for the past eight years was out of reach and might never exist again.

Her daughter was still missing. Smeaton was dead.

Wyatt lay next to her in the queen-size bed. She'd insisted that they share; there was no need for him to sleep on the floor. They were exhausted. Of course they would sleep—only sleep—there was no doubt.

Until the need to feel something, something good, something entirely physical, overcame her. She'd tucked herself against him, her hands sliding over his chest, and tentatively kissed him. At first, he resisted—"We really shouldn't," he whispered—but they didn't stop. He slipped her T-shirt over her head, lowering his mouth to her breasts as he pulled her closer, his body hot against hers. She lost herself in him. And he needed it as much as she did—to forget the guilt he felt over Smeaton, at least for a little while. That was how she convinced herself it wasn't a mistake.

She slid out of bed, glancing back at Wyatt, who rolled over on his side to face her and gave her a sad smile as he recited softly, *"And wilt thou leave me thus? / Say nay, say nay, for shame / To save thee from the blame / Of all my brief and grame."*

Nan turned his words around in her head. While she'd been surprised when he'd told her he moonlighted as a poet, after last night, she understood. She looked closely at her face in the bathroom mirror. Even though she hadn't slept much, she didn't look tired but, rather, refreshed. Wyatt had been good for her, despite the stresses of the past few days.

There had been a couple of men at home, men who helped her pass the time, reminded her that she was still alive and very much a woman who enjoyed a man's company—and his body. But they were nothing special, no one she wanted to bring into her life—Harry had never met them.

But Wyatt was different. Under other circumstances, not to mention that she had a life across the ocean, she would be tempted to see what might develop between them. She hadn't felt such symmetry with anyone in a very long time, not since Hank in the beginning.

When she emerged after her shower, dressed in jeans and a T-shirt, Wyatt quietly slipped past her and shut the door behind him.

She wasn't sure what the plan was for today. The kidnapper hadn't texted again after their warning. Time was running out. It had already been three days since Lizzie went missing.

Nan's impatience rose. She opened the bathroom door to see Wyatt shaving. He wore a towel around his waist. For a moment, she allowed herself to admire his broad shoulders and remember how his arms had felt around her, but then she pushed the memory aside.

"We need to come up with a plan," she announced.

Wyatt continued to shave, but she saw his eyes shift slightly to look at her in the mirror's reflection. "We're meeting the reporter in half an hour."

"When did that happen?"

"You didn't give me time to tell you last night." A smile appeared, and his hand slipped a little, the razor nicking his chin. "Damn," he said, reaching for the hand towel.

"Do we need to talk about it?" Nan said.

"Is there something to talk about?"

Nan rolled her eyes and crossed the room, settling in on the bed against the pillows. She grabbed her phone off the bedside table. No new messages. She itched to send a text, but that would be a bad idea, so instead scrolled through headlines, looking for more about Kate Parker, but there was nothing. Hank was probably doing what he could to keep it out of the news.

Wyatt's phone pinged. Just as she was debating looking at it, he came out of the bathroom in the towel. She looked away as he took off the towel and pulled on a pair of jeans and a button-down shirt. She didn't need any more distractions. "I think you got a call or text," she said.

"Voicemail." He was one step ahead of her, as he already had the phone against his ear, listening. After a moment, he looked up at her. "I'll be right back." Without waiting for a response, he went out the door.

It was one of those motels with a long, covered walkway in front of the rooms. The car was parked right outside. Wyatt had paid for the room in cash after a stop at an ATM—they didn't want anyone to track them via a credit card. They assumed Gardiner was aware Smeaton worked for Wyatt's firm, and it was possible he'd called around to area motels and inns looking for him, so they'd checked in under different names. The clerk hadn't even looked up when Mr. and Mrs. John Smith took their room key.

Nan watched Wyatt pacing outside on the walkway as he spoke to someone on the phone. Was it the reporter? She hoped he wasn't canceling on them.

Nan busied herself with packing her bag, and when Wyatt still hadn't returned, she packed his bag for him as well.

The bags were next to the door, ready to be loaded into the car, when Wyatt finally came back. She could tell from his expression that something had happened, and possibly something positive from the look on his face. They could certainly use good news.

"What is it?" she asked.

"Remember I told you we were checking out the title of the *Perseverance*? To see if we could find out who owned it before it was registered in your name?"

Smeaton had been looking into it, but it now seemed Wyatt had found out something without his associate.

Wyatt didn't wait for her to answer. "It's an LLC based in Delaware."

That wasn't unusual. Delaware was a popular tax haven, and as Nan understood it, businesses could be registered anonymously under someone else's name with no documentation or identification papers. Because of this, she failed to see why Wyatt was so excited. That LLC would be untraceable. She said as much.

"Ye of little faith," he said. "You see, there's a tax loophole that allows LLCs to avoid corporate state taxes by setting up a subsidiary where they can transfer intangible assets that aren't taxed."

This was going over her head. "I'm a restaurant cook," she reminded him, "not a finance person."

Wyatt ignored her interruption. "The subsidiary is where she screwed up, but it's easy to miss for anyone not looking closely." He paused for effect before saying, "You were right about her. Catherine Tudor. She owns the LLC."

Nan caught her breath. Now she had proof. Proof that Catherine really was after her. She could hardly believe it. Catherine had always been so smart, so business savvy. But the more she thought about it, the more she wondered if Catherine hadn't made a mistake after all. "What if she set it up so I would find out?" she asked. "She wants me to know it's her."

Wyatt nodded. "Possible. But there's something else. Something I'm not sure she thought we'd find." He paused a moment. "There's another boat."

56

Nan fidgeted in her seat at the corner table of the coffee shop. Wyatt was a couple of tables away, nursing a cup of coffee and nibbling on a muffin. The reporter was late.

The other yacht, called *The Aragon*, was in Long Island Sound, just off the coast of Old Saybrook at the mouth of the Connecticut River, not too far from Essex. When Wyatt had shown her the map on his phone screen, Nan had touched the small location indicator and a window popped up, confirming that it had originated in Edgartown on Martha's Vineyard.

"Two yachts? It's the perfect move," Nan had mused, exactly how Catherine would play it.

Nan had worked for Catherine; she'd been her assistant. She understood the way Catherine's mind worked. The woman was always planning and plotting to negotiate the best deals to one-up the competition. While Catherine might be even smarter than Hank, she had stumbled after Hank's eye wandered. Hank was her Achilles' heel. It would be just like Catherine to now try to prove how shrewd she was by taking down Nan once and for all.

"Do you think Lizzie's on that boat?" she'd asked Wyatt, who was focusing on his phone and didn't seem to hear her. She touched his arm. "Wyatt?"

He'd turned the phone so she could see the news story they'd read about Kate Parker's disappearance. "Her car was found at the Edgartown boatyard," he said.

That was too much of a coincidence. Wyatt had drawn the same conclusion she had: Lizzie may or may not be on that yacht, but it was more than possible that Kate Parker was.

"We should alert someone," Nan had said. "Who handles this type of thing? Marine police? Coast Guard?"

"We can tell the reporter. Let's have him call and keep you and me out of it." He'd emphasized the need for a low profile, especially because of Smeaton and the newest text threat Nan had received. Neither of them were in a position to reveal themselves. It would put them in jeopardy. They were already taking a risk meeting with the reporter.

Nan glanced over at the door, but no one had come into the coffee shop. She worried that they couldn't trust the reporter. She had spent too much time away, concealing herself, to have a journalist turn her world upside down.

"You don't have to come," Wyatt had said when she raised her concerns. "He doesn't know about you. When I emailed, I indicated I might have information, but I never indicated who I'm working for."

But she wanted to be there, which was why they were sitting separately. If Wyatt felt it was safe for her to approach, he'd give her a nod.

But the reporter hadn't shown up yet. He was fifteen minutes late. Nan went to the counter and asked for a second cappuccino. While the barista was making her drink, she tapped the floor with her foot, one eye on the door.

The jangle of the bell came while she was paying for the coffee. She forced herself not to turn and look but finished the transaction and carried her cup to the table, one eye on Wyatt, who'd stood and was shaking the reporter's hand.

He was tall and lean, his hair graying a little around the temples. He had a wide smile as he introduced himself.

"Tom Seymour." He didn't apologize for his tardiness.

She and Wyatt had done a little dive into Seymour before they left the motel. He'd slept with a source and was on the outs with his publication because of it, moved from his political beat to general assignment. From her vantage point, Nan could study him without being noticed. He had a roguish, bad boy look about him; the beard stubble didn't conceal a handsome jawline. She could see how he could get into trouble.

Wyatt had ordered two coffees, and he indicated one was for Seymour. She was sitting close enough to easily hear their conversation.

"Thanks, man. Just flew in this morning from the Vineyard. Haven't had much time to think." Seymour's jovial, relaxed demeanor seemed at odds with the serious story he was pursuing. He took his phone out of his pocket and put it on the table. "Mind if I tape this? I've got a lousy memory and even worse handwriting." He hit the record button before Wyatt could answer.

Wyatt reached over and took the phone, ending the recording that had only just begun. "Yes, I mind." He got down to business without giving the phone back. "You've written about Kate Tudor's disappearance. Do you know any more than what's been published? Do you think it's tied to Lizzie Tudor's kidnapping?"

Seymour shifted slightly in his seat, clearly not happy that Wyatt still held his phone and turned the interrogation around, but then he surprised Nan by saying, "Why don't we ask the former Mrs. Tudor to join us? It'll make it easier for her to hear our conversation."

Nan's head snapped up to see Seymour staring at her.

"Don't pretend you're not her," Seymour said. "I saw you on the carousel with Kate. She said it wasn't you, but you are definitely the same woman."

It wasn't worth trying to deny it. He was more astute than she gave him credit for. Nan picked up her coffee cup and bag and slid into the chair next to Wyatt, making it easier for the two of them to tag team Seymour, who took a sip of his coffee as though it didn't matter. Maybe it didn't.

"You somehow got that backpack out of the carousel and left it in your rental car," Seymour began, addressing Nan. "The police found it with some help from Tudor's people. But what I haven't written is that there was also a head in a bag."

Nan caught her breath.

"I can tell from the look on your faces that this is news to you."

"Was it the woman they found at the marina?" Wyatt asked. Nan was glad he did, because she couldn't find her voice.

"The police think so. So far, no ID. It's not Kate, though."

Nan saw genuine relief in his expression. He cared about the woman.

"What about my daughter?" she asked. "Have you discovered anything about her? Where she might be?"

He looked straight into her eyes, and she could see his were a bright blue, almost too blue. "No, but I found out about your"—and now he shifted his gaze to Wyatt—"associate."

Wyatt didn't react, just took a sip of coffee.

"That's not a surprise to you," Seymour said. When Wyatt didn't respond, he continued. "You know, if you wanted to stay under the radar, you shouldn't have checked into that Vineyard motel under your name."

Nan had thought she was protected by taking a room as Louise Savoy, but she hadn't realized that Wyatt wasn't using an alias. They were seen together by the motel staff—and they were using his car. So much for leaving her rental behind as a smokescreen. It was pure luck that Gardiner hadn't gotten to them yet.

"You might want to know that Hank Tudor is on his way here, along with his lawyer and his ex-wife," Seymour was saying.

"Catherine?" Nan asked before she could stop herself.

Seymour smirked. "No, not that one. Anna Klein."

Why on earth would Hank bring his fourth wife? Nan pushed it aside. It didn't matter. Seymour didn't know anything about Lizzie. He also didn't know about the other yacht, but it was time to tell him. He could prove useful, after all.

"We think we might have a lead on where Kate Tudor is," Wyatt said, beating her to it.

Seymour's posture shifted; his eyes widened.

"There's another yacht. It left from Edgartown yesterday."

Seymour put it together more quickly than they had. "Can you give me the details?" He now had a notebook out, pen in hand.

"It's called *The Aragon*. The last we knew, it was off the coast of Old Saybrook in the Sound."

Seymour was scribbling. "Okay, okay," he said, nodding.

"When you call marine patrol, keep our names out of it, all right?" Wyatt asked.

Seymour's head snapped back, and he looked from Wyatt to Nan. "You haven't called?"

"It would be best if you did," Wyatt said, his voice steady, calm. "And when they ask, just tell them you got this from an anonymous source."

Seymour shoved back his chair and stood. "Right. Sure. Let's just hope it's not too late."

57
KATE

Something was happening outside the door. Footsteps back and forth, murmurings. She couldn't make out what they were saying, but the tone was frantic.

Kate had managed to sleep a little after Gage brought her to this stateroom, but only because she was exhausted—mentally as well as physically. Seeing Lizzie had been a shock—and then learning about Joan. The body they'd found at the marina had to be her, considering what Lizzie had overheard.

Kate hadn't known Joan very well. The only extended period of time she'd spent with Anna's wife had been earlier this summer in Greenwich at their inn.

Anna would be devastated—both to find out that Joan was involved in Lizzie's kidnapping and that she really was dead, although only recently, and it now appeared that Joan must have staged her own disappearance.

Anna had told Kate that she thought she'd seen Joan at the house. While Anna thought it was a hallucination, discovering that Joan had been on the *Perseverance* meant that it most likely hadn't been. What had happened to cause Joan to vanish—and end up the way she had? Joan and Anna had been devoted to each other; the way Joan had looked at her wife indicated that she truly loved Anna. Was that why she'd risked trespassing on Hank's property and allowing Anna—and anyone else—to see her? Because she wanted to see her wife one more time?

Kate wondered if that would be a comfort to Anna, despite Joan's actions. Could Anna ever forgive her wife after this?

It was easier to think about Anna than her own circumstances. Seeing Lizzie had distracted her, too. But as she looked around her, locked in by a man with a gun, she began to tremble with fear. She'd seen Gage, seen his face, knew his name. Could he let her go with that knowledge? Probably not. So, what would become of her? Would he kill her, like Joan? Her heart raced even faster.

She took some deep breaths, forcing herself to calm down. She had to think logically. How could she get out of here? Kate laid her hand across her abdomen. There were two of them here—no, three, counting Lizzie. There had to be a way.

She raised the blinds on the window and saw that it was early morning, the sun shining in the cloudless sky. It was almost a crime that she was locked in on such a beautiful day.

This stateroom was larger and more opulent than the one where Lizzie was being held. The teak paneling and gold sconces gave it an elegant flair, and although it wasn't really to Kate's tastes, she could appreciate it. A large en suite bathroom had a full shower and sleek marbled tile. If she had to be held captive, it wasn't awful.

Lizzie's stateroom was just next door, on the other side of the bathroom. Kate wished they'd kept them together, but supposed that wouldn't be realistic, from a kidnapper's point of view.

If only she'd been able to conceal that phone better. Her only hope was that they'd passed through the dead zone, and that Gage had reached out about the car and the backpack with the money inside it, alerting Nan that she was in danger.

Kate sighed. That was a pipe dream. She'd been suspicious of Nan, and she assumed Nan must also be suspicious of her. After all, she'd told Nan that she found the phone in Hank's car. Why would Nan have any reason to trust her? Nan might well think Kate was part of the plan to trap her.

She peered out the window again but realized they must have moved in the night because the yacht was closer to land now than it had been. She gauged the distance—could she make it if she swam? She thought about Lizzie's fear of sharks. While it was doubtful these waters were shark-infested, she had heard reports now and then of an attack off Cape Cod. Right now, she might risk it just to escape.

She wished she knew where they were, exactly. Not that it would help, but just to get her geographical bearings.

It helped keep her fear at bay to think about these things.

More heavy footsteps passing the door. How many people *were* there on the yacht?

She heard fumbling at the lock, then suddenly the door swung open. Gage stood in the doorway, his gun trained on her.

Kate took a step back. Another flashback of being held at gunpoint crashed into her. Will Stafford hadn't hesitated to shoot her; would Gage shoot her, too?

"Where is she?" Gage demanded, waving the gun in front of her face.

Kate took another step back. "Who?"

"The girl. Where is she?"

Kate frowned. Was he asking about Lizzie? "In her stateroom, I imagine. You did lock us in." But as she spoke, it dawned on her that he wouldn't be asking if Lizzie was still next door. Where could she have gone if she'd gotten out? Was she hiding somewhere on the yacht? It was large enough so there were probably places for a preteen girl to hide. And then Kate had a purely selfish thought: If Lizzie had gotten out of her room, why hadn't the girl unlocked her door, too?

She shook it aside. There must be a reason, although she was hard-pressed to think of any at the moment. It couldn't be that Lizzie was kidnapped—wouldn't that be ironic, being kidnapped from her kidnapper?

"You're hiding her," Gage said.

"How on earth could I do that? You locked me in here," Kate said.

Gage moved swiftly toward Kate, grabbing her as he pressed the gun to her temple. "Where is she?" he repeated.

The gun was cold against her skin, and she closed her eyes, waiting for the shot. She shifted involuntarily; his grip tightened. She was pressed up against him, his musty body odor filling her nose, and she could feel the hardness of his muscles. She didn't stand a chance against him under any circumstances.

But then she felt something else. A phone in his front jeans pocket. There was no way to get to it without sticking her hand inside. She wasn't a professional pickpocket, after all. How could she get him to relinquish the phone—and put the gun away?

"I could make a call," she said. "I could get you that million dollars. Maybe more, if you'll release me. It could be between you and me. No one has to know. My husband is a billionaire; I'm sure he'll make a deal."

He took a quick breath, and for a second, she thought she had him. Instead, he pressed the gun harder and said, "You must think I'm really stupid."

As if in slow motion, out of the corner of her eye, Kate saw his finger reaching for the trigger.

58
ANNA

Steve Gardiner met them at the airport. Anna got the sense it was unexpected, him being there, because Hank sent Anna and Cromwell to find the car while he spoke to Gardiner. One of the two security guards who'd accompanied them on the flight followed; the other stayed back with Hank, although he gave Hank and Gardiner space to talk.

"What do you think that's about?" Anna asked. She didn't expect Cromwell to answer and was surprised when he did.

"He was supposed to meet us at the marina. Not here." Cromwell's tone was clipped. He was annoyed as well, but Anna supposed it had more to do with the rivalry between Cromwell and Gardiner than anything else.

The driver was loading their bags into the back when they got to the parking lot. It was a very small airport surrounded by woods. Anna had never been to this part of Connecticut before and wondered how long it would take them to get to the marina.

When Hank and Gardiner joined them at the car, Anna sensed a tension between them, not dissimilar to the one between Cromwell and Gardiner. It was more than possible that Hank held Gardiner responsible for the ransom drop-off screwup: Gardiner had been in charge of it, which did not bring back Lizzie and resulted in Kate's disappearance. Hank held his people to the highest standards and expected nothing less than perfection from them. Gardiner was failing on all fronts.

Cromwell held the car door open for her, and Anna climbed in, the three men after her.

An uncomfortable silence filled the car as it maneuvered its way on back roads. Anna had never traveled with Hank like this before, even during their short marriage, which was more a business arrangement: she would stay with the children while he attended to his companies. He preferred to keep his wives at a distance when it came to his businesses. Ironically, he'd married Anna to acquire her father's company's newspapers, which she'd been running after his death.

The car eventually turned up a driveway in front of a white Colonial. When she stepped out of the car, Anna could see a wide, green lawn that stretched down to the water. Unlike at the Vineyard, though, this was a river inlet, not the ocean. Anna was uncertain whether this was a property rental or if Hank owned it; it was more than possible it was the latter. Hank had houses everywhere and seemingly bought and sold them with the ease of someone playing Monopoly.

The security team brought their bags into the house after checking everything out and giving the all clear. Anna was directed to a bedroom at the top of the stairs, and she found it easily. Her bag sat on the queen-size bed that wore a cozy patchwork quilt. She wished they were staying here under better circumstances. Lizzie and Ted would love that yard outside.

Hank poked his head inside the doorway. He wore a worried expression. Was he afraid he'd lose yet another wife?

Anna went over to him and touched his arm, compelled to try to give him some kind of comfort. "We'll find both of them," she said softly. As she spoke, she wondered how she could bring up Tom Seymour's meeting with the investigator. Somehow it seemed important that Hank be aware of it. But she'd have to approach it carefully. He would not be happy that she was talking to a reporter.

Hank covered her hand with his. It was large and warm, and she was reminded of the early days of their courtship, when Hank was attentive and remarkably affectionate. Few people saw that side of him, which was why there was so much speculation as to how he managed to keep finding women who would marry him. Anna had seen the way he was with Kate, and she'd never doubted the feelings between them. But both were being stubborn, refusing to make things right. Sometimes Anna just wanted to shake them both out of it, remind them how much they loved each other.

"When we find them, I won't take either of them for granted again," Hank confided, as though reading her mind. "I'll make things better with Kate—and Lizzie."

Anna hoped so. He seemed sincere, but it might be too easy for him to fall back into old ways.

The moment passed, and he was all business again. "Gardiner has some sort of lead that we're going to follow up on. Can you stay here? I'll have one of the guards outside."

Would she ever get her freedom back?

"What's the lead?" she asked before she could stop herself.

Hank snorted. "It's all very mysterious. It could be Gardiner just talking out of his ass so he'll get back in my good graces."

Anna was certain Gardiner was talking as fast as he could.

Now was the time to warn Hank that Tom Seymour was going to be in town, too. If he found out she'd known and didn't tell him, there would be hell to pay. She still wasn't quite sure how to broach it, but she might as well just rip off the Band-Aid and get it over with.

"I have to tell you something—" she started, when she heard the buzz of a cell phone. Tom Seymour really needed to leave her alone, especially now.

But she'd forgotten she'd turned her phone off. Instead, Hank took his out of his pocket and frowned at the number. It looked like he wasn't going to answer but then changed his mind and accepted the call.

"Yes?" he asked.

Suddenly, his face transformed, shock registering in his eyes. "Kate?"

PART V

59

KATE

The second Gage moved his finger toward the trigger, Kate, in one swift knee-jerk reaction, twisted and brought her elbow up toward the weapon. She knocked it askew.

The gunshot rang in her ears, deafening her. She watched Gage's body fall as if in slow motion, blood spilling from the wound in his temple and across his cheek.

Gage lay splayed on the plush carpet, his eyes open yet unseeing.

Kate stared at his body, her heart racing as the realization of what had happened settled in.

She didn't mean to kill him. She was only trying to save herself. Protecting herself. He was going to shoot her. He was going to kill *her*. Justifying it made it far easier to accept.

Kate tried to pop her ears; it felt like she was on an airplane that was descending too fast. She hummed to test whether she could hear herself, and it was as though she were underwater. This was a definite disadvantage, under the circumstances. She might not hear footsteps or voices.

She had to rely on her vision.

Kate glanced around to see if anyone had come in, if anyone had heard the shot, but so far, she was still alone. Her eyes strayed to Gage's jeans pocket, where she could see the outline of the phone. Another glance at the door, and she stooped down, swiftly pulling the phone from his pocket. She stuck it in her own, then reached for the gun.

It wasn't very heavy, not unlike the one she'd owned, although it was bigger. She knew how to use a gun; when she'd bought hers, she'd taken lessons to protect herself from an ex-husband who'd stalked her. Will Stafford had gotten his hands on it and used it against her. She'd vowed never to own a gun again, but this was different. She needed it now for the same reason she'd bought hers.

Gripping the gun, she tiptoed to the door and, with her other hand, turned the knob. She opened the door a crack and peered out into the hallway, which was empty, but that didn't mean someone wasn't waiting to ambush her. Someone must have heard the shot. Known Gage had gone to the stateroom.

The hallway ran along the side of the yacht. Windows overlooked the water, and peering out, Kate saw land. It wasn't as far away as it looked on the other side.

On the off chance that Lizzie was still next door, that Gage might have been mistaken or lying about her being gone, Kate pushed open the door to the other stateroom. The bed was unmade, the covers bunched up, two pillows on the floor. But no Lizzie.

Kate went into the room and slipped behind the door, closing it so if anyone were to walk past, they wouldn't see her. Still holding the gun, she used her other hand to reach into her pocket and retrieve the phone. It wasn't easy with one hand, maneuvering so she could make a call, but she managed to tap in Hank's phone number—thank God she'd been his assistant and knew the number by heart—and hit the CALL icon.

Her hand holding the gun began to shake as the adrenaline began to wear off. She almost dropped it but managed to readjust her grip.

Answer, answer, she whispered to herself. She had the volume on so low, even if she could hear properly, she might not hear it ringing, but she saw that the call was finally picked up.

"Hank?" she whispered, holding the phone against her ear. "Hank?"

She strained to hear his voice, and through the tunnel effect, she heard him say her name. She didn't have time to explain. She got to the point.

"I'm on a boat. A yacht. It's called *The Aragon*. Lizzie's here, too. I don't know where we are. You have to help us. Please, find us."

No response. Had he hung up on her? Was he that angry with her? Kate's head was spinning, unable to think straight, but when she looked at the phone, she saw that there was no signal. Another dead zone. Had he heard her at all? What if the call had cut out before she told him the name of the yacht? She was certain if he'd heard her, he could track it; that's how he'd found the *Perseverance* at the Vineyard marina.

She stuck the phone back in her pocket. There wasn't time to speculate. She had to find Lizzie. It was obvious she had managed to escape her room, and since there was literally nowhere else to go, she must be hiding somewhere.

Kate held on to the gun as she crept along the hall. Her ears popped a little, but she couldn't hear anything. Was she still impaired or was there nothing to hear?

Ducking her head into yet another stateroom, she saw it was immaculately made up. No one had disturbed it. She swiftly went to the closets and peered inside. No Lizzie. A quick look into the en suite told her the same thing: Lizzie wasn't here.

Did she dare climb the staircase to the next deck? Someone might be lying in wait for her there. But she had the gun, which gave her a definite advantage. She slowly went up, one hand on the gun, the other on the railing to steady herself. She pictured the layout: she'd come up next to the open dining and salon area, the outside deck was through the sliding glass doors.

So far, she saw no one. Was the yacht abandoned? Had Gage been the only one on board? It wasn't moving, so perhaps they were anchored and everyone else—captain, crew—had left?

Kate was halfway across the salon when she heard it. Her first thought was, *I can hear again*. But then, she understood what that meant. She wasn't alone after all.

The voice drifted up from below.

"He's dead."

They'd found Gage—and knew she was gone.

"She's got to be somewhere, but it doesn't look like she's down here."

Kate scurried up the stairs and went around past the dining table to the other side of the yacht. She spotted another set of stairs. It all went in a circle. If they'd already searched downstairs, that might be a good place to hide—as long as she didn't meet anyone coming up while she was going down. But luck was on her side. She heard muffled voices above her. They must have gone upstairs another way.

She was glad for her canvas shoes, which didn't make a sound as she made her way back to the stateroom where Gage's body still lay sprawled on the floor. She gently opened one of the wardrobe doors and saw a white terry cloth robe hanging from the rod. Pushing it aside, Kate slipped inside, glad that whoever owned this yacht felt the need for a large closet. She pulled the door shut after making sure she'd be able to get out if necessary. She kept one hand on the door latch; the other still held the gun.

Kate was betting that hiding in the same room as Gage's body was the safest place for her. They wouldn't think she'd stick around, would they? She nestled back into the closet, sinking down in a squat, ready to move if she had to and hoping that call to Hank went through and that Lizzie was safe somewhere.

60
CATHERINE

"They're both gone."

This was not the news she'd been expecting.

"What do you mean, gone?"

"Just what I said. They must have had help."

What help? Catherine had put too much money into this to have anyone "help" anyone. "What about the cameras?" she asked.

"Offline."

So, there had been help after all.

Someone else was pulling the strings. Catherine was at a distinct disadvantage. How could the girl and the wife get off a yacht without being seen?

"We've searched everywhere."

Clearly not everywhere, Catherine thought. Maybe they'd decided to swim for it. She would admire that tenacity. But it was more likely that they were still on the yacht somewhere.

"The wife killed Gage, and she might have his gun."

This news surprised her even more. Who was Gage? The wife killed him? It was getting worse and worse. Catherine didn't want to get pulled into this mess. Just the fact that they'd called her was hitting too close to home.

But she couldn't let them know she was in the dark. "Have they seen you?" she asked.

"No. Just Gage."

And Gage was conveniently dead. There was only one option.

"Get rid of him," Catherine ordered.

"What?"

"Get rid of him." She shouldn't have to repeat herself.

"How?"

When she'd devised this plot, it had been far simpler. She found herself unexpectedly missing Joan, who had been reliable and loyal for years. *She* wouldn't have hired incompetents who allowed the wife to kill anyone and then go missing—much less taken orders from someone else. She also wouldn't have lost the daughter.

But Joan had crossed a line. She'd gone back to see her wife—and Anna Klein had seen her, too. Catherine couldn't trust that Joan would stay away, could no longer be assured that Joan would keep her secrets. She pushed aside any regrets. What was done was done, and there was nothing she could do about it now.

"You're on the water. Use some creativity."

"What do we do if we find them?"

For goodness' sakes, who were these people?

Again, she wondered who'd authorized taking the wife. It had to be Gardiner. She wouldn't have played it this way. Catherine worried that rather than split Hank and the wife up, it might bring them together again—and that was definitely not the plan. Gardiner had acted rashly and, by not considering the possibilities, left Catherine in an uncomfortable position.

Catherine ended the call without answering the question. They could call Gardiner. She was washing her hands of this particular situation. She'd come all the way out here with a plan in place, but she hadn't expected to leave a trail of bodies. Why had Gardiner left that private investigator on the *Perseverance*? Since the yacht had been searched thoroughly and the girl not found, it had been perfect to lure That Woman there. Now, however, that marina would be crawling with police and security. Her trip here had been for naught.

Then there was this situation on *The Aragon*, not to mention that she'd gotten a notification that someone had gotten into her account associated with her LLC and was poking around. To her chagrin, she realized she'd made a mistake and left herself vulnerable. Had they discovered it? She couldn't risk it. With a few keystrokes, Catherine was able to extinguish any link between the LLC and herself, praying it wasn't too late. No one could know her connection to either the *Perseverance* or *The Aragon*.

Catherine settled into one of the chairs by the window, absently studying the cheerful red roses on the wallpaper as her mind wandered. *The Aragon*. Hank had no idea she was the one who bought it when he put it up for sale. He'd bought it for That Woman, but she didn't appreciate the gift. All she'd done was complain about it, how it didn't fit in with their new lives as parents. Catherine and Hank had had a sailboat when Maril was born, and they'd raised the girl on the water during her summer holidays. They sailed up and down the East Coast, to the Caribbean, Bermuda. Those were some of the happiest days of their marriage. For That Woman to take away Hank's opportunity to relive those times—albeit, not a sailboat and not with Catherine, but that was beside the point—was wrong.

When she found out Hank had to sell the yacht, she bought it, quietly through her LLC, naming it after the region in Spain where her parents had been born. She would surprise him with it when they reconciled.

The Aragon had been her alternate plan. But that was impossible now.

She considered abandoning her scheme, but she might never get this chance again. That Woman had a habit of slipping through her fingers, and she had to see it through. The only silver lining was that while someone else had been giving orders, if she changed course now, she would be working unilaterally. There would be no more communication with anyone. She was perfectly capable of executing the plan without any interference.

She had to focus. There was too much at stake, and when it was over, she'd take care of whoever was impersonating her, too. Catherine had had enough of being underestimated.

It didn't matter anymore that the girl was gone. That Woman didn't know what had happened—although she had to act fast, in case the girl reappeared soon, safe and sound.

Catherine took out the burner phone and texted an address, adding:

Come alone.

61
LIZZIE

Robert Dudley and I are in the back of what he says is the engine room—"the heart" of the yacht. It's a little loud; fans are blowing. The steps down were really steep, and I slipped a little on the way, but once we were on firm ground, I was okay. It's really tight, and we're around a corner, tucked behind all this mechanical and electrical stuff and out of sight if someone comes down the stairs. Problem with that is we can't see the stairs, but Robert says we'll be able to hear if the door opens. Anyway, there's a lock on the inside, so it would take some doing to actually get in. I worry a little that we're trapped back here, but Robert tells me that he turned off some sort of camera surveillance system so no one would be able to find us—at least not easily.

"You know how to do that?" I ask.

He shrugs. "It's a gift." And then he adds, "My dad showed me."

"Is he here?" I ask.

He looks at me with an odd expression. "He's dead," he says, like I should know this already.

I think about my mom, but I don't know for sure that she's dead. I'm pretty sure about Joan, though. I wonder if he knew her, since he took me from that other boat. So I ask him.

He gets a funny look on his face. I'm pretty sure he does know who Joan was. And that he knows she's dead now, too.

"I lived with Joan and Anna," I tell him.

"Yeah, I know."

He does?

When we hear a loud crack, I stiffen. It sounded like a firework.

"Gunshot," he whispers in my ear.

For a moment, I can't breathe. Did the man with the gun—Kate called him Gage—shoot her? I knew we should have brought her with us, but Robert said there wasn't time, he'd go back and get her once the coast was clear. Well, it didn't seem like that was going to happen now.

I have no idea how long we've been crouching here. My legs are all pins and needles, and I try to move them but it's tight and I'm not all that successful. I can see Robert is doing the same thing with no more success than me. I want to ask him how long we'll have to stay here, but I'm afraid to talk because I think they'll hear me, even over all the noise.

After what feels like forever, Robert moves. He stands and reaches for my hand. I take it, my legs wobbly. I wriggle my toes and move my ankles, trying to get feeling back. It doesn't take too long.

"Wait here," he says, moving past me and disappearing around the corner. I hurry after him and see he is already at the top of the stairs, pushing the door open. He sticks his head out first, then goes into the hall, shutting the door behind him.

Okay, so I'm an idiot. That stateroom was a lot more comfortable than this engine room. I should have stayed there if I was going to be locked in somewhere.

But then the door opens, and I see a hand indicating I'm to come.

I don't waste any time.

"There's no one on the yacht," he says.

"But what about Kate?"

"I don't know."

I hope she's not dead. It's bad enough about Joan.

We get to the first stateroom, and there's a big smear of red on the carpet. The sheets are off the bed. I don't like the look of this.

But then I hear something from inside the wardrobe. Robert and I look at each other, uncertain. It could be Kate—or it could be one of the kidnappers. He indicates I should move away, and then he yanks the door open.

He stumbles back as Kate emerges, a gun pointed right at him. I shout, "Don't shoot! Kate! It's me!"

But she doesn't lower the gun. It's like she hasn't even heard me, doesn't even see me. She's staring at Robert Dudley with a weird expression on her face.

"You're supposed to be dead," she says.

62
KATE

What on earth was Will Stafford doing on this yacht? He'd died two months ago in a car crash—after shooting her and leaving her for dead. He'd killed Caitlyn Howard. But here he was, standing in front of her—with Lizzie?

Kate's hand began to shake, and she lowered the gun, no longer able to keep it leveled and steady. She couldn't stop staring at him, and the longer she did, the more she realized it wasn't Will Stafford at all, but a younger carbon copy of the man. In fact, he was a boy, not much older than Lizzie, who was pleading with her not to shoot.

Her whole body began to tremble, and she moved to the bed, sitting down and placing the gun next to her.

"It's okay," she told Lizzie. "I'm not going to shoot him." But her brain hadn't quite caught up yet. "Who are you?" she asked the boy.

"This is Robert Dudley," Lizzie said. "I told you about him. He helped me. We hid in the engine room. Everyone else left. We're alone."

Lizzie shouldn't have to be the grown-up in this situation, but it seemed that she had taken on that role. Kate attempted to shake herself out of her shock, and as she did so, she saw the smear of blood on the floor where Gage's body had been.

"You look a lot like someone I used to know," Kate said, forcing herself to ignore the blood. "Someone named Will Stafford. Did you know him?"

The boy—Robert—looked at the floor, but Kate had caught his expression. He knew Will Stafford. She would bet on it.

She shifted a little and felt the phone in her pocket. A rush of relief washed over her as she pulled it out. But there was still no signal.

"We can call for help from the pilothouse on the bridge deck," Robert Dudley said, starting out the door. He was moving fast, probably faster than he needed to, but Kate suspected he didn't want to face any more questions.

"He's okay," Lizzie said quietly, and after a slight hesitation added, "He knows Joan."

Kate didn't have time to ponder the implications of that as they followed a trail of blood out of the room and into the hallway that ran along the side of the yacht. Kate tried not to think about what had happened to Gage's body, but she could guess.

The boy was nowhere in sight. Kate's sense of direction was off; had she even seen the pilothouse, much less know how to find it now?

"Are we sure no one else is on board?" she asked Lizzie.

"That's what Robert said."

But the boy hadn't come back. Perhaps Lizzie was wrong about him. Should they have stayed in the stateroom? Locked themselves in? She'd faced men with guns twice now, and she couldn't risk a third time.

"Come on," she said to Lizzie, leading her to the other stateroom, the one that wasn't splattered with blood, and locked the door from the inside. "He can find us in here." She still held the gun and wasn't about to give it up just yet.

"You know you're covered in blood, right?" Lizzie asked in a small voice.

Kate looked down at her clothes and the sight shocked her. She'd seen Gage's blood on the carpet but hadn't given a thought as to how close she'd been when he was shot, that the blood would splatter on her as well. She had a sudden urge to take off her clothes and stand under a hot shower, and while the en suite was merely steps away, she couldn't do it. She'd be vulnerable; Lizzie wouldn't be able to hold off anyone trying to get to them.

Robert Dudley still had not returned.

"I don't think he's coming back," Lizzie said, voicing Kate's own thoughts. She scooted around on the bed and lifted up the window curtain. Kate peered around her to see the strip of land she'd noticed earlier. Where were they?

Lizzie jumped down. "I'm going to go look for him."

Kate grabbed her. "No!"

The girl yanked her arm away. "We can't stay in here forever, Kate." She ran to the door, unlocked it, and disappeared outside.

Kate scurried after her. Panic rose in her chest when she stepped into the hall and didn't see the girl, but she pushed it down. Lizzie had to be close by. She found the stairway going up, and when she emerged, she was in the main salon. Lizzie was standing on the outside walkway, watching an approaching boat.

There was lettering on the side. It was a police boat. Kate felt an overwhelming sense of relief, closing her eyes and taking a deep breath in and out. They were going to be all right, she and Lizzie were going to be all right. She blinked back tears and made her way to Lizzie.

"Are they coming for us?" Lizzie asked when Kate joined her.

"Seems so," Kate said, putting her arms around the girl and squeezing her tight.

"See, Robert Dudley did call for help," Lizzie said, squirming out of Kate's grasp.

He must have, but where was he?

The police boat was getting closer to the yacht. Besides the two marine patrol officers on the craft, she saw a third person, a man. For a moment, her heart lifted, thinking it was Hank. Maybe it hadn't been Robert Dudley who had alerted them; maybe her call had actually gone through.

But then she recognized him. Tommy Seymour.

What on earth was he doing here?

She didn't have time to sort it out, because Lizzie was already running across the deck to meet them—Robert Dudley forgotten in the moment. By the time Kate reached them, the police boat had pulled up next to the swim deck, and one of the officers was tying it to the back of the yacht.

Kate was close enough now to catch Tommy's eye. The relief in his face mirrored her own.

The officer who'd already come aboard stepped between them. "Ma'am?" he asked. "Are you harmed?"

That's right. The blood on her clothes. "Yes, I'm fine. This isn't mine," she said softly.

The other officer was now on board, nudging Kate and Lizzie to the police boat. "Stay here while we check out the yacht," he said.

"We're not sure anyone else is here," Kate said.

"Except for Robert Dudley," Lizzie interrupted.

"Who is that?"

"A boy who helped us," Lizzie continued. "He's the one who called for help from the pilothouse."

The officers looked at each other. "We never got that call. Mr. Seymour here"—he indicated Tommy—"was the one who told us where we might find you."

Tommy? How had he known where they were?

Kate wasn't sure how he'd managed it, but it wasn't a surprise that Tommy had convinced them he should accompany them on this rescue mission—thus, getting his story after all.

63

NAN

It was Lizzie. Her daughter.

She looked like her. And like Hank. She was tall for her age and thin, her limbs long and a little awkward, like a colt's. She was growing into herself, into the woman she'd eventually become.

Nan felt a rush of love for this beautiful girl who had no idea her mother had come for her—and she might never know.

She and Wyatt lingered on the dock, watching the scene unfold. Tom Seymour had texted that they'd found the yacht, that Lizzie and Kate were safe, and they'd be bringing them back. He also let them know that Hank was coming to meet them. Nan wondered how the reporter would handle that, if he'd tell Hank that the tip about the yacht came from them—or from an anonymous source. She didn't entirely trust him, but Wyatt said either way, it didn't matter so long as Lizzie had been rescued. He was right.

Nan was certain that Catherine was behind this; the yacht was the key. The problem was, when Wyatt pointed the reporter to the evidence, it had already vanished behind a maze of documentation with no indication that Catherine Tudor had ever owned an LLC, much less a yacht. Wyatt's associate had not thought to screenshot anything, believing the online records were safeguarded. With no solid proof, it would be difficult to convince the police—not to mention the skeptical reporter—that Catherine Tudor, who had not ventured out of her own home for years, was the mastermind behind an elaborate kidnapping scheme.

Nan had gotten the latest text right after she and Wyatt met with Seymour. *Come alone*, it said, its meaning clear. But Catherine must know by now that the moment Lizzie stepped off that yacht, her plans had gone awry. That there was no longer any need to threaten, because her daughter was safe and her father had come for her.

Nan caught her breath when she saw Hank walking along the dock, his stride as smooth and strong and confident as he'd always been. His auburn hair had mostly gone gray, but it was still full, his face only more handsome despite the age lines, giving him a distinguished look. If he had given in to any plastic surgery, it was not noticeable and had only enhanced his appeal. This man was the man she'd fallen for.

Nan hadn't seen him in more than eight years. Those last days slipped away as she remembered how it was in the beginning. The way he danced with her when she was Perseverance, the champagne kisses stolen in dark corners. How he left her gifts, a strand of pearls, a battered copy of Voltaire, all to woo her, to make her fall in love with him. And how she had loved him.

Catherine had thought she could win Hank back by outlasting his affair. She'd had no idea what she'd been up against.

Wyatt had had his hand on her arm, but now she pulled away, an old instinct kicking in until she realized what she'd done and gave him a small smile, slipping her hand into the crook of his elbow.

"Old habits die hard," she said.

It was like watching a movie from the back row: Hank reaching for his wife and daughter, taking them both into his arms. She could see him whispering to them. *Are you all right?* she imagined him saying. The relief at having them back was obvious. Nan had never seen him like this, so openly emotional. Maybe he'd changed since she'd left. Maybe if she'd just stayed a little longer, she could have seen that side of him. Maybe her son would have a father.

She didn't realize she was crying until Wyatt handed her a handkerchief.

Nan had imagined a reunion with her daughter, but the longer she stood here, the more she realized she had no place here. She spotted Tom Seymour hovering from a distance, just like her, watching Kate Parker be embraced by her husband, her own expression mirrored on his face. He'd lost a love, too, but he'd done the right thing.

Nan stiffened slightly as Cromwell approached with a woman she recognized as Anna Klein. She caught her breath again when Lizzie ran toward Anna, throwing her arms around her with more emotion than when she'd hugged her father. Lizzie loved this woman like a mother, Nan could see that, and it ripped her heart in two.

She wiped her eyes and started to turn to go. As she did, Cromwell lifted his head and looked right at her.

Nan stared back at him, their gaze unbroken for a long moment. He gave her a short nod, and then she tossed back her hair, standing up straighter before giving him a salute.

"Time to go," she told Wyatt.

They walked hand in hand back up the dock.

"Will I see you again?" he asked when they got to the rental car they'd picked up for her.

Nan reached up and cupped his face with her hand, meeting his eyes. She wanted to say yes; she hoped he could see that. But she couldn't make promises. Her life was a long way from here.

"*And wilt thou leave me thus / And have no more pity / Of him that loveth thee?*" he recited, his voice soft, caressing each word before he leaned over and kissed her.

For a moment, she allowed herself to get lost in him, to think that anything might be possible. And then she pulled away, dropping her hand, and said with a sad smile, "If you ever find yourself in the Côte-d'Or, look me up."

"You underestimate me, Ms. Savoy," Wyatt said with a wink as he opened the car door for her. "I'm a private investigator. I don't give up easily."

She certainly hoped he wouldn't.

As she drove away, taking one last glance at Wyatt in the rearview mirror, she turned her thoughts to her son and the new puppy she'd surprise him with when she got home.

64

KATE

They were staying at the New York penthouse until Lizzie and Ted went back to their boarding schools. Kate had tried to talk to Hank about keeping them home and going to school in the city after all they'd been through, but he wasn't having it.

"It's best to keep their schedules," he argued. "Routine is good for children."

Lizzie hadn't wanted to leave the Vineyard. She'd confided to Anna that even though her mother hadn't been waiting for her, she still felt her presence in the house. Kate wondered about Nan Tudor. The woman who'd come looking for her daughter seemed to have disappeared. She was glad she hadn't said anything to Lizzie about meeting her; it would have been devastating for her to find out her mother left her again.

Robert Dudley had never reappeared, either, much to Lizzie's chagrin. She'd been convinced that he was trustworthy—and felt betrayed that he'd vanished. He'd never told Lizzie anything about himself, except that his father was dead.

"His last name was Dudley," Anna mused when Kate told her about the boy.

"What of it?"

"Will Stafford's real name was John Dudley. That's the name Joan had for him in our records at the inn."

Kate recalled her first impression of the boy, the resemblance to the man who'd shot her. "Will could have been Robert's father. He told Lizzie his father taught him how to dismantle surveillance systems." Will Stafford, who'd been a computer expert, had been in charge of Anna's security team—and it hadn't been Anna who'd hired him; it had been Joan. "So, Joan knew who Will really was." She must have had a strong tie to Robert, too, since Robert Dudley had been on the yacht. But what was that tie? Would they ever know? And where was the boy now?

There had been others on the yacht, too, but they were gone by the time police boarded—and two dinghies were also missing. Presumably, Robert Dudley had taken one of them; an extensive search turned up the other, along with two bodies—a man and a woman—in the marshes of Great Island. The police determined it had been a murder-suicide. While it was a relief to know no one else would be coming after them, Kate was disappointed that there were questions that might never be answered—unless Robert Dudley resurfaced.

When Kate wondered out loud why Joan would have involved the boy in Lizzie's kidnapping—because of his age, he was as much a victim as Lizzie—she immediately realized her mistake. Anna's lip trembled as she struggled to keep her tears at bay.

"Joan was . . ." Anna paused a moment before she cleared her throat and started again. "I have to come to grips with the fact that the woman I was married to was a complete fraud. She used me to get to Hank and the people he loved."

"But why?"

Anna shook her head. "I have no idea."

Anna was staying with them, not wanting to return to her house in Greenwich, which was filled with memories of Joan. After a summertime of thinking Joan might come back to her, the loss of her wife was now all too real since the body at the marina had been positively identified. And learning that Joan had played a part in Lizzie's kidnapping had been heartbreaking. Anna roamed the penthouse as if a ghost, barely speaking, just like Ted when Lizzie was missing.

"Do you think she'll ever get over it? Joan was the love of her life," Kate asked Hank.

He hesitated a moment before responding. "I'm not exactly one to give advice about love and marriage," he said.

Kate didn't think she could, either, since she still harbored doubts about her husband. Even though the phone that she'd found in Hank's car belonged to the driver who took her to the boatyard and Hank insisted he'd been set up, just like Kate had been, she couldn't shake her suspicions that there was more to it than that.

Tommy Seymour had written several stories so far about the kidnapping of Hank Tudor's wife and daughter and the murders of Joan Carey and a private investigator named Mark Smeaton. Smeaton's employer, a man named Thomas Wyatt, had no comment about the case Smeaton had been working on at the time of his death, citing confidentiality. Tommy's story indicated a "person of interest" had been interrogated but released due to lack of evidence. It wasn't long after that that Gardiner showed up at the penthouse and he and Hank disappeared behind closed doors.

"He had met with the investigator who was murdered at the marina," Cromwell told Kate after she mused out loud what they might be discussing. "Gardiner was asking him about Nan," he added, surprising her with his candor.

Kate frowned. "Why?"

"Because the investigator had been seen with her."

As Hank's investigator, Gardiner had to follow up on any leads to Nan's whereabouts, since Hank hadn't hidden the fact that he felt Nan had played a part in Lizzie's kidnapping. How far would Hank—and Gardiner, by extension—have gone, though, to find Nan Tudor? It had come out that the investigator had been tortured before being killed. Gardiner might not be as innocent as the evidence suggested, and while Kate didn't want to believe that Hank would condone anything like that, she knew him well enough to know he might.

That investigator wasn't the only one who'd been seen with Nan. Hank hadn't been happy to find out that Kate had lied about talking to her. He tried texting and calling the number Kate had found in the phone, but the service had been disconnected. Hank believed that meant Nan was guilty, even though she hadn't taken the money and there was no proof she'd been involved at all outside of being at the carousel. He seemed to let the matter drop once it became clear Nan wouldn't be making another appearance in his life—yet his meeting with Gardiner might mean that he wasn't ready to move on.

"We won't be seeing Gardiner again. His job is done," Cromwell told her. His statement was definitive; he knew what was going on behind closed doors. Of course he did. He was Cromwell, and Hank rarely made a move without him. Kate noted a sense of relief in his tone. She was relieved, too—and hoped he was right. Gardiner didn't seem like the kind of man who'd go away quietly.

Neither did her husband, but that was exactly what he did. Hank slipped away shortly after Gardiner left the penthouse, his carryall missing.

Kate hadn't hidden her feelings, and Hank had a pattern of disappearing—he'd done that with Catherine, with Nan, with Caitlyn. In each of those cases, the separation was permanent. No contact, save for Cromwell, who picked up the pieces and handled all the legalities.

Kate touched her abdomen. The doctor had confirmed that the baby hadn't been harmed, despite the trauma she'd been through. She was now almost twelve weeks and no longer ambivalent about her condition. This baby was a survivor, just like her. If she had to be a single mother, she could do it.

She had to move past what had happened and look to the future, whatever it might hold. For now, she was safe—and despite Hank's absence, she was confident, with Cromwell's assurances, that he would make sure she and the baby were protected.

But there were nights when Kate awoke in the dark, her heart pounding with nightmares about Gage and Will Stafford and she remembered Nan's warning about Catherine.

"She's a killer."

65
CATHERINE

She didn't think the woman would come. After all, her daughter was safe now. There was no more threat. Catherine had lost her last chance—or so she thought.

But here she was, standing in the doorway of Catherine's Greenwich house. Catherine thought about how Lourdes was still not back from her trip to see her sister. How *she* was alone—and how that could work to her advantage.

"Hello, Catherine," she said.

Catherine's eyes skirted around. She didn't see anyone else with her, but it was possible that private investigator was lurking somewhere nearby.

"I'm alone, like you wanted," the woman said. "It's just you and me. Wyatt doesn't know I'm here."

Before Catherine could respond, she stepped inside and shut the door behind her.

Catherine studied the other woman. She was older now, her face lined with the life she'd chosen, no longer a young woman ready to seduce. But she still had that confidence, that way of holding herself that made men look. That had made Hank look—and more.

The anger slipped between her bones, a physical sensation that she welcomed. This was what she needed, what kept her strong.

"Your daughter was not harmed," Catherine said, a steely tone in her voice. No need to be friendly. This was not a friendly visit.

"No thanks to you," the woman said.

She couldn't prove anything. Gardiner would keep his mouth shut; if he didn't, all the evidence would point to him. She'd made sure of that—and made sure he knew it. As it were, he was richly compensated for his part. Catherine had covered her bases, as she had with Will Stafford—and Joan. Even the text asking the woman to come would not be able to be traced to her.

"What do you want from me? He doesn't love me anymore. I'm not a threat. So, why? Why take her? Why bring me back?"

She couldn't be foolish enough to think that she wasn't a threat. Every woman was a threat—but not every woman had borne him a child.

"He loves her, you know. Kate Parker," the woman continued when Catherine didn't speak.

This is what she'd been afraid of. Gardiner had been confident he could take the wife down—that reporter was the best way—but by taking her, Gardiner's plan had backfired, although he continued to claim that was not his fault. Someone else had given the order, but he refused to say who. He was protecting someone; Catherine would eventually get it out of him. She had her ways.

"He's not coming back to you."

As the words settled between them, Catherine felt a pressure in her chest, a familiar weight. No, not now.

"You lost him a long time ago. He was lost to you even before I met him. You have to accept that."

She was right, of course. Ironically, she and this woman were both in the same boat: divorced from the same man, neither of them Mrs. Tudor now. Yet Catherine still used his name, and this woman still answered to it. What did that say about either of them—continuing to tie themselves to Hank Tudor despite the pain he'd caused?

That pain crept through her upper back now, and Catherine struggled to breathe. She couldn't give in to it, but she needed her pills. The anxiety replaced the anger.

"Are you okay?" the woman asked, her kindness unexpected, considering.

She couldn't find the words.

Catherine felt the woman's hand under her arm. She was leading her to the great room, settling her in on the sofa. Her prescription bottle was on the coffee table, and the woman saw her glance at it. She picked it up and studied the label, giving a short snort before shaking out two pills and handing them to her.

"Do you need water?" she asked.

Catherine hated herself for shaking her head and swallowing the pills dry. Never show weakness, she'd told herself. Yet here she was.

The woman perched on the edge of the armchair across from her, watching her closely.

The pills were doing their job. Catherine's strength began to return. She could feel it spread through to her fingertips, her toes, as the weight on her chest lifted.

"You could have let me die," she said.

The woman laughed. "It's a panic attack. It won't kill you."

The sound of her laughter revived Catherine's anger. She stood, shifting her gaze behind the woman to the sword that hung on the wall. Could she be successful where no one else had been?

Catherine lunged toward it, but the woman was faster, grabbing the sword and holding it aloft.

"Stay back," the woman said, the sword gleaming as a sunbeam hit it through the window. Catherine imagined it slicing against this woman's neck, how satisfying it would feel.

The woman spoke, interrupting her fantasy.

"I'm going to go now, and I won't be back. But I know what you did. If you ever threaten my children again, I'll come for you. And I'll make sure Hank comes for you, too."

The woman held on to the sword as she walked to the door. When she opened it, she tossed the sword back onto the floor. It clattered as it slid across the tile, landing at Catherine's feet. She could pick it up now; she could finally have her revenge.

In one movement, Catherine had the sword, whipping it around, piercing the air.

But the door had slammed shut. The woman was gone.

"You should have killed her."

Catherine swung around to see her daughter standing behind her. How long had she been here?

Maril went over and gently pried the sword from her mother's hand, running her finger along the edge of the blade as she smiled conspiratorially.

"Next time, we'll work together. It'll be easier."

EPILOGUE
MARIL

She was invisible. It didn't matter that she'd spent the past year working more hours than she ever had before, bringing in millions—possibly billions—in a merger acquisition that would position her father's company as one of the most powerful in the world. He'd scoffed when she said the words *artificial intelligence*, not believing his eldest daughter could have a vision that he hadn't already explored. And then, when it did happen, he took the credit, posturing in front of the cameras, giving the interviews—as though he had made the deal himself.

Her mother didn't understand. *She* had always allowed her husband to be in the limelight, stepping back to take her place offstage, even though she was just as responsible for the company's success.

So, when she'd confronted her mother, finally told her what she'd done, she'd expected some thanks. Some appreciation. Because what she'd done was for *her*, to bring some dignity back to the woman who'd had to watch the man she loved marry woman after woman, without so much as a thank-you for what she'd done for him through the years.

Her mother had never wanted her involved, she knew that. Her mother had always wanted to protect Maril, shield her from the anger within her. But Maril had been hurt, too, by her father's indiscretions—and this latest wife's pregnancy. Yet another sibling to stand between her and her father was just too much to bear.

He had to lose something. He wouldn't lose the company; she'd unwittingly made its future even more secure. No, he had to lose something much more personal.

So, she brought in the investigator, deftly dropping his name to her mother as someone who would be willing to do anything for a price. The ransom had been his idea—"We both might as well get paid for this" was his reasoning. He'd been invisible as well, her father forgetting about the work he'd done in trying to discredit the wife he wanted to shed. His failure, however, relegated him to routine duties. Until Maril maneuvered him back into her father's orbit, turning him into a double agent of sorts, proving yet again that she was no ordinary daughter.

Maybe someday he would recognize that.

The reporter, however, had proven to be a problem. He was more competent than she'd expected. She was aware her mother thought he should be used more subtly, especially since her father's marriage seemed to be hanging in the balance. But the pregnancy changed all that.

No, the woman had to be taken—and taken care of. Her father's history with dead wives had become almost comical. Would they suspect him? She hoped so. It had been her idea to leave the phone in the car. The authorities would search it when the wife went missing; it was her father's car. Explain that, they would demand.

Except something had gone wrong. The wife wasn't dead. She didn't even lose the baby. And now her mother had failed in her effort to finally get rid of the woman who'd started it all.

Her mother looked at her as though seeing a stranger. Even her mother didn't know who she was. What she was capable of. She'd been pushed into the shadows for too long.

She would show her. She would show everyone.

It was her time.

AUTHOR'S NOTE AND ACKNOWLEDGMENTS

Bringing historical characters into contemporary times has been a challenge. I've had some say I have stayed too close to history, while others have said I have moved too far away from it. In this sequel to *An Inconvenient Wife*, I have done more of the latter. Anne Boleyn and Katherine Parr, Henry VIII's second and sixth wives, respectively, never met or corresponded—for obvious reasons—but they were very similar: Both were Reformists, deeply religious, incredibly intelligent, and well-read. They were both fashionable, fun-loving, and cared deeply for Elizabeth. They most likely would have been friends, under other circumstances. In these pages, I wanted to explore that, to give the reader a "what if." The poet Thomas Wyatt, who was in love with Anne Boleyn; Thomas Seymour, who married Katherine Parr after Henry died; and Bishop Stephen Gardiner, who played a part in the fall of Anne and attempted to take down Katherine, are also a part of this story.

While I have taken a lot of liberties with the actual history, I hope to pique readers' interest in the Tudor period if they are not as familiar with the stories. Joanna Denny's *Anne Boleyn*; Nicola Tallis's *Young Elizabeth*; Tracy Borman's *Anne Boleyn & Elizabeth I: The Mother and Daughter Who Forever Changed British History*; John Guy and Julia Fox's *Hunting the*

Falcon: Henry VIII, Anne Boleyn, and the Marriage that Shook Europe; and Joanne Paul's *The House of Dudley* are all remarkable reads and good places to start if you want more of Anne and Elizabeth. Linda Porter's biography about Katherine Parr, *Katherine the Queen: The Remarkable Life of Katherine Parr*, is excellent.

I have to thank Claiborne Hancock and Jessica Case at Pegasus Books for again taking on this next Tudor retelling, allowing me to continue the wives' stories. Their publication list is a veritable wish list for anyone who wants to take a deep dive into the Tudors, so I know these books have found the exact right home. Many thanks, too, to my editor, Victoria Wenzel, whose thoughtful edits helped to better shape my Tudor world; publicist Nicole Maher for her myriad connections in the book world; Maria Fernandez for another terrific interior design; copy editor Lisa Gilliam; and proofreader Erica Ferguson. A big shoutout to Addie Lutzo at Faceout Studios for yet another amazing cover design.

Josh Getzler is my agent extraordinaire, an excellent first reader and editor and cheerleader. I am eternally grateful for his support and belief in my work. Shivani Doraiswami's faith in the fact that "the Tudors are evergreen" convinced me that she would go above and beyond to get my characters on the screen—and she has done so, tirelessly. I am so lucky to have both Josh and Shiv in my corner.

When I needed to know if a boat could be tracked like a plane, I turned to my dear friends Patty Smiley and her late husband, Bill Solberg, long-time sailors. Bill was eager to share his knowledge, and we had a rousing conversation about the Coast Guard and tracking systems. I will forever miss his humor and wisdom—and our discussions about grammar.

My friend and neighbor Kate Hagmann Borenstein, aka *Boater Girl*, regaled me with stories and photographs from her yachting adventures on Martha's Vineyard and other environs. She gave me yachting magazines and answered my questions, pointing out the app where I could track boats online.

I spent a lot of time on YouTube, watching video tours of mega-yachts, as well as on Zillow, to see how the other half lives. The internet has forever changed research since I first began writing novels more than twenty years ago.

While much of the book is set on Martha's Vineyard, I wanted to also send my characters to Essex, Connecticut, which is one of my favorite small towns along the Connecticut River. Our dear late friend Gordon van Nes had a large, rather famous sailboat called the *Yankee* docked there, which was where I got the idea that it might be a good place for the *Perseverance*.

So many thanks to the usual suspects for their friendship and support while I labored with getting Kate, Nan, and Catherine back onto the page, especially Nancy Lyon, Dorothea Halliday, Liz Medcalf, Patty Smiley, Clea Simon, Liz Baldwin, Kerri Pedersen, Judy Bobalik, Clair Lamb, and my summer Ridge Top Club ladies Diane Alderman, Judy Campbell, and Ruth Kleinfeld.

And thank you to all the readers, librarians, and booksellers who have enjoyed my books and helped me get them out in the world. You've made this journey so much fun—and I hope to keep telling stories to entertain you for a long time.

I couldn't do any of this without the love and support of my husband, Chris. We've had more than thirty years together, and here's to many more, full of laughter, travel, good food, and, of course, cocktails. Our daughter, Julia, and her husband, Mitchell, make our family complete. Love you all.